THE COWBOY

Also by

THE COWBOY

VONNA HARPER
P.J. MELLOR
NELISSA DONOVAN
NIKKI ALTON

APHRODISIA

KENSINGTION BOOKS
http://www.kensingtonbooks.com

KENSINGTON BOOKS are published by

Kensington Publishing Corp.
850 Third Avenue
New York, NY 10022

All Kensington Titles, Imprints, and Distributed Lines are available at special quantity discounts for bulk purchases for sales promotions, premiums, fund-raising, and educational or institutional use.

Special book excerpts or customized printings can also be created to fit specific needs. For details, write or phone the office of the Kensington special sales manager: Kensington Publishing Corp., 850 Third Avenue, New York, NY 10022, attn: Special Sales Department, Phone: 1-800-221-2647.

Aphrodisia and the A logo are trademarks of Kensington Publishing Corp.
Kensington and the K logo Reg. U.S. Pat. & TM Off

ISBN: 0-7582-1528-2

First Trade Paperback Printing: August 2006

10 9 8 7 6 5 4 3 2 1

Printed in the United States of America

Contents

Wild Ride

Vonna Harper

1

The bulls had arrived.

Fighting the knot in her belly, Jordan Shore gripped the corral railing as the massive stock truck made its way through the night-darkened rodeo grounds. Whinnies from the nearby horse barn mixed with bellows from the soon-to-be unloaded Brahmas.

Like many competitors, she'd arrived at the county fairgrounds the day before the rodeo was set to begin. But where her fellow barrel racers, as well as the bronc and bull riders and ropers, were primarily concerned with getting settled in, she'd come early so she would have time to study the Brahmas.

So she could come face-to-face with her fears.

Whoever was driving the stock truck handled it as if he'd been jockeying the unwieldy thing for years, expertly backing until it was only a couple of feet from the corral where the bulls were contained until their event. Shivering, Jordan sensed the animals' impatience at being penned up. If she had the brains of a gnat, she would leave right now. But even with her heart pounding and her surgically repaired right leg aching, she held her ground.

If she didn't, she might never win the biggest round of her life.

Mercury lights illuminated much of the grounds, but back behind the outbuildings, deep shadows provided the perfect opportunity for her nightmares to breed. And, boy, were they breeding, making her hands and between her shoulder blades and in the small of her back sweat.

Then the driver opened the door and jumped down from the high cab, and she couldn't breathe.

Cougar Lighthorse.

A sharp pain turned her attention to her right palm. Damn! She'd been gripping the railing so tight she'd forced a wood sliver into her flesh. Yanking out the splinter with her teeth briefly distracted her from the reality of Cougar's presence. By the time she'd turned her attention back to him, the tall, solid Indian, and whoever had been in the passenger's seat, had moved to the stock door.

Wiping her sweating hands on her well-worn jeans, she hurried around to the rear of the corral. Her riding boots thudded dully on the packed earth, echoing her heartbeat. Given his need to concentrate on what he was about to do, she doubted Cougar was paying attention to his surroundings. Good. This way she had more time to come to grips, to comprehend, to resign herself. And, if truth be known, to ogle.

She was asking herself if two men on foot really could unload who knew how many two-thousand-pound bulls, when several mounted cowboys appeared. They spoke briefly with Cougar, but the bulls' continual bellowing made it impossible for her to hear anything.

One of the men on horseback opened the corral gate. A minute later the rear door to the stock truck swung open. Heart in her throat, she frantically looked around. If one of those monsters broke loose, where could she run? The barn? Could she reach it in time?

Stop it! Damnit, get over it!

To her surprise, although the bulls fairly charged down the ramp and exploded into their temporary home, they almost immediately calmed down without giving her so much as a glance. Of course, finding hay and water waiting for them had a great deal to do with things. In less than five minutes a dozen Brahmas had been secured in the sturdy enclosure. It was so dark in there she barely glimpsed their massive forms, but morning was soon enough for that stroke-threatening task.

Male voices tore her attention from the bulls. Cougar and the others had gathered near the truck cab. Occasional laughter told her the conversation was less than serious. Although thoughts of being surrounded by so much testosterone intimidated her, she wanted to laugh with them, to absorb their strength and competence, to thank Cougar for holding her tight and strong and safe during that memorable day a year ago when pain and panic chewed at her sanity.

Heat touched her nerve endings. Unsettled, she closed her hand around her throat. If a bull—no! What she felt spoke of something far different from danger, at least the kind of danger she'd experienced, thanks to one of those beasts. This was a hell of a lot more carnal. If she didn't—

Cougar had left the others and was walking toward her.

Her legs trembled. She wanted to run. She needed to stay. Watching him, she concentrated on a body carved from a lifetime of physical labor. His jeans barely contained powerful thighs, and yet what she could see of his ass was tight and minimal. Like most true cowboys, his belly nestled between prominent hip bones. If this was rodeo day, he'd be sporting a handtooled leather belt complete with decorative brass buckle, but tonight he hadn't bothered with flash. He'd tucked in his long-sleeved Western shirt and had rolled up the sleeves, exposing hard forearms capable of handling the wildest bronc. His shoulders were broad enough for any task. Midnight hair so long he'd contained it with something at the nape of his neck spoke of his Native American heritage.

Although he was now so close he might see what she was doing, she couldn't stop herself from glancing down. There. Wrapped tightly in denim, the bulge she'd thought about more times than he would ever know.

"Jordan? Jordan Shore?" His voice hit her nervous system like a drumbeat.

"Cougar."

He held out his hand. In the uncertain light, she couldn't see all the details, but memory told her of long, strong bones and sun-weathered flesh. Although her hand shook, she closed her fingers around what she could of his. She felt small and feminine. Turned on.

"I heard you were going to be here," he said, still claiming her hand. "Is this the first time you've competed since . . ."

"Just a couple of local events. Nothing as big as this."

"Or with my bulls around."

The statement weighted the air. Although robbed of breath, she mustered the strength to pull free. Before she could think of a response, one of the men called out.

"I have to go," he said. "But we need to talk."

"I don't—"

"Where are you staying?"

She pointed toward the parking lot reserved for participants. "It's a double horse trailer. Faded blue and white, sleeping area."

"I'll find it. You'll be there later?"

"Yes. But you don't—"

"Yeah, I do. We do."

Although she was tired after the ten-hour drive from the family ranch in Harney County, Oregon, Jordan hadn't undressed. In the hour since she'd spoken to Cougar, she'd checked on her trained quarter horse, Trixie, dropped by the trailer of a woman she'd competed against for several years, and read the local newspaper. Now, because the night was hot, she was sitting in a lawn chair in front of her rig, boots off, attention shifting between the moths swarming around the lights and the comings and goings of those around her. She could have joined the large group in the next row but didn't because experience had taught her that someone would bring up her accident. She understood their curiosity but wasn't interested in rehashing the details. Besides, there were certain questions she didn't want to try to answer.

For the second time that night, something hot shocked her nerves. She didn't have to look to know who was walking among the many vehicles, but she did. Cougar still carried himself as if he had limitless strength, but his steps were slow. Either his day had been as long as or longer than hers, or he wasn't looking forward to this.

"I'm here," she said.

He nodded, came closer, stopped when maybe four feet separated them. She'd known this man all her life, but there'd always been a certain awkwardness or awareness or something between them, and the years hadn't changed that. Telling herself it was the civilized thing to do, she pointed at a lawn chair she'd propped against her trailer. Nodding, he set it up so he could sit across from her. Because she'd left a light on in her sleeping/eating quarters, the night only nibbled at his edges. He'd always been quiet, while she'd been what her parents called the ultimate chatterbox. Now, however, she couldn't think of a word to say.

You're making me crazy, Cougar. I've been attracted to you since I was old enough to know the meaning of the word. Why the hell do you have to look so damn sexy and feel so dangerous?

"Long day?" she brilliantly came up with.

"Long. At least these bulls are accustomed to traveling."

"You've really gotten into stock contracting, haven't you?" She tried to lean back, but her body refused to relax. Her skin jumped and hummed, and she couldn't keep enough air in her lungs.

"It's working out."

"Do you enjoy it?"

"Yeah, I do." He smiled, revealing perfect white teeth in contrast to his deeply tanned face. "Those years of working for your father taught me a lot about handling livestock."

Except for those few minutes a year ago. "What about your father?"

"He's doing good. He and Mom are in Arizona for some kind of powwow."

"I've been meaning to thank him. When your dad retired, mine finally admitted he couldn't run the ranch without his foreman—and that maybe his kids really were capable of taking over the operation."

"That's what you're doing? Running the ranch?"

Despite the wear on her emotions, she'd been meeting Cougar's black eyes. Now she looked down at her right leg. "Not really. The truth is, I'm addicted to competing. At least, I was until I did a number on this. Fortunately my brothers aren't the incompetents I accused them of being all the time we were growing up."

"You didn't mess up your leg. One of my bulls did."

There. The truth laid out between them.

"All right. Your bull. Rampage. He's aptly named."

"He's here."

The heat he'd pumped into her just by breathing flowed out to be replaced by ice. She didn't remember lifting her head, but now that she had, she couldn't tear her gaze off those high cheekbones and broad nose. "Oh."

"I wanted you to know. Reporters might pick up on it. The announcer's probably going to say something."

"I know." She started to shake. "But thanks for the reminder."

"That's not the only reason I came looking for you."

Through the years she'd seen countless mares backed into the corner by countless stallions. She'd taken bulls to cows and watched the sometimes violent servicing. Why those images came to mind right now escaped her—or, at least, she told herself she had no explanation for the comparison.

"Why did you?"

"To see how you're doing. And to apologize."

Quit looking at me like that! As though you want to throw me onto the ground and bury yourself in me.

Forcefully reminding herself that she was putting her own spin on his gaze, she shook her head. "You didn't open a gate and let Rampage out when he was having a bad hair day in spades. You didn't plow into my mare and send me flying."

Now it was his turn to jerk his head. "I've relived the accident a thousand times. No matter how hard I try, I can't make it come out different."

Realizing she wasn't the only one who hadn't been able to let go of the past shocked her. But, then, if she'd had to hold a frightened and bleeding accident victim, the memory would have stayed with her, too. "At least it's behind us."

He stood, the movement both weary and effortless. "Is it? We'll know better once this rodeo is behind us."

Us? She might have questioned his word use if he hadn't held out his hands. Not giving herself time to ask what the hell she thought she was doing, she let him draw her to her feet.

"Funny how life turns out, isn't it?" He continued to grip her fingers. "While we were growing up we were pretty formal around each other. There you were, my dad's boss's daughter. I knew there'd be hell to pay from my old man if I was anything except respectful toward you. I understood my place."

"Your what?" Why did his hands have to be so warm and strong, his body so close, her libido so in overdrive? "You scared me."

"Scared?"

She looked up, up, shaken to realize how much taller and substantial, more everything he was. "Every time I saw you, you were doing something physical. You were so muscular." *You still are.* "I'd watch you on horseback and envy you because you made it look effortless."

"You ride as if you were born to it."

"Hardly." She laughed more as an attempt to calm her nerves than anything. "It took countless hours in a saddle for it to become anything close to second nature, while you . . ."

"What?"

Stop holding my hand. Give me back my space, because if you don't, I'm going to jump your bones. "I was going to say that your being Indian made your horsemanship instinctual, but that's stereotyping."

His chuckle rumbled up from somewhere deep inside and slid over her skin. Her breasts tightened, and her nipples hardened. She struggled not to acknowledge the moist heat between her legs. Damnit, a man's laugh shouldn't have this impact on her.

But Cougar Lighthorse wasn't just any man.

2

Jordan's living quarters while on the road were what a horse-trailer salesman might label efficient. She was more inclined to call the combination eating/living/sleeping area cramped to the max, but her primary need had been for something large enough to haul her horses and gear. She'd joked that she could sit at the table and cook dinner on the doll-sized stove. A cloth curtain separated that space from the bed, which, although only double-sized, took up so much space she had to walk sideways to get around it.

At the moment, she and Cougar were standing in front of the red and black cotton, which not-too-effectively hid her bed. If pressed, she couldn't say why she'd invited him in; maybe the truth was she didn't want to admit what had motivated her.

"A little smaller than mine, but not by much," he said. Only a few inches separated them, and her skin was telling her that wasn't nearly enough. Other areas of her anatomy wanted to get a hell of a lot closer. "I have more storage room."

"I keep most of my belongings back with the horses," she

explained. "Since I take only two mares with me, I have the space." The light that had barely touched him when they were outside now played over his features. If he'd been born two hundred years ago, surely he would have been selected as his tribe's chief. There was something commanding about his strong facial bones, especially the large and deep-set eyes that reminded her of polished obsidian. No wonder he'd intimidated her while she was growing up.

And now she'd brought him into this cramped space.

"W—well"— she stammered over the word— "that's pretty much it. Not much of a tour. And I—I imagine you need to get back to your stock."

"Jordan?"

Don't say my name that way. "What?"

He leaned against the metal wall; then, when it creaked, he pushed himself off. The move brought him even closer. "Every time I think about the day Rampage attacked your horse, one thing stands out."

"What?" She licked her lips and tried again. "My screaming?"

"You only did that once." He rested his hands on her shoulders as though he had every right to her body. "The way you felt in my arms."

Rampage, who'd shattered a section of the bucking chute he'd been placed in, had charged into the arena while she and her mare were in it. Rampage had run right at Trixie and knocked Jordan to the ground, trapping her leg under Trixie's weight. Fortunately Trixie had suffered only bruises and a blow to her less-than-calm nervous system. Unfortunately, while her mare scrambled back onto her feet, Jordan's attempt to stand had resulted in a piercing cry and teeth-loosening pain. To make matters worse, Rampage wasn't finished.

"You're shaking." Cougar's fingers clamped down around her shoulders. He drew her against him.

Back up. Stay in control.

But she could feel his heat, his strength, his cock. "I—I guess I am." Determined to regain control, she dug her toes into the sad excuse for carpet. "Sorry about that."

"Memory lane?"

"'Fraid so. Fortunately it's nothing I can't live with."

"Maybe." When he relaxed his grip she told herself he'd done his good deed by the traumatized barrel racer with the pinned-together leg bones. That was before he wrapped his arms around her back and pressed her against his chest, before her own arms found their way around him.

He smelled of the cowboy way of life. He might not yet be in rodeo regalia, but the impact was there. This was a man who made his living much as those who'd settled this land once had. He was in tune with the environment and understood the vital role horses and other livestock had once played. His ancestors once hunted with bows and arrows and fought their enemies with knives and spears. They'd prayed to the sun, moon, rivers, bears, and eagles.

And tonight a great-grandson of those proud and resourceful people was holding her.

"Do you want me to leave?" His breath heated the top of her head.

"No."

"Because if I stay . . ."

Just like that. No fumbling, no awkward exploration of her limits.

"I want you to."

He leaned back, putting space between their upper bodies but keeping the pelvis-to-pelvis contact. "I'd like to see your leg."

Taken aback, she could only stare. She'd been so sure that sex was on his mind—just as it was with her. "It, ah, isn't the most beautiful thing in the world. The scars are going to fade

some more, but I'm afraid my days as a runway model are behind me."

Instead of responding to her lame excuse for a light note, he
unfastened the snap on her jeans, and then stopped with his fingers on her zipper as though he had every right in the world to
do so. "Not many people have seen this, have they?"

Trying not to tremble, she shook her head.

"Any men?"

None of your damn business! "No."

"Why not?"

"Look, my life is none of your—"

"Yes, it is. An animal I own altered that life. I need to see the
full extent of that alteration."

Oh. Well, in that case . . . "Maybe I should have sent you the
bill."

"I tried to pay it but was told your insurance covered everything."

In other words, he'd been willing to assume financial responsibility for something that wasn't his fault; it had been
determined that the boards Rampage had shattered were rotten.

His fingers still rested over her navel, warm life seeping
through denim to heat her flesh. "I, ah, I just shaved my legs."

Apparently taking her lame comment as approval, he pulled
down on the zipper tab. Because the jeans were snug, they remained in place, but he'd exposed her practical panties. Truth
was she loved the sensual feel of a hip-hugging bikini, but experience had taught her that long hours in the saddle or behind
the wheel weren't compatible with tight underwear, not that
she would ever tell him that.

Eyes on hers but unreadable, he tugged on her jeans until
they clung to her thighs, and then told her to sit down. She
pushed aside the curtain and slumped onto the end of her bed.
Then, while he finished the disrobing, she stared down at the
skin creases around her waist.

Kneeling before her, he placed her foot on his thigh and began running his hands over her leg. Her tibia had been shattered in two places and tendons torn. Surgical pins now anchored the compromised bone, the pins' positions identified by small round scars. His fingers lingered there.

"Are you still doing physical therapy?"

"No. Thank goodness that's behind me. By the end of a day it aches, but much of the time I don't think about it."

He ran his knuckle over her shin, prompting her to grind her buttocks into the bed. "About the break at least."

What do you mean by that? "Are—are you satisfied?" It took all she had to remain sitting instead of collapsing back onto the bed. The instant the words were out of her mouth, she regretted them. Satisfied couldn't be further from how *she* felt.

Instead of answering, he rocked back and looked up at her. He rested his hands over her knees, holding her in place, letting her know how easily he could spread her legs.

"It could have been worse. At least Rampage didn't gore you."

He does in my nightmares, which is why I can't get past doing whatever I have to to end them. "No, he didn't. Cougar. . . ."

"Do you want me to leave?"

"No," she blurted. "No. Do you want to?"

"No."

He stood, healthy muscles effortlessly bringing him to his feet. His legs pressed against hers. She had to place her arms behind her and look up in order to see him. How could this man she'd known nearly all her life be so intimidating, so overwhelming?

Because he is.

Not asking if she wanted this, he took hold of her shirt and tugged. The snaps gave way. With her gaze still locked on his face, she nevertheless knew what he was looking at: practical white bra designed to minimize the jiggling caused by a galloping horse. He pulled the shirt away from her breasts and as far off her shoulders as the fabric would stretch. Although she could have finished the job, she continued to let her arms support her while he gazed at her newly exposed flesh. Pinpoints of energy flickered over her throat, breasts, belly. Beneath the layers of clothing waited a woman too long denied her sexuality. Nothing else mattered.

"You're beautiful. When you started changing from a child to a woman, every time I looked at you, it hit me anew."

"You never said anything."

His mouth curled upward, and he rested his hand at the back of her neck. "We hardly ever spoke to each other, did we?"

"No, we didn't."

"Because you were the boss's daughter."

"No." When she shook her head, his hand shared in the journey. "That wasn't it. At least, I never felt that way."

"Then, what?" He leaned over, brought his mouth dangerously close to hers. His grip on her neck increased.

"You intimidated me! All right? You intimidated me." *Just as you're doing now.*

"Did you think I was going to scalp you?"

"Don't go there! Maybe it was your name." Thinking had gotten so hard. She couldn't find the words for what she needed to say. "Cougar. A prey animal."

Still holding his body all but suspended over hers, he started tracing the top of her bra with the side of his thumb. Each step of the journey resonated through her. Beyond caring about the consequences, she spread her legs and welcomed him in. He pressed his knee against her crotch, the touch saying everything.

Once again his mouth turned up. "My mother wanted me to have a white-bread name, something she thought would make it easier for me to fit in when and if I moved away."

His family and various relatives and friends lived in a sparsely populated section of the county in what she'd always thought of as an informal reservation. Although the children attended the small district school, for the most part, whites and Indians stuck with their own kind. His relatives and friends wouldn't think twice about a black-eyed and -haired boy named Cougar, but that boy couldn't spend his entire life in that closed-in world.

"I'm glad she didn't win. Your name is right for you."

"Even if it intimidated you?"

I'm still intimidated—only, maybe what I feel now has everything to do with being a woman and you a man.

3

She loved the sound of snaps popping. Even more rewarding was the sight of his dark chest. Although she was still trying to wrap her mind around the reality of what she'd just done, she wasted no time running her tongue over his flesh, because a bold and hungry creature had taken control of her.

Apparently Cougar had no objection to being treated like her personal boy toy because as she continued bathing his silken and yet hard flesh, he explored her arms with callused fingertips. She'd taken a few seconds to shuck off her shirt and unhook her bra. The loose garment still covered her breasts, frustrating her and hopefully tantalizing him.

These moments of exploration were about foreplay, nothing else. She'd think later, question later, maybe regret later.

Embracing her decision, she clamped her knees around his thighs and wondered if she could keep him there forever.

Maybe not. One moment she was sitting upright; the next he'd pushed her back on the bed and was looming over her. Much as she wanted to say something, anything, she couldn't.

Her legs still hung over the edge. Because he continued to

stand within the shelter of her knees, she might have told herself she had some control over what was happening, but she didn't want that. She wanted to be used, worshipped, fucked.

There. The single word that says it all.

Her cunt heated. Moisture built from deep inside, softening and preparing her.

"My panties. Get rid of them."

Grabbing the elastic, he tugged them off, the effort made easy because she arched upward and lifted her ass off the mattress. Still only half believing what was happening, she reached for her bra straps. Shaking his head, he pressed her arms onto the bed. His gaze warned her not to move. Her lips both numb and swelling, she nodded.

He closed his fingers over the straps and guided them out to her shoulders, and then directed her to lift her arms. Although she had to grit her teeth to keep from begging him to hurry, he took what seemed to be forever to uncover her breasts. The bra landed on the top of the rest of her clothes. Folding his arms across his chest, he stared down at her.

Naked. Exposed. Ready.

By contrast, he still had on his boots and jeans.

"You're making me crazy!" she gasped.

"Not nearly as crazy as you've made me for years."

"What?"

"You think I've never wanted to do this?"

She reached up, but then fell back again onto the bed. Inch by maddening inch, he unfolded his arms and let them dangle by his sides. Furious, she ground her knees against his legs. The effort earned her a chuckle.

"All right. All right." She licked her lips and tried again. "Do you want me to say I've wanted to have sex with you?"

"Only if you mean it."

"Yes. Damnit, yes!"

"Why?"

"Why wouldn't I?" Her belly clenched. It took every bit of self-control not to offer her pussy to him like some mare in heat. "You have a killer body. Strong, rugged, masculine."

"That's the only reason?"

"What do you want me to say?"

"Nothing. Nothing at all."

Bothered by his pensive tone, she tried to concentrate on his expression. But maybe he knew what she was doing and had no intention of letting her succeed. And maybe he'd grown weary of talking. Eyes half closed, he pressed a hand down on her mons. His other hand sought and found her cunt.

"You're wet."

"Yes."

If he'd asked permission, she would have granted him full access. Instead he claimed her. His work-roughened finger slid in and along the wall of her vagina. Although she fought to stay silent, a long, low groan rolled out of her. Tilting her pelvis upward, she lifted her head so she could watch.

He made her vagina his playground, sliding in and out repeatedly. She clutched the coverlet, and sweat coated her throat and the small of her back. The muscles had been stripped from her legs. Her lower body became so weak she couldn't think how to move.

Drifting in a sea created by her need for sex, she was slow to comprehend that he was no longer finger-fucking her. Instead he'd taken hold of her labia and was drawing the loose flesh toward him. Intrigued by her imprisonment, she clutched the hand still pressing on her mons. "So fast. So damn fast."

"You don't want this?"

"Yes, damnit. I do."

"So do I."

On the tail of his admission, he grabbed her hips and pulled her closer. With her being robbed of his hands on her sex, she started to sit up. "Don't play games! Don't tease me."

"I don't intend to," he said, his strong fingers pressing her back onto the bed. "But I've wanted to do this for a long time. It's going to happen—my way."

My way.

An image of being tied and at his mercy flooded her mind. She who barely tolerated being indoors, and who had nearly lost her mind while in the hospital, reveled in the thought of being his to do with what he wanted. He would rule her world and body, keep her teetering on the brink. In that world of her imagination, she would do whatever he commanded of her. Her reward would be a forced-upon-her climax, and she would worship him for it.

His mouth on a breast pulled her back to the reality of a cramped enclosure. He sucked, licked, circled, nibbled her rock-hard nub and bathed her until her breast became as wet and warm as her cunt.

Her now-ignored cunt.

"Take off your clothes." Given his greater strength and control, her order was laughable. "I want to see you. All of you."

"A warning," he said and shifted his attention back to her pussy. This time his fingers seemed to care only about her clit and the space between her vaginal opening and anus. "Once I'm naked, sex is going to come quick."

"Sounds—sounds good to me."

A fingernail feathered over her clit, forcing out a shiver. She grabbed his hand but made no attempt to pull him off her. Her cheeks were on fire. Her thigh muscles had melted.

"No more foreplay?"

"Cougar! Damnit, do me!"

By way of response, he slid his hands under her buttocks and leveraged her upward. Out of the corner of her eye, she saw that he'd slumped down so that he was on his haunches, his mouth close, so close to her cunt.

His breath! Warm. Alive. Skittering over her pussy and heating the fluids that had leaked out of her.

"Please, please."

"This is it?" He blew on her. "Your world doesn't go any further than this?"

"No. No. Oh, god, please."

"You feel whole?"

Whole? "Damnit, Cougar! Get out of those clothes."

Straightening, he cocked his head to the side. For so long she all but squirmed under his scrutiny, he studied her from the top of her head all the way down to her toes. His gaze lingered longest on her blatantly displayed pussy, yet although she felt more exposed than she ever had, she didn't close her legs. After all, he'd touched her nearly everywhere, blown his breath over nearly every inch. Need lashed her, but she clamped down on her plea for his cock and waited him out.

Displaying more of the grace that had already stolen her breath, he stood, bracing one hand on her belly as he did. The other swiped her inner thighs, making her jump. Not taking his gaze off her, he unfastened his jeans. Then he sat beside her so he could remove his boots. Once again he ran his fingers over her, this time his knuckles dragging along her entire vulva. She cried out in need. In want.

Through a haze, she recorded the last of his undressing. Then he positioned himself between her legs and lowered himself onto his knees. She tried to sit up only to be flattened against the bed again.

"Stay there," he ordered. "This time it's my show."

This time.

The fear that he might deny her release caused her to dig her nails into his forearms, but if she hurt him, he gave no indication. Yet again he explored her breasts, drawing circles around them, taking hold of her nipples and drawing them up. Embracing and fighting the sensations, she caressed his hips with her legs.

Just as she entertained thoughts of surging up and closing her teeth around his nubs, he gripped her pelvis and tugged, pulling her so far off the bed that only his body kept her from sliding to the floor.

His cock held her in place, pressed against her labia, insisted on being granted entrance. "Wait," she gasped as he thrust toward her. "Wait. I'll—let me—" Thinking to pull apart her heated flesh to expose her opening, she tried to slide her hands between them.

"No." Grabbing her wrists with so much strength he cut off her circulation, he held them in the air. "Not yet."

"I can't—damnit, don't make me beg."

"I have—I have to . . ."

He was gone. Scrambling away from her on his knees, reaching for his jeans, pulling out his wallet, opening it, extracting a rubber.

How could she have forgotten something so essential! Berating herself, she watched him slide it over a cock so large and hard and hot-looking she wasn't sure the protection was up to the task. Then he was back where he belonged—between her legs.

Her inner thighs ached, forcing her to acknowledge how long she'd been spread like this. Even with the flimsy door open a crack, the air was stuffy. She could hear the livestock; indistinct, mostly male voices; truck tires crunching over gravel. Those sounds were part of her world, and yet tonight they meant nothing. Only Cougar did.

This time he had no trouble finding her entrance. This time he slid home with the first thrust.

How did this happen? Why am I having sex with this man?

Her questions faded under the pure and basic sensation of having her entrance filled. They'd captured each other in the most elemental of ways, and nothing else mattered. Again he slid his hands under her pelvis and lifted. Instead of holding him in place with the strength in her legs, she kept them splayed. Her restless fingers found his forearms, and she held on, her sweating palms recording muscle, bone, hair, veins.

Eyes locked on her face, he thrust, pulled back, thrust again. She quickly learned his rhythm, making it possible for her to match him attack for attack. The bed rocked under her, prompting her to wonder—briefly—if the vehicle itself might be in motion. It didn't matter. Onlookers could draw their own conclusions.

She wanted to fuck. Needed to fuck.

Lived to fuck!

Her back and legs bore most of her weight, and she became aware of the coverlet abrading her skin. Still, the need to pull him into her as deep as possible made the discomfort pale in comparison. Looking at him, sensing how naked her expression must be, she imagined his buttocks contracting over and over again. Artificial light glinted off his sweat-soaked chest. The hair at his temple broke free of the leather cord designed to contain it, sliding forward and darkening his features even more.

This man, this man she really didn't know, was fucking her. Driving into her offered cunt. Watching her breasts shake and pushing against her pelvis.

Heat. Building. Sensation powering her forward.

He pounded deep into her. But suddenly, instead of retreating, he remained in place, his muscles stonelike and yet trembling. "I can't—can't."

"Can't what?" she gasped.

"Wait. Too fast, damnit."

No! She wasn't ready for their union to end. As he pulled back, she went deep inside herself, left rational thought behind, and focused on her body's messages. She burned from both the effort of matching his frenzy and from the heat boiling out of her. A little more, and she'd reach that sweet explosion.

"I'm going to come!" she sobbed. Thrashing her head from side to side, she dug her elbows into the bed to keep herself from sliding away from him. Again his cock slammed into her, sliding hotly along her inner tissues, wetly sanding countless nerve endings. "Damn, damn."

"Already?"

Not caring whether she might hurt him, she dug her nails into his flesh. Close. So damn close! Release just out of reach.

No! He couldn't be leaving her! She needed him; her pussy demanded him. Both terrified and angry, she gripped his elbows and tried to pull him close again. He'd clenched his jaw. His eyes were the barest of slits, and his nostrils flared.

Empty. Nearly deserted.

No!

Hot, wet bulk plowed into her, sliding home like some conquering hero. Beyond anything civilized, she wrapped her legs around his hips and buttocks and made him part of her. When he tried to pull away, she refused to release him. He was hers! She couldn't climb the mountain without him.

His cock shuddered, twitched, strained.

"Yes!" she gasped. "Yes!"

"Yes!"

Although the damnable rubber caught and contained his cum, her cunt didn't care. It drank of the gift and grew strong. Took her to the edge. Threw her over.

"Shit. Shit."

Her muscles still felt as though they'd run a marathon as she watched Cougar dress. She stared at him, not just because she loved the look of him, but because she needed to try to make sense of what had happened. She'd never, absolutely never jumped in bed with a man like this. There'd been no seduction, no candlelit dinner, no whispered sweet nothings. Instead they'd fucked like animals. He was a stallion, a bull, she a mare or cow in heat.

But as powerful as it had been, their fucking hadn't entirely quieted her need. If he didn't leave soon—

"You really have to go?"

"Yeah. The bulls—"

"Ah. When will I see you again?"

"Tomorrow." He stood over her with his unzipped jeans hugging his hips and his shirt open. "Jordan, I didn't want it to be over so fast, but it's been a while since I've . . ."

"'Didn't want'? Have you been planning this?"

4

Trixie shivered under Jordan. Although she'd anticipated her mare's nervousness, Jordan couldn't put her attention fully on distracting the horse from everything going on around them. No matter how resolutely she tried to focus on her upcoming ride, her mind refused to stay in the here and now.

It was evening. Time for the first day of the rodeo to begin. She'd survived the opening ceremonies by making sure she stayed in the middle of the barrel racers where, hopefully, reporters and photographers wouldn't spot her. Cantering into the arena dressed in her show-only deep red shirt and hat had damn near been her undoing, for one simple reason. The bulls, although not yet loaded into the bucking chutes, were so close she'd smelled and heard them. The usually laid-back, eight-year-old Trixie had bugled and tried to buck. Jordan had had her hands full and might not have been able to keep her mare under control if a couple of men on horseback hadn't ridden up on either side, effectively squeezing Trixie between them. Their presence must have calmed Trixie because she'd stopped prancing and whistling. The men's black shirts had identified them as stock handlers, Cougar's employees.

"Cougar said you might have a bit of trouble with her." The man on her right had indicated about Trixie. "Asked us to keep an eye on things."

"I appreciate it. She has more of a memory than I hoped she would."

"Cougar told us what happened."

But had he told his men everything? she pondered as she waited for her turn to compete. It didn't matter—at least, not now, because she was about to do her damnedest to put her own demons behind her. After a year devoted to almost nothing beyond getting to the point where she could compete again, the time had come. That's what was important, not asking herself for the umpteenth time why she hadn't seen Cougar so far today. Of course, she'd gone out of her way not to be where she thought he would be, but a considerate man did something to acknowledge the woman he recently bonked, right? Of course that worked both ways, or it would if she had a better handle on her emotions.

Let it go! You're here to ride.

From where she and the other barrel racers waited just outside the arena, she could barely glimpse the woman currently guiding her galloping horse around the barrels, but yells and clapping left no doubt that the woman was doing well against the clock. A little more than a year ago she had been one of the top competitors and had her share of awards to prove it. But thanks to the damage to her leg, she'd missed the rest of last season and the start of this one. Making up for lost time wasn't going to be easy—nearly as hard as getting the Brahma-sized monkey off her back.

"Damn that Crystal!" the racer next to her exclaimed. "Thanks to a daddy willing to fork over for the best horses, she's always going to be a pisser to beat."

"It's not just her horses," another competitor observed. "Crystal goes all out. The damn broad is fearless."

Fearless? What did that feel like?

When Crystal came cantering back, her face flushed and her smile showing a mouthful of perfect teeth, Jordan applauded. Inside, however, she warred with equal compulsions to rip out Crystal's hair and beg her to give her some of her fearlessness. Here. Now. Finally. Goal number one met. Number two coming up.

"You'll do fine. All you have to do is believe in yourself."

Cougar's voice rolled over her. For a moment the earth-sized knot in the pit of her stomach eased. Turning toward him, she took in his black outfit, especially the form-fitting shirt with its silver snaps that played up the silver band on his cowboy hat. Even his boots carried out the same theme. Of course his horse was black and a stallion. Not many rodeo participants risked having a tetesterone-charged mount under them, but Cougar easily controlled the wide-eyed, prancing beast.

"I didn't expect to see you," she said when, finally, she remembered how to make her voice work. "I thought you had enough to do behind the fences."

He guided his horse a little closer, and then reined up, keeping the stallion a safe distance from Trixie, who obviously wasn't in the mood for a suitor. "How are you feeling?"

Pretty much like I'm going to fly off in a million pieces. "Rusty. Practicing at home's hardly the same as the real thing."

"At least you're doing it." He dropped his gaze to her leg.

"Cougar!" Crystal exclaimed, urging her gelding between Cougar and Jordan. "Fancy seeing you. Are you going to ride? No matter what bull you draw, my money's on you."

That's right, Jordan reminded herself. Cougar had started out in the rodeo business as a bull rider and twice had qualified for the finals. He'd finished high both times, and Harney County residents had boasted of the local boy who'd made good. He hadn't competed in a while, and she'd assumed it was because the contracting business took too much time.

"Put your money away." Cougar had been looking at Crystal. Now he returned his attention to Jordan. "Riding's behind me."

"You sure you won't reconsider? There's nothing like a stud riding a bull to the bell to ring my chimes, if you know what I'm saying."

Just then the announcer called out the name of the next rider, Kari. Knowing she was set to go after Kari, Jordan shut everything else out of her mind. She'd practiced endlessly on the ranch and had been relieved to learn that she hadn't lost her skill or timing. Actually competing wasn't that different from circling the barrels she'd set up herself.

Liar. Cougar wasn't watching you then. And Rampage wasn't a short distance away.

Because she rode two-handed when she competed, Jordan had kept only one hand on the reins as she'd walked Trixie in circles prior to entering the arena. The switch had prevented Trixie from anticipating what was coming up. Now, however, the sturdy mare shivered under her, prompting Jordan to sit back, which shifted Trixie's weight onto her hindquarters. At the same time, Jordan pressed her calf against Trixie's right side, indicating she wanted Trixie to continue circling. Then a nod from the timer prompted her to stop. Heart hammering, she waited.

The flag dropped. Leaning low, she urged Trixie into a full-out gallop. *The first barrel. Close in on it, slow, lean as much as you can without losing your balance, circle, straighten, aim for barrel number two.*

Even as the wind created by Trixie's hard gallop grabbed her hat, something snagged Jordan's attention. She couldn't say what it was, couldn't make sense of the blur. *Bull!* her insane instinct insisted. *Horse and cowboy*, her rational side countered.

Rampage *hadn't* gotten loose again. He *hadn't* charged into the arena, wasn't pounding toward her and Trixie. There would be no collision, no terrified and squealing horse being knocked to the ground, no sound of snapping bone.

Ride, damn you! Ride. Barrel number two coming up fast. Slow. Slow. Lean and turn. Straighten. Find number three and head for it.

Once again a blur of movement slammed at her nerves. Once more time buckled back on her. Although it couldn't be, she *heard* Rampage bellow, *felt* herself flying, hitting the ground, Trixie's weight crushing her. And then, worst of all, staring up at the great Brahma's churning hooves, thick curving horns, and impossibly powerful chest, knowing she couldn't move, knowing she was going to be killed.

"Give our young lady a round of applause, ladies and gentlemen!" the announcer yelled. "This is her first time to compete since a serious accident last year, and I know she would appreciate your encouragement."

Fighting tears and self-disgust, Jordan glanced up at the illuminated time clock. She'd never ridden that slow. Surely there'd been a malfunction. The hell there had!

Her fellow racers applauded when she returned to them, and she forced a rueful smile. Dismounting, she loosened the cinch around Trixie's belly and rubbed the heavily breathing mare's forehead. "You done good, old girl. A hell of a lot better than I did. And tomorrow can only be better, right?"

Trixie turned her head to the side and gave Jordan a look she interpreted as *It's up to you. I did my part.*

"I know you did. Just be patient with me. There's something about a head trip that—"

Trixie suddenly back-stepped, compelling Jordan to grip the reins. When the mare stopped tugging, she turned to see what

had startled her. She supposed she shouldn't have been surprised to see Cougar and his black stallion, but tell that to her
heart. The way it pounded could only be attributed to shock,
right?

"I'm going to be tied up until late tonight." His too-dark
eyes bore down on her, powering through the protective layers
she tried to throw up. "You know which is my rig, right? I'll
leave it unlocked. Wait for me."

*Wait in that too-small space smelling of you? Feel your pres-
ence on my skin and think about what you're going to say—and
do?*

"What for?"

"We need to talk."

She swallowed. "Just talk?"

"It's your call."

Cougar's personal area had to be twice the side of hers,
which helped defuse her claustrophobia. Only, if she was being
honest, fear of enclosed spaces had nothing to do with the state
of her nerves.

After putting Trixie in her stall and mounting her other
mare, she'd returned to the action. Her reason had been two-
fold; she wanted to get three-year-old Misty used to the sights,
sounds, and smells of a rodeo, and watching the other events
made it possible for her to take at least part of her mind off her
poor performance and what Cougar thought they needed to
discuss.

All right. There'd been a third reason. She'd watched Cougar.
He'd been in constant action, one moment behind the chutes so
he could supervise those people handling the bulls during their
event; the next riding pickup in the arena. Like his stallion, he'd
seemed tireless. In an environment filled with the most masculine of men, he stood out.

And no matter how hard she'd tried, thoughts of the body beneath the clothes stalked her.

Is that why you're here? she asked herself. At the moment she was looking through a folder filled with newspaper clippings about the various rodeos for which Cougar supplied bulls. He appeared in only a handful of the photos, too often at a distance. But there was one close-up of him being interviewed, with a pen full of milling Brahmas behind him. His hat was pulled low on his forehead, so she could barely make out his features, but his sweaty shirt clung to every muscle and rib. Damn, she could feel his heat just looking at him.

A sound outside spun her around. Heart hammering, she peered out. Cougar and a short, slim man were standing a short distance away. Cougar glanced at her, and then he turned his attention back to his companion.

"If you can find better hay, see if you can get it delivered tomorrow," he said. "But I'm guessing this is the best we can do."

"I'll get on it at first light." The sparse and weathered man was looking at her, but she couldn't guess if he was surprised to see a woman waiting for Cougar. Probably not. "Anything else, chief?"

"Get some sleep."

"More than you will, that's for sure," the man said as he walked away.

"Who was that?" she asked when the silence threatened to drive her crazy.

"Todd Little Deer, but we call him Slim. Not too original. He's been with me since shortly after I got into the business. He knows what I'm thinking before I do."

"That's good, I guess."

"Sometimes. Let's go for a walk."

Although he'd presented it as a simple statement, she recognized the undertone of an order. Instead of refusing, she closed the door behind her. As before, the moment the distance between them disappeared, she felt his power and strength, the testosterone rolling off him. If she'd been a mare in heat, she would have turned her back to him and lifted her tail, signaling her readiness to be bred.

Bred. Carrying Cougar Lighthorse's child?

"Where—where are we going?"

"To where we both belong."

5

When he first stepped into the large barn with its multitude of stalls, she nearly told him that although *he* might belong in the space smelling of hay, horses, wood, and leather, there was more to her than a cowgirl. Then the atmosphere closed in around her, and she knew he was right because barns had always been part of her existence. She'd cleaned out countless stalls, repaired or replaced countless boards, hauled in tons upon tons of hay. She felt comfortable here, at home.

"Have you ever wanted anything else?" he asked. The double doors hung open. Faint light slid in through the opening to touch the stalls on either side of the center space. Every stall was occupied, but only two of the horses acknowledged their presence. The rest, worn down from their long day, couldn't care less.

"Other than being involved with the ranching life? When I went to college I thought a lot about my options, but too many entailed spending my days in an office, living in a city."

"And you need space."

"Yeah." *And the chance to prove I haven't lost my nerve.* "What about you?"

He hadn't touched her tonight. Instead of feeling safer and more self-contained, she ached for the brush of skin against skin. Every molecule of her being was tuned in to him, so much so that she half believed he could see beyond her clothing to breasts, belly, hips, and, mostly, what waited between her legs. Even after her eyes adjusted to the muted light, she still felt isolated from the outside world. There was just them and the unconcerned, warm-bodied horses.

A horse stomped his hoof, shaking her mind loose of whatever spiderweb it had sunk into and reminding her that she'd asked a question that hadn't been answered. "I'm sure it goes without saying that you need to be where you can see the horizon." Her voice seemed to echo off the weathered wood.

"Because I'm Indian?"

"Because you grew up surrounded by nature." Because she had no choice in the matter, she touched his forearm. Just like that, her flames were fed. "I think it gets in our blood. No matter what people like us do with our lives, we're not satisfied unless we are surrounded by what was embedded in us as children."

"You're philosophical tonight."

Either that, or something was driving her to lay more of herself before him. Someone might be in the barn, maybe bedded down in a stall with his or her horse, but she didn't sense the presence of another human. Just him. "It hasn't been an easy day for me," she admitted.

"No, it hasn't."

She forced her hand back to her side, but it was an uneasy separation. Maybe she wouldn't have been this aware of him if they hadn't fucked, but she wouldn't take bets. Very possibly, he'd touched her hormones in ways they'd never been touched.

"Is—is that what you wanted to talk about?" she asked. "Why the hell my time was so bad?"

"I don't need to ask. I know why."

His words were still echoing around her when he took her hand and lifted it to his mouth and touched his lips to her knuckles. A rolling shiver ran from her fingers up her arm and from there down, down until it settled between her legs. Her knees nearly buckled.

"You—you do?"

"I've been there."

His fingers now laced in hers, he lowered their hands so her knuckles brushed his thighs. His warmth, his pulsing warmth, nipped at her.

"Do you recall what the announcer says when he introduces the riding events?"

Incapable of concentrating on anything beyond pounding need, she shook her head.

"He tells the bronc riders to check their gear—and for the bull riders to go behind the chutes and puke."

Suddenly restless, she drew him into the dark. Hay and wood chips crunched underfoot as they walked, and the scent of animals and weathered wood grew stronger. The barn closed around them, sheltered them and fed her flames.

"Is that why you no longer compete as a bull rider? Because you'd done enough puking?"

"That's part of it."

Of course it was. Even the biggest, strongest cowboy looked like a helpless child next to a ton of Brahmas. The bulls were peaceful enough when they were left alone; some became so docile that they could be led around by a halter. But rodeo Brahmas were bred to buck, to demonstrate in spades that they were more powerful and dangerous than any human being. The moment a cinch tightened around their gonads, fury drove them to twist and turn, pound the ground, and throw back their heads with those awful horns, trying to dislodge the fool clinging to their backs. Only a minority of cowboys remained for the endless eight seconds a ride was supposed to last.

And then the real danger began. Whether they'd been thrown or made it to the bell, they had to get out of the arena alive. She didn't know a single bull rider who hadn't had bones broken or muscles torn or flesh bruised—or all three.

"Only part of it?"

"It's a young man's sport, Jordan."

She could point out that some of the best bull riders were in their thirties, but he was right. Age and years of physical punishment caught up with all of them. So instead of playing the odds, with his health and life as the ultimate stake, he'd become a stock contractor. Fortunately the physical demands were less on barrel racers.

"Do you regret your decision?"

He'd been matching her slow walking pace, but now he stopped, bringing her to a halt as well. He spun her toward him as effortlessly as if he held her reins and wordlessly ordered her to look up at him. He drew her so close that her breasts brushed his chest. Instead of keeping what distance she could between them, she leaned forward until she found his cock

Deny this, the bulge seemed to say. *Tell me you don't want it.*

I can't.

"Regret?" he said. "Sometimes, like now, yes."

"What do you mean?"

"You need to get back on your horse and into the arena tomorrow. And for as many tomorrows as it takes. If you're going to get your head on straight, you have to face down your demons. But how can I tell you that when I'm not willing to do the same thing?"

"Barrel racing isn't going to kill me. Bull riding might destroy you."

"Yeah." His breath dampened her eyelashes. "The only thing you have to worry about is Rampage getting loose again."

Damn, but she hated hearing him speak that bull's name!

"You're shaking," he said. "What is it?"

I don't know! Or, if I do, I'm not willing to admit it. His bulge twitched and began to swell. Panic assaulted her. She'd turned into a wild animal last night, lost all control and rational thought. It wasn't going to happen again! It wasn't.

Propelled by fear of what she'd become last night, she jerked free and spun away. She actually made it halfway to the door before she stopped. Because her back was to him, she couldn't be sure, but she didn't believe he'd come after her. This was her decision, her choice.

Even more upset than she'd been a moment ago, she turned and faced the human shadow in the shadows. "I'm afraid," she whispered.

"Of me?"

"And of me. Of what came over me when we . . ."

"When we fucked?"

Fucked. Had sex. Screwed. "Yes."

"Do you regret it?"

Damn him and his hard questions! Energy pooled in her thighs and sent her back toward him. Not a molecule of her being didn't cry out for his touch.

"Do you?" he repeated.

"I don't know, damnit." Less than a yard separate them. His body, now magnetized, called to her. But not yet. Not until— "Had you decided to seduce me last night? Is that why you came to see me? Because you knew how horny I was?" *And am again.*

"The seduction was deliberate, but it had nothing to do with you being horny."

How dare he speak in riddles! "Then my needing to screw and be screwed was a bonus?"

His hand snaked out, grabbed an elbow, and pulled her close. "Don't talk like that."

He was right. In the household she'd been raised in, words like *screw* and *fuck* were never spoken. But something had changed her. It had everything to do with the electrical charge coursing through her and the man responsible. "It's the truth."

"I know."

His whisper, his soft, low, magical whisper, ran through her like warm water. She'd known this man most of her life, and yet she didn't know him at all. She certainly had had no inkling that she'd respond like this or that he'd be able to see beneath her protective layers.

"What do you mean by deliberate?" They were standing so close that his features had blurred.

"The first time I saw you here, I sensed your tension. Because I've been there, I knew what you were going through. I wanted to do what I could to take your mind off it."

"I appreciate you going out of your way to—"

"Stop it!" He shook her. "My bull nearly killed you. That's what it all boils down to."

And he'd decided to have sex with her as a way of making up for it? No. That was too bizarre to think about. They stood so close; every time one or the other shifted position, their bodies sparked. Did an electrical current run through him? Whatever it was, she hadn't had enough of the accompanying heat and energy. Neither did she know how to keep it, or herself, under control.

"We keep going round and round about this, don't we?" she said. "I didn't sue you, so you're off the hook."

The words were barely out of her mouth when he shoved her back but kept his hands on her. "I don't want to be off the hook, got it? You're going down a road I know all too well. I'd like to help you find your way off it so you can give some thought to the rest of your life."

"How can you know about my road? I seem to be making it up as I go along." *I can't even think about my future.*

His grip relaxed, and he began running his hands up and down her arms. With each stroke, the electricity became more intense. She needed to get away from him, go outside and take a few deep breaths, jump into a cold shower, bury herself in a snowdrift if she could find one.

But even more, she needed to stay and feed off him.

"You didn't hear about it?" he asked. "No, I don't suppose you did, because it happened in Texas."

She closed a hand around her throat. The other rested on his hipbone. "What did?"

"I got thrown. My hand hung up in my rigging, and I couldn't get loose."

"Oh, no. The clowns—"

"They did their job. But for too damn long, they couldn't get close enough to free me."

The image of Cougar being thrown about helplessly was almost more than she could handle. He was warmth and life, the epitome of the rugged cowboy. But during those terrifying moments when he and a bull had been one, he'd been at the beast's mercy. "What—what happened?"

"They told me that a rider got close enough to use a knife on the rigging."

"They told you? Had you been knocked unconscious?"

"Yeah. Probably by his hooves, although they said I hit the ground several times, and once the bull ran me into a fence."

You could have died! "No! I, ah, I guess it's a good thing you didn't remember. Did you have a concussion?"

"Among other things."

Growing up, her youngest brother had been a tough kid who wouldn't admit if he was bleeding to death or scared out of his mind. She'd seen a lot of cowboys like that, macho men unwilling or unable to admit to any weakness. Maybe she should respect that in Cougar, but this was about more than one acquaintance telling another about an accident he'd been in.

"Sit down." She indicated a tarp-covered bale of hay behind him. He shrugged but obeyed. Then, well aware of the risk, she pushed his knees apart and planted herself between them. Hoping she was giving off a no-nonsense air, she placed her hands on his shoulders and forced him to look up at her. "Tell me everything."

The "everything" didn't take long. Not only had he wound up in the hospital with a concussion, he'd cracked a bone at the back of his neck. For two days he hadn't been able to move. Despite his pounding head, he'd been awake and aware.

"You were paralyzed?" She nearly gagged on the word.

"Obviously not permanently, but long enough to get my attention."

"Get my attention" had to be the understatement of the year. She couldn't imagine anything more terrifying than losing control of one's body. The thought of Cougar confined to a wheelchair for the rest of his life made her blood run cold.

"Thank god you're not," she whispered. Her fingers on his collarbone tightened, but she couldn't relax them because she needed to feel his strength. "Did feeling come back all at once?"

"It took a couple of months because of the bruising to the nerves."

The nightmare was getting worse. Only knowing how it came out kept her sane. Or was she? Last night he had been the aggressor, the one who'd taken them over the edge. Although she'd been more than ready for sex, she'd happily gone at his pace.

Not tonight. Tonight she needed to say things with her body that she had no words for.

"I've always thought of you as, I don't know, more something than the average man. Physically superior, maybe."

"I'm not."

Tell that to my body. Her hands were sweating, and she didn't trust her legs. Her bra had suddenly become too small for her heavy breasts, and her pussy—a single touch there, and she would probably explode.

The power behind her need to have sex with Cougar frightened her, and yet she was already too far gone to walk away. She would drink from him, and the act would serve as affirmation of how healthy and whole he was.

Thank goodness his shirt came with snaps. Otherwise she would have popped all the buttons, the way she was yanking on the shirt. When she'd exposed his chest, he reached for her, but she pushed, forcing him to balance with his arms behind him on the hay, much as he'd done to her last night. Leaning forward, she ran first her lips and then her tongue over his newly exposed flesh. The salty, masculine taste raced through and became part of her. Fed her need.

Moving to his side, she rested her cheek against his right nub. One hand went to the back of his neck. The other slid toward intimate territory. Damn his jeans!

Men had this thing about being in charge. They were protective of the family jewels and hesitant to give a woman unmonitored access to them. She might not be a well-traveled sex partner, but she knew those elementary things.

And didn't care.

Contain him somehow. Let him know who's in charge. Show him how much you want the body he came too close to losing control of.

Most of all, drink from everything he has to give.

Sliding his shirt off his shoulders so it bunched around his wrists like makeshift handcuffs solved the immediate problem of keeping his hands off her. At first his jeans' snap resisted her efforts, but she kept after it. The zipper put up much less resistance.

"Just like that?" he asked.

"Just like that."

"What if someone comes in?"

"I'll tell them the joint's taken and to mosey on down the road."

She'd dropped to her knees and tugged off the first boot before what she'd said registered. Any number of people had every right to come in here. What would they think if they ran into a couple fucking?

Let them deal with it. Let them beat a hasty retreat.

Both of his boots now rested near the hay bale. Cougar hadn't moved.

I'm not going to think. And I hope you don't either. We need to do this. That's all that matters: the need.

"Stand up," she ordered.

He did, shaking off his shirt at the same time. She barely managed to wait until he was done before yanking down on his jeans. *Don't talk, please. Don't make me explain what I'm doing.* Only a long sigh from one of the stalls broke the silence, and no outside sounds reached them. There was just the two of them and insanity.

Crouching, she drew the jeans over first one raised foot and then the other. Eyes closed, she stroked his calves. Relying on her hold on him to keep her from losing her balance, she began working her hands higher. His knees were remarkable, bone and cartilage masterfully created. But much as they fascinated her, she needed to feel his thighs even more, to embrace his cock.

His briefs. Damnit, she hadn't—

Biting down on her frustration, she willed her fingers to glide to the back of his thighs. He shivered, and she laughed, the sound full of power and animal need. Dizzy, she again lowered herself to her knees. Despite the roaring in her head, it was now easier to continue her upward journey. She needed to embrace his cock, but that could wait, because even the backs of his legs carried the same message of strength under smooth flesh. Downy hairs grew at the juncture of thigh and buttocks, and she gently ran those hairs between her fingers. His hands rested on the top of her head.

She couldn't keep her hands off his briefs, or, more precisely, out from under them. As she slid past the thin layer, the mark the elastic had left at the base of his buttocks held her interest. She might have spent a long time exploring the thin indentations if he hadn't twitched. Ah, the man was sensitive there.

And there, too, she discovered as she inched northward. His ass was compact but nicely curved, with layers of skin and muscle and just enough fat between her and bone. Buried in there was the strength that would come into play during the sex act. Strange how modest his muscles felt now, strange how urgent her need to have them work her.

"Damn you, Jordan. You're driving me crazy!"

"I intend to."

"Not if I have my way. Someone could come in. If we're going to—"

"We are. Now."

"No, not yet. Your clothes."

Much as she hated ending her exploration of his ass, she leaned against him and pulled off her boots. He reached for her jeans, but she shoved him away.

"No. This time I'm in charge."

"Are you?"

Hell, no. But until or unless he made a liar out of her, she would strip for him and give herself up as a gift to this man who'd nearly lost his life, or, if not that, his physical freedom. Too excited to attempt a slow seduction, she dispensed with her jeans and panties at the same time. As she did, he shrugged out of his briefs and perched on the edge of the covered bale. His cock waited for her, impatient and strong, barely a shadow.

She managed to unfasten her blouse before need gripped her. Something between a growl and a cry escaped her. Then she was on him, pushing him onto his back. He reached up, his hands gripping the sides of her neck and forcing her forward. Straddling him, she stood on her toes and started to lower herself, seeking the union of cock and cunt.

"Wait. Stop!"

"What?"

"I need a rubber."

Oh, shit, shit. But even as she gathered her thoughts to tell him she didn't care, she knew she wouldn't say the words. Dizzy, she tore his hands off her. "Stay there. I'll get—"

"In my wallet."

Fumbling in the near dark for his jeans took an unreal amount of time. She tried to make sense of her naked belly, ass, pussy, and legs as she dug through his wallet, but finding the damn rubber was more important than shedding her blouse, which still hung half off her. When her fingers closed around the small package, she snorted in triumph. Tearing at the wrapping with her teeth, she stumbled back to where she'd left Cougar.

Hard as it had been to locate the necessary protection, closing her hand around his cock felt like a homing pigeon returning to its nest. But the instant her fingertips stroked the soft, potent flesh, what little strength she'd held on to deserted her. She couldn't stop shaking, couldn't help but wonder at the near miracles that had brought them to this point.

She was going to have sex with Cougar. Take him into her flesh. Share that deepest of intimacies.

As for why she needed this so much—

"Jordan?"

Jerked out of her knotted thoughts, she forced herself back to reality. She was standing beside this prone Indian cowboy with her hands cupping his penis and the rubber caught between her fore- and middle fingers. If they were going to fuck—which she needed in ways that rocked her to her soul—she had a task to perform. But once she had, she would no longer be able to feel his sensitive and sensual flesh.

If they were married, if they were trying to make a child, nothing man-made would stand between them.

"Yes, yes," she muttered. But instead of doing what she'd committed herself to doing, she lay the rubber on his belly. Then, more frightened, overwhelmed, and eager than maybe she'd ever been, she cradled his meat between her palms. So big. So strong. And hot, so incredibly hot and alive.

Hers. For this brief time, hers.

"Oh, god," he hissed. "Damn. Damn."

Those could be her words as well, would have been if the utter intimacy of what she was doing hadn't rendered her mute. Much as she loved sex—who didn't?—she'd always been torn between having a climax rock her and the core, deep vulnerability that went with release. She'd had no longtime lovers, no fiancé, no husband, no one she felt utterly safe with.

And now she was about to close her cunt around this most challenging of men.

So, for moments that had no meaning, she cradled and controlled.

"Jordan? I can't . . ."

Of course. She was asking the impossible of him, playing and delaying while expecting him to lie there like some specimen under scrutiny. Besides, as wonderful as his firm and smooth head felt between her fingers, she'd been clenching and releasing her pussy muscles in a pitiful attempt to feed its need.

She'd never put on a rubber. As a result, an act that shouldn't have been that difficult took forever. Finally, however, she'd sheathed him. Now there was no reason to put off the inevitable, was there?

Placing her legs on either side of his feet, she straddled him. Attention fully on what little she could see of him, she slid closer, calves brushing calves, thighs kissing thighs. Again he settled his hands along the sides of her neck and pulled her toward him. If only she could read what was in his eyes!

No. Not enough.

Overwhelmed by the awesome responsibility she'd given herself, she nevertheless reached between her legs and parted her lips. Then, guided by primitive instinct, she lowered herself over him. His tip kissed her clit, and she sobbed. Down, down she went, knees bent, his hands keeping her close. Despite the burning in her thighs, she remained suspended over him with her hands on his chest for support. Skewered. Gifted.

"Home. You're home," she muttered.

She couldn't quite call his response a chuckle, but even if he was laughing at her, she didn't mind because he was where he belonged. Where she needed him to be. Instead of beginning the friction she craved, she closed her muscles around him and embraced all of him. Explored his contours. Acknowledged what she'd accomplished.

Using a gliding motion that nearly rattled her teeth, he ran his hands from her neck to her bra, which he yanked up over her globes. For a moment he simply held her newly freed breasts. When he stroked the pebbled area around her nipples, she thought she'd start crying. Desperate not to expose herself that way, she straightened slightly and took him with her. The idea of being about to move with his cock buried in her was nearly more than she could handle. She settled herself against him, gasping as his bulk consumed even more of her. He gripped her nipples and pulled as if trying to hold her in place, but she fought him, fought the demon in her that screamed for her to attack him.

Barely containing her fury, she began a pumping motion that caused her legs to burn and her mouth to open. "Got you. Got you. Won't let you loose."

"Who says I want to be free?" Arching off the bale, he powered into her. His hold on her nipples kept her in place.

Up and down. Up and down. Leg muscles on fire, forced to remain hunched over, her fingers digging into his chest, and his features a mix of black and red.

"I can't!" he gasped. "Jordan, I can't!"

"What?"

"Move. You're pressing on . . ."

How could that be when she felt weightless? But by concentrating, she felt his effort throughout her. His cock slid against her rear wall. Although she loved the sensation, she needed more.

When she tried to stand, he refused to release her nipples, but she continued to pull, oblivious to any discomfort or perhaps driven by it. Finally he let her go, and she straightened a little, fingers still digging into him, his cock deep and true.

Then she locked her knees and stood. The effort allowed his cock to slip out. Empty and hating the sensation, she turned so her back was to him. With a hand around his cock to stabilize it, she easily swallowed him again.

Mine . . .

He opened his stance and braced his feet under him. Doing so decreased their connection, but she reveled in the feel of his tip just inside her and the danger of losing him. Then he gripped her elbows and pulled her back toward him, held her in place, reclined, as he pounded into her. Her blouse fell back, revealing her breasts with the bra pressing against them. With one hand she feathered his balls. The other claimed her breast.

Unexpected pressure on her back made her wonder if he was trying to push her off him. Then she realized he wanted her to lean forward. She did, swallowing a few more precious inches of him, joining them, feeling his hot bulk. She managed a crude rhythm that brought her down just as he strained upward. Her cheeks burned, heat rolling down her neck to heat her breasts. Hunger gnawed at her, and she ground her knuckles against her breast.

Fuck him, fuck him. Eat him.

"Not—not going to work."

She tried to look over her shoulder at him.

"I still can't—move enough."

She nearly told him that she would happily fuck his brains out, and all he had to do was lie there and enjoy the ride, but just as she couldn't stay still, obviously neither could he. Besides, she *was* crushing him under her.

Before she could guess what he had in mind, he pushed with all his strength, forcing her up and off him and leaving her pussy empty. He stood, grabbed her around the waist, and forced her onto the bale, much as he'd just been.

"There. Now we'll do it my way."

What did she care? As long as he silenced the terrible ache, he could do anything he wanted. His expression unreadable, he closed his hands around the back of her knees and forced them into the air. Keeping her splayed, he crouched over her, aimed, housed himself. He leaned closer, loomed over her, trapped her under him. She felt small and helpless, desirable, wild.

This wasn't simply sex. He repeatedly came at her as if determined to pound her into submission, but instead of being frightened, she fed off his strength. Lifting her right leg as high as she could made it possible for him to close in on her even more, to splay a hand over her throat and keep her motionless.

No fear. Nothing except the thundering in her temple, her melting, flowing cunt, crying out as she raked her nails over his arm.

Every thrust threatened to knock her off her perch. As he drew back for yet another attack, she sucked in a frenzied breath and silently pleaded with him to hurry, hurry!

The pace quickened, giving her no time to prepare for the next assault. Movement and hunger flowed together. On fire, she grasped his shoulders. Holding him over her, she strained for his mouth. He answered her plea by crushing his lips against hers, attacking, not kissing. Much as she craved the savage union, her neck couldn't handle the strain, and she fell back down, whimpering.

A deeper moan rolled out of him. Straightening slightly, he again gripped her legs and held her open and exposed. He rode her like a strong, young cowboy with endless energy. The long, stressful day flowed out of her, and she became an animal, a bronc fighting for freedom.

Only, she didn't want to be free.

Much as she tried, her fingers only brushed his belly, but she kept after him. Touching and tantalizing him, like spurs rolled over a bronc's sides, propelled him to another level. He came at her, came over and over again, branding her entire cunt. Flames consumed her, scorched her, shook her as she'd never been shaken.

"Oh, shit. Oh, shit. Oh, shit, shit, shit."

"Got you. Doing you. Oh, shit!"

A climax rushed over her. Always before, the downhill slide came fast on the heels of the explosion, but this time the fireworks hit over and over until, maybe, she passed out.

Spent. Worthless. Twitching. An accident victim trying to make sense of what had happened.

Cougar's muscles trembled as he drew her into a sitting position. As long as he kept his knees bent, the union held, but then his cock grew limp. The thought of losing him unnerved her, and she wrapped her arms around him. He started to straighten, prompting her to lock her legs around his hips. Resting her head against his hot and sweating chest, she concentrated on his heartbeat, his breathing, his skin.

I love you, Cougar. I don't know how long this feeling is going to last, but for this moment, I love you as I never have loved anyone.

7

She woke to the sound of Cougar's faint snoring. Her first thought was that she needed to ask him what she was doing in his bed, but then she remembered.

While still in the barn, they'd thrown on what clothes were absolutely necessary. He'd asked if her rig had a shower, and she'd said it didn't, and they would have to use the grounds' facilities, but he'd offered to let her use his. After dropping by her place for a change of clothes, they'd walked barefoot and hand in hand to the huge gas-guzzling truck and sleeper trailer in which he hauled his bulls. A discussion about who merited the first shower had led to him flipping a coin. She'd won, which meant she hadn't taken time to study his quarters until she was clean. She'd been envious of his larger refrigerator and considerable storage space, and the twin recliners looked comfortable enough to sleep in. But what had held her attention had been the queen-size bed.

That's where she was. In a bed that smelled of the man next to her.

It was just getting light, but although she tried to bury herself in sleep again, her bladder wouldn't allow her to. By the time she'd finished in the bathroom, he was awake, propped up on his elbow, naked chest slowly rising and falling. She hadn't bothered with a nightgown.

"What are your plans until the rodeo gets going tonight?" he asked.

To have sex with you over and over again until we can't move. "I'm not sure. What about you?"

"Unfortunately my day's full."

"Of course." She sat on the edge of the bed and turned so she could look into his eyes. With every passing second, more daylight was slipping in. Knowing Cougar most of her life had conditioned her to accept his toasted complexion, but he seemed even darker than before. At least being Indian kept him from having a farmer's tan.

"You're smiling. What are you thinking about?"

"Never mind." She covered her hand with her mouth. "Believe me, it isn't worth sharing."

He grunted and slid off the bed. Not looking back at her, he trudged naked into the bathroom, which gave her ample opportunity to study the smooth roll of leg and ass muscles. She'd long admired a strong young horse's taut flanks, but her admiration centered around appreciation of how fast and long the animal could run. Cougar's flanks spoke of another kind of staying power.

"I'd like you to trail along with me today," he said when he returned. His cock was morning hard, although she chose to believe her presence had everything to do with its condition. "Watching the bulls sling snot and poop should go a long way toward dispensing any mystique they have for you."

"You aren't responsible for the head trip I've done on myself—if I have." It felt unreal and wonderful to be sitting buck naked on a man's bed while he, equally naked, leaned against a wall. "I don't need a shrink." *Just a hard kick in the butt every time a particular nightmare tries to latch on to me.* "And I don't need you worrying about me, if that's what you're doing."

"Worry? It's not that."

"Then what is it?"

When he held out his hands, she placed hers in them and let him pull her to her feet. There was a pillow crease on his cheek, and his hair needed to be combed and contained—something she would love to do.

"I need to ask you something."

She looked up at him.

"Do you think I'm a coward?" he asked.

A chill ran through her. "What?"

"For not getting back on a bull."

"You—you were in the hospital. How could you?"

"I'm talking about later, after I'd recovered."

Much as she wanted to shrug off the question, she couldn't, because it was too important. "Cougar, only a few men out of millions have ever ridden a bull—or tried to. That's a hell of an accomplishment."

"A lot of people would call me crazy."

Was he aware that he was rubbing her arms? Although she wasn't cold, a shiver shook her. If he kept up what he was doing, she'd be hard-pressed to carry on any conversation, let alone this vital one. "Of course bull riding is crazy, but it was something you wanted, or needed, to do. Has that changed? You no longer feel you have anything to prove?"

His hands stilled. A moment later he pushed her away but continued to hold her. Although his gaze ran down her, she wasn't convinced he was looking at her body. How strange. All those years of being ships passing through each other's lives, and they'd never had a serious talk. Now it was all coming at once—along with a physical attraction more powerful than anything she'd experienced.

"No." He sighed the word. "I don't feel I have something to prove."

Although she was glad he'd found his peace, a part of her wanted to remind him that, damnit, she had gotten back in the saddle after her accident and made coming to grips with her head trip her priority, her only priority. Her life's goal, even. If she was that committed, that insane, he should be, too. Shouldn't he?

"You have problems with that, don't you?" he asked.

"Damnit, Cougar! I'm not going to tell you how to live your life."

"I didn't ask you to."

Were they fighting? And if so, why? "Fine. Fine." Pulling free, she looked around for her clothes. "It's a hell of a lot better if people don't dictate to each other." Spotting her jeans, she sat back down and started pulling them on. Too late she realized she'd forgotten about her underpants. "I, for one, have enough to do running my own life."

"What are you going to do?"

Damn him for asking such a complex question! And damn him to hell for standing there without a stitch on and his cock long and dark and jutting. Reminding her of how it felt inside her.

"Today I'm going to catch up with some of my fellow competitors, compare horses, and tell tall tales, that kind of thing."

"Have you talked to any of them about what's going on inside you?"

"What do you care?"

"Don't."

She'd stood up so she could attend to the zipper. Unfortunately that brought her breasts—and the rest of her—too close to him. "Don't what?" The moment she'd said the words, she wished she could take them back.

"Push me away. Jordan, I didn't have anyone to talk to when I didn't know whether I was ever going to walk again. I'm offering you that."

His gift included much more than his muscles, his cock, his cum. When all the layers had been knocked aside, that's what it came down to, didn't it? He'd more than walked in her shoes. He'd taken the journey before she had, only his had been more dangerous, the outcome drawn out, his nightmares—he had to have had nightmares—surely more vivid.

"I don't know what to say." Leaning forward, she ran her lips over his chest, in part to give herself time to blink back her tears. "I downplayed what I was going through with my family, and although my older brother kept studying me, he didn't ask. In other words, you aren't the only one who kept things locked inside."

He was stroking her hair, soothing her, presenting her with his warmth, his life. Tears again burned her. "I—I don't want you feeling sorry for me. I don't."

"I didn't either when it was me on the receiving end."

Fine, she nearly said. *That's noble of you.* But before she could make that mistake, reality rolled over her. Although she wouldn't call him the silent and stoic Indian, he was a macho man in a macho world. Hadn't she seen countless riders puke before getting on the bull or bronc they'd drawn? None of them ever talked about the fear clamped around their bellies— just as Cougar hadn't told anyone he was afraid he would spend the rest of his life in a wheelchair.

"It's so complicated, isn't it?" she said and straightened. Let him see her tears after all. "That's why I'm going to compete tonight, so, hopefully, I can make things less complicated."

Instead of pointing out that she hadn't made any sense— which he had every right to do—he pushed the hair back from her cheek and planted a kiss on her forehead. "It's all right if you don't get out there again. That's what I want you to hear. I won't think any the less of you."

Instead of feeling strengthened by his words, he'd, maybe unwittingly, lain the most important thing on the table. He might not think less of her if she hung up her barrel-racing saddle and put her horses out to pasture, but she would.

And she wouldn't be able to hold up her head around him.

"What is it?" he prompted. "Are we back to where we started? You're comparing the way each of us faced our injuries?"

"I don't know where we are!" Much as she wanted to be in a different hemisphere from the one he was in, even more she wanted to give his cock a home. Her home. "Damnit, it doesn't have to be this complicated."

"No. It doesn't."

He was bringing her closer, pressing her against his body and making her terribly aware of the fabric she'd placed between her sex and his. Maybe he knew what she was thinking—and regretting—because he ground himself against her, forced her to back up, forced her to deal with frustration.

"I—I thought you had a lot to do."

"I do, starting with you."

"Just like that?" Torn between trying to shove him off her and leaving no doubt of her sudden and powerful need, she clung to him.

"Yeah, Jordan, just like that. You came on strong last night. It's my turn again."

She? Strong? On the brink of calling him a liar, images from the barn pushed past her barriers. He was right. She'd been the aggressor, right up until the time he threw her on the hay and took her missionary style. "What do you want?"

"You. Goddamnit, you."

Like him, she, too, was torn between the need that was taking huge chunks out of her sanity and the undeniable fact that they were taking things too fast. But when he lifted her and laid her out on his bed, nothing else mattered.

She reached for her jeans, but he grabbed her wrists and placed her hands over her head. He stretched out beside her, the pressure on her wrists making her feel small and helpless and desirable.

"You're an incredible woman with an incredible body."

"It's—it's standard issue."

"The hell it is. The way you turn me on—" Rolling toward her, he closed his mouth around a breast.

He nipped, nibbled, licked, and sucked. Within seconds she was writhing on the tangled sheets. He took her breast into his wet, warm cave. Lightning tiptoed from her mound to her pelvis. Then the sensation spread out, closing around her pussy and making her think of a wilderness storm with thunder booming, rain pounding down, lightning shattering the night.

What was it she'd always believed about needing lengthy foreplay? What was it she'd maintained about not being a cheap lay?

What the hell did either of those things matter?

"Cougar, Cougar, Cougar." The chant echoed off the metal walls.

He released her wrists, but she remained the way he'd positioned her, lost in the fantasy of being at his disposal. Pain in her captured nipple lifted her pelvis off the bed. But instead of trying to free herself from the sharp nip, she arched toward him and offered him everything. He closed his lip-covered teeth around her nipple and drew on it. Looking down at herself, she regarded the pale and stretched breast tissue. There was a grinding sensation in her pelvis, and her fingers kept reaching for something, anything. Her head rocked from side to side, and she sounded as if she were strangling.

When he released her breast, she cried out. He quieted her

by pressing his palm over her wet flesh. Then he turned his attention to her other breast. His weight held her down, kept her where and how he needed her to be.

"Yes, yes, yes," she chanted. "Oh, yes."

Her other breast was subjected to the same mix of pleasure and pain as the first. He bathed her, chewed lightly, suckled, drew her so deep inside him that she half believed he was fucking her there.

"Yes, yes, yes."

This time when he backed away, she found the courage and promise to wait with her body turned toward his and her vision rose-tinted.

Finally—yes, damnit, finally—he removed the garment she'd foolishly put on. The disrobing seemed to take forever, slow inch by slow inch being revealed. He was a powerful man, strong in ways that went far beyond muscle and bone. Next to him she felt like a feather, when she'd always believed herself equal to any man. She didn't want that anymore. She wanted to be imprinted with his masculinity, to be allowed to house him and maybe, please, to hear his secrets.

To trust him with hers.

When he dropped her jeans to the floor, she thought he would climb on top of her. Instead he ordered her to sit up. Obeying, she knelt on the bed and hugged herself. He stretched out a few inches away, his cock rising above his body.

"I have a rubber in the night stand."

I don't want to put it on. I need to feel you, to take your cum into me. But she did as he ordered. Once he had come, she would lick his cock and taste his offering.

Wondering at the wanton turn her mind had taken, she sat back on her haunches and waited for her next order.

"Get on top of me."

That she could do. Slowly—as slowly as she could, anyway—she straddled him, with his cock resting against her belly and her ass kissing his thighs. She clenched her fists to keep from touching him.

"Put my cock in you."

Just like that? Yes, she answered her own question, just like that. Made uncomfortable by his scrutiny, she nevertheless sheathed his cock with her hand while she inched forward and up. Running his tip over her labia nearly drove her crazy, but she did it again—and then once more. He was giving himself to her. She was presenting herself to him.

And nothing else mattered.

In the distance a diesel truck started up. She heard the faint murmur of male voices so deep that the tones became part of what she and Cougar were doing.

"Now. Do it."

Yes. Yes. Her fingers strong around his base held him in place as she skewered herself on his cock. Despite the pounding need to rush the union, she took him slow and smooth, all the way. When she couldn't absorb any more of him, she cautiously lowered herself until her buttocks closed around his crotch.

He grabbed her shoulders and pulled her forward. His cock shifted inside her, pressing where it had only touched before, demanding she concentrate on the change.

Down, down, down he guided her until she was afraid she would hurt him, but his relentless hold brought her even closer. Her hanging breasts brushed his chest. Then they were flat against him, and his hands were around her neck, and she was reaching behind her ass, and they were kissing—for the first time truly kissing.

Nothing mattered except the tender and intimate gesture. These were her lover's lips, the breath of a man unlike any she'd ever known, barriers knocked away, honest and vulnerable.

Then animal need slammed into her.

Growling, she sat up. He slapped her breasts with a stinging blow that fed the animal. Teeth clenched, she pressed her pelvis against him as though she could power through him to the bed. With his own teeth bared, he grabbed her nipples. Fighting and yet not fighting his control, she growled again. He started pumping into her, but it wasn't enough! More times than she could count, she pistoned herself. His relentless hold on her nipples added to the volcano boiling out of her.

Twice more he pulled her down so their bodies fused. By turn she struggled for freedom and wrapped herself tight around him. She sobbed and gasped, sounds she'd never before made exploding from her. Twice more his grip slackened enough to allow her to straighten. When she did, she pressed her palms against his chest while he did the same to her thighs.

And they fucked. Fucked until her every muscle screamed and darkness invaded.

She came, yelling out her joy. Instead of letting her rest, he thrust and pressed and pressured until, shuddering and sobbing, she came again.

The lights went back on. She'd started to be aware of more than her cunt when he rolled her over onto her side and then onto her back. Straddling her with his hands fisted in her hair, he relentlessly slammed her. His face turned red. He shoved, held the position, exploded.

So did she.

"I'm not going to be worth shit today," Cougar said. At the moment he was standing in the doorway between bath and bedroom, hair dripping, a towel dangling from his fingers as if modesty was the last thing on his mind.

Still in bed where her beaten and rewarded body insisted on staying, she stared at him. For the first time she took note of his scars. A small round one on his right knee spoke of arthroscopic surgery. A long, thin streak of white on his left forearm looked like something left over from a battle with a barbed-wire fence. He'd had stitches taken just below his collarbone. She debated asking him to turn around so she could take a complete inventory but wasn't sure she could count beyond five.

"I can't move," she admitted.

Lifting his muscular arms, he toweled his hair and dried his face. Hot damn, but he was put together like every woman's fantasy of a stud. "Seriously?" He threw the towel at her.

"Seriously."

"Then get some sleep. I'll check on you later and make sure you get ready in time—if you're going to compete."

Compete. Close the door on the fantasy I've been in since last night since the first time we'd touched. Face the Brahma that has taken up what might be permanent residence in my mind.

She could tell Cougar she'd changed her mind and know he would support her decision. In fact, he would probably applaud it.

But he hadn't run away from what surely had given him nightmares. True, he no longer risked getting killed by bull riding, but his life still revolved around the beasts. A careless move could place him too close to those deadly horns and hooves. No matter how careful he was, there was no way he could anticipate every danger.

"Think about it," he said. Walking proud and naked over to her, he leaned down and kissed her. Just kissed.

"Go," she finally managed. "You have to get to work."

"What you have to do is more important."

"Sleep? That's hardly—"

"No." He placed a finger over her mouth. "I don't think you're going to do much of that. Whatever you decide, I'll support it."

Will you? Can you really? If I can't face my demons, will that destroy what we've started?

8

Rampage and the other bulls were in the same corral Cougar and his men had unloaded them into the other night. Fortunately she'd overheard a couple of the hands talking about the tight time frame to get the stock to the next rodeo, and how their boss had decided to go to town for supplies now so they would be ready to roll. Right now she needed to be alone with the damn Brahma.

"How do you like living on the road?" she asked Rampage as she peered through the fence at the dozing bull. "Do you ever wish you were doing something else? Of course, maybe looking forward to grinding cowboys into the dirt makes up for everything."

If Rampage heard, he gave no indication. The longer she studied the massive but unmoving body, the harder it was to remember that this hay-burner was hardwired to attack—and, if possible, kill. Pushing her hair off her neck, she ambled around to the far side of the corral to get closer to her nemesis. When she was as close as she could get without wriggling under the fence, she placed her arms on the railing and rested her chin on the back of her hand.

"You look bigger than you did a minute ago," she informed Rampage. "Pretty much the damn biggest creature I've ever seen. Do you remember me?"

Another Brahma headed her way. If it came much closer, she would back away. Instead, after snorting at her, it turned toward Rampage. When maybe ten feet separated the two, Rampage's heavy head swung up. The two regarded each other, making her wonder about their brain capacities. These two lived together. Surely they were familiar with each other.

Familiar but not friendly, as witnessed by the mutual ground-pawing and bellowing. Cougar wouldn't keep them together if there was real danger of their attacking each other, but watching the bulls circle each other like playground bullies brought home the reality of their capacity for destruction.

"They're something else, aren't they?"

Startled by the woman's voice, she turned. Her fellow barrel racer Crystal was standing behind her.

"I do a little calf roping," Crystal said. "Throwing a calf to the ground and tying it is as close as I want to get to the big boys. I don't care how many times I see them"— she indicated the Brahmas—"they scare the hell out of me. What are you doing?"

"Watching." Deciding to get it all out in the open, she pointed at Rampage. "He's the one who got to me."

"No shit." Crystal joined her at the fence. "Look at that monster. He could have killed you."

"I know."

"Will you tell me why those damn macho bull riders do what they do? We women, we're smart enough not to jump in front of a charging locomotive. But not a man. Give them a challenge to their manhood, and they lose what brains they have."

"You really think so?"

"Not all men, but what other explanation is there?" Lips pressed together, Crystal shook her head. "Do you see women standing in line to climb on the back of these dung-caked beasts? Hell, no. We've got more sense."

Rampage and the other bull butted heads, backed off, and glared at each other.

Crystal gave her a rueful glance. "Basically we know enough to be scared shitless."

She hated spying on Cougar, but what Crystal had said compelled Jordan to study him as he and several other men moved the bulls to the rear of the bucking stalls in preparation for the evening's event. Although she'd seen this done before, the potential for danger still tightened her chest. True, the bulls had spent the day doing next to nothing instead of hell-bent determined to dislodge the idiot trying to ride them, but how could the handlers be sure something wouldn't set them off?

Cougar, astride his stallion, watched his bulls, his expression alert but calm. Even when someone spoke to him, he didn't turn his attention from the beasts. His quiet strength seeped into her.

This was a man who knew what he wanted to do with his life and had found a way to do it. In the wake of his own accident, he'd gone through a vital decision-making process. Instead of lamenting his reckless youth, he'd acknowledged that the life of a bull rider was no longer for him and had embraced the future.

And he deserved a woman who had also gotten her act together, instead of one incapable of seeing past finding a way to get her damn monkey off her back.

Shaking her head, she tried to convince herself that their relationship was too new for her to be thinking about spending the rest of her life with him, but she would be an idiot not to want to be bedded by—and bed—him. But that wasn't enough. There was a little thing called the future. Her plans and goals, whatever they were.

Her boots thudded on the packed dirt behind the arena, the sound seeming to echo what her heart was doing. But although she might be giving herself a heart attack, she kept going. She knew this world of strong men and leather, of horses and ten-gallon hats, and right now she couldn't imagine any other existence.

Was this why she'd decided to do this insane thing, because she didn't know how to be anything else?

No, damnit! She *had* to adjust and adapt just as Cougar had. She just wanted it to be her decision, and not something fear had forced her into.

Secure in the knowledge that no one would think twice if she climbed the wooden fencing and looked down at the bulls, she did so. Unlike the spacious corral they'd been in earlier, this enclosure kept the Brahmas closely bunched. They were restless and short-tempered, undoubtedly because they knew what was coming up. She became part of them, a small life-form caught in their current.

"You think you're pretty damn tough, don't you?" she asked Rampage. His heavy head swung up, and he stared at her. His small eyes were wet and reddened, his horns impossibly large. "You would love nothing more than kicking this cowgirl's butt again, wouldn't you? You've got her shaking in her boots and messing with her mind when she should be thinking about—about her future and a certain cowboy."

Feeling a tug on her ankle, she looked down to see Cougar staring up at her. The sounds, sights, and smells of the rodeo faded away. Even Rampage no longer mattered.

"What are you doing?" he asked.

"Ah, talking to an old friend."

Climbing effortlessly, he joined her. The time might come when her skin didn't heat when he came close, but that was far from the case now. She needed to feel his fingers on her, his damp breath between her breasts. He'd changed into his show outfit, which only added to the impact.

He indicated her own outfit, consisting of bright blue jeans and shirt, accented with a silver belt and buckle and a silver band in her blue hat. "You're going to compete tonight, aren't you?"

"Old habits die—" she started, and then she stopped herself. "Yeah, I am."

"Will you be able to go full out? Or will memories get the better of you?"

A loud snort spun her head back toward the bulls. Rampage was closer than he'd been before, head high and horns pointed at her. "I hope not. I need to replace them with something new. Something better."

He blanketed her hand with his, the gesture telling her he understood what she was going through. "Like what? Your fastest time ever?"

"No. I want to ride Rampage."

Nine hundred and ninety-nine people out of a thousand would call her a fool and refuse to let her—flat out, no argument. Instead, Cougar studied her with his midnight eyes. "A lot of cowboys have tried. Most have failed."

"I know. Believe me, I know. Cougar, I don't mean I want to try to ride to the bell. I don't have a death wish. But if I could sit on him while he's squeezed into a chute, if I could accomplish that simple thing . . ."

He lightly kissed her fingertips. "I understand."

Of course he did. He'd been down the same road. "You'd—you'll help me?"

"I'll make it happen. As for whether it'll help, only you can determine that."

* * *

A few minutes later Rampage had been loaded into one of the bucking chutes. Although several cowboys had shaken their heads, they hadn't said anything. If they'd asked her why she was doing this right before the night's events began, she would have explained that what she had in mind wasn't going to take long—but the ramifications would last the rest of her life.

"There's no cinch on him," Cougar explained. "He'll be less agitated without that pressing against his gonads."

"I know. I just want—hell, I don't know how to explain it."

"I'm not asking you to."

From her perch right above Rampage's back, she struggled to remind herself that she wasn't looking at some supernatural beast, but she'd never been this close to her nemesis before. She knew what the Brahma was capable of, damnit. Knew that no one, least of all his owner, trusted him.

"Whenever you're ready. He's not going to be able to move around much, but that won't stop him from trying to climb out of here. It's one of his favorite tricks."

If you knew this, why didn't you warn me?

Because you believe I need this.

She'd seen enough bulls leap, actually leap straight up, in the small enclosures. If a cowboy was on its back when that happened, the cowboy either rode out the explosion or bailed off by diving for the fence. She didn't want to do that.

"Jordan?"

"What?" With an effort, she took her attention off the bull. Cougar's gaze left no doubt that he was looking beneath her surface. Perhaps he could see all the way to her heart and nerves. She loved him. Just like that, she understood the meaning of the word in ways she never before had understood.

"Something is happening between us." He caressed the side

of her neck, leaving electrical sparks in his wake. "Something that goes beyond some incredible sex."

"Yes."

"I want to explore the possibilities, and I believe you do, too."

"Yes, I do." *If I can deal with this head trip of mine.*

"Take all the time you need." Leaning over the highest railing, he grabbed Rampage's horn and shook it—at least, he tried to. When Rampage didn't so much as twitch, he gave her a rueful smile and then winked.

The wink helped. A lot.

Knowing he would understand if she blocked him out of her mind, she swung a leg over the top of the corral. No matter how far she stretched, she couldn't get it over Rampage's back, so she kicked off and let go of the railing at the same time. Her butt landed on a hard spine, and her inner thighs made contact with what felt like pure muscle. She had nothing to hold on to. Nothing to do except think about the incredible thing she'd just done.

Rampage, under her. Rampage, squeezed into an enclosure designed to immobilize him, but still deadly.

She, her heart pounding like a jackhammer. She, scared and excited and in awe of the monster.

The bull's thick skin shuddered, putting her in mind of a horse trying to dislodge a fly. Rampage pawed the ground.

"Do you know who I am?" She tapped Rampage's shoulder to make sure she had his attention. "Maybe not. You have so many grudges against so many humans."

Rampage snorted, the sound rumbling up from deep inside his great chest. She thought of thunder rolling through the night.

"I'm impressed. Got it? I'm impressed. You're an amazing creature."

On the tail of his second bellow, Rampage flung his head back. Because she'd sensed what he was about to do, she leaned away, evading the horns. *Shit! Shit.*

"All right," she whispered, once she'd remembered how to breathe. "Duly noted. I won't take anything for granted."

Yet another bellow rolled through him. The sound seemed to press against her buttocks and thighs. She wondered if an avalanche felt and sounded like this. What would it be like to try to outrun tons of deadly free-falling snow?

"Magnificent. Absolutely magnificent, big boy."

Her thighs were starting to ache from being forced into a near split, but she barely paid attention because Rampage's heat was soaking through her jeans and imprinting her with the reality of his strong heart.

"Do you know you have a heart? Maybe you're all instinct. Sleeping, eating, fucking, fighting what you don't like. Does that sum it up?"

Once again a subtle tightening of his neck muscles alerted her. This time when he flung back his head, his horns came so close she could have grabbed them. Although he was only a few years old, she thought of the centuries his kind had been on the earth. Someday there might not be any more rodeos, but Rampage's children and grandchildren would still be here—oblivious to man's self-importance.

"I envy you. I never thought I'd say that, but I do. No one's ever going to push you around. You are what you are. You exist, simply exist."

Rampage repeatedly pawed the ground. His muscles rolled under her like some amusement-park ride. The difference was that she had no brakes, and the ride wouldn't end when the operator decided. This was real life, heart, muscle, bone, a tiny brain that wanted nothing to do with humans who foolishly believed themselves his equal. The moment Rampage and the other bulls were free of this man-made prison, they became the aggressors and sometimes killing machines.

"I'm thinking too much. Hard to believe, given the need to concentrate, isn't it? You know, I think I want to be like you, the neighborhood bully. Feed you, and leave you alone, and you're a happy camper. Mess with you, and you take no prisoners."

Still pawing, Rampage started rocking from side to side, perhaps trying to smash her legs against the boards. Lifting them, she rested them along the back of his neck.

"End of the ride, old buddy." With that she dove for the railing. Just as her hands closed around it, Rampage reared, his front hooves inches from her. His bellow made her ears ring.

Strong hands gripped her and pulled her out of the way. Her belly dragged over the railing, and she kicked to help propel herself forward. Her boots struck Rampage, but she didn't stick around to discover where she'd landed a pathetic blow.

"Had enough?" Cougar asked. With one hand he clung to the railing. The other held her against him.

"Oh, yeah. Quite enough."

A few feet away, Rampage pounded the ground like some out-of-control jackhammer. She'd sat on him! Sat and talked and felt. Discovered.

"Thank you," she whispered and rested her head against Cougar's chest.

"You learned what you needed to?"

Straightening, she looked into the eyes of maybe the one man on Earth who understood. "Yes."

"Now what?"

"Now I get ready to ride."

There was more than one kind of ride. The first had occurred earlier when she'd ridden Trixie to a second-place finish, secure in the belief that she could coax an even faster run out of her mare during tomorrow night's final.

As for the second—

"Jordan?"

Cougar's voice turned her around. The bridle she held started to slide out of her hand, prompting her to clutch it. Believing she wouldn't see him until long after the show was over, she'd bedded Trixie down but had taken the bridle with her so she could work some lubricant into the leather. Instead of going to her place, she'd wandered back toward the arena complex. Although the fans had left, most of the participants were around the concession stand drinking beer and dissecting everyone's performance.

"How did you find me?" she asked.

"Maybe instinct." Taking the bridle from her, he looped it over his neck. Then, obviously not caring who else saw, he took her in his arms and bent her back until she clung to him to keep from falling. Her legs slid between his, and she felt cradled by him.

Alive.

Instinct closed her mouth in on his. The same primitive reaction propelled her pelvis toward his. He was aroused, as turned on as she felt. When he parted his lips, she did the same and welcomed his tongue into her. It circled her mouth and then rolled in and out, igniting memories of another kind of invasion. Familiar heat spun through her.

"Get a room!" a man yelled.

"Do it fast," another added. "Looks like the two of you are going to be busy all night."

"Are we?" Cougar asked as he helped her straighten. Instead of releasing her, he pressed on her buttocks and kept her close. If not for their clothes, they already would have been fucking. "Going to be busy all night?"

Taking his face in her hands, she looked up at him. Even as her pelvis gave out a message she intended to explore for as long as the two of them lasted, she faced the world beyond this moment. "You're going to be leaving as soon as things wind up tomorrow, aren't you?"

"I have to. The bulls are—"

"Committed to the next rodeo. I know."

"Not just that one. They're booked clear up to the finals. And depending on how they perform through the rest of the season, I might be taking a couple of them to the finals."

"Living on the road."

"It'll quiet down some during the winter, but I'm going to be traveling some, looking to replace some of the stock."

"Not Rampage?"

"No." His smile lasted no more than a second. "He'll be around for several more years. What about you? Are you going to try to qualify for the finals?"

A few days ago she hadn't dared look beyond trying to face her demons. But she had, damnit. If she was ever going to make her mark in the barrel-racing world, this was the time to do it.

If.

Not caring who saw, she rested her hands on his hips. They hadn't said anything about a future together. This thing between them was too new, and she'd had too much personal baggage to get rid of.

"Don't," he warned and removed her hands.

"You don't want—"

"I don't trust myself where you're concerned."

"You don't want—"

"Oh, I want, in spades." His hard and hot gaze left no doubt of his meaning. "But if I go to one rodeo and you go another, the only way I'm going to handle it is by walking away from you, now. I'm not going to stop you, Jordan. Not even going to try. I pulled my life back together, so I think I know what you've just gone through. I don't want your effort to be for nothing."

"You think I should—"

"I think you should do what you want to with your life and not be pulled from it by what's been going on between us. If you do, the time will come when you regret it—and resent me."

Epilogue

It was probably close to three A.M. Because she hadn't bothered with anything except her socks, Jordan's feet were silent on the packed gravel. Although the small rocks dug into her heels, she gave the discomfort scant attention.

She'd tried to sleep. Damnit, she really had.

But as she'd suspected, the answers she'd been seeking had kept her awake. As for whether she would learn more now—

He wasn't in his rig after all. Instead Cougar was sitting in a lawn chair near it. Only a few lights had been left on to illuminate the grounds. As a consequence, if she hadn't memorized his contours, she wouldn't have known that the shadow belonged to him.

Maybe he knew the same thing about her, because he nodded when she drew close and indicated she could sit in the chair next to him. He was barefoot and shirtless.

Had he put out the other chair because he knew she would come? Maybe he'd only been hoping.

"I love this time of night," she said, sitting down and stretching her weary legs. "The world has gone away, leaving me with my thoughts."

"You aren't the only one who's been thinking."

"And?" How she wanted to touch him! But not yet.

"No matter what I want, the decision is yours."

"Which gets down to what do I want to do with my life, right?"

"Right. You faced your demons. You can go forward."

"Thanks to you. If you hadn't let me get on Rampage's back—"

"I believe you would have gotten to this point without me or Rampage. All he and I did, maybe, was get you there faster."

"You really believe that?"

He didn't answer. Unless she'd been mistaken, he hadn't moved a muscle since inviting her to join him in the dark.

"It's strange," she said. "Ever since Rampage rearranged my leg bone, I've thought of little else. But not tonight while I was trying to fall asleep." Although her legs threatened to collapse, she stood and moved in front of Cougar. "Tonight I thought about you. Us."

Gazing into the eyes of the man lost in the night, she unsnapped her shirt and pulled it off her shoulders. Then she held it out, not breathing until he accepted the gift. She hadn't bothered to put back on her bra after getting out of bed. Neither had she bothered with panties, a fact made clear as she stepped out of her jeans.

"I've been doing the same thing," he said and took the jeans from her.

"If you want me, if you want to explore this *thing* between us, I'd like to follow you and the bulls." Her voice was thick with unspent tears and fear more powerful than she'd ever felt. What if he rejected her?.

He dropped her clothes to the ground. "What about competing?"

"If I can get entered in time, I will. But it isn't a priority."

Instead of asking what her priority was, he took her hands and pulled her close. "It's an insane life. I don't really have a home."

"I don't need one." Tears trickled down her cheeks. "Just— just you."

"What about your life?"

"You—you're my life. As long as I have that, everything else will fall into place."

Standing, he lifted her in his arms. Clinging to his neck, she pressed her cheek against his chest as he carried her into his sleeping quarters. A nightlight in the bathroom was the only illumination.

"Welcome home," he said and laid her on his bed.

Cowboy in Paradise

P.J. Mellor

Special thanks to Jody Payne, at Evensong Farms, for sharing her knowledge of horses. Any mistakes are entirely mine.

1

―――――――

"So tell me, just how drunk do you have to be to have sex in a PortaPotti?"

Tyler Last swallowed and set his longneck bottle on the bar, the thought of his excesses forming a knot in the pit of his stomach. "Too damn drunk." He fixed his gaze on the rodeo clown's smiling face. "I'm through. With everything. As of right now. I already sold my ranch and packed my truck." He picked at the label on the sweating bottle. "I'm only thirty-two, and I'm the old man of the circuit." He shrugged. "And I'm sick of getting my ass kicked, hardly able to crawl out of bed the next morning."

"You're never in the same bed the next morning."

"Yeah, well, there's that, too." He tipped the bottle to his lips again and then returned the smile of the redhead at the end of the bar. Maybe outright quitting was too hasty. Tapering off might be easier. Throwing money on the smooth surface, he said, "See you around," and headed toward the woman. After all, a guy had to ease into the turning-over-a-new-leaf thing.

* * *

Tyler rolled out of bed and walked naked into the bathroom. With a cautious glance at the redhead sprawled across the mattress, he closed the door until it clicked and then turned on the light.

Damn. He scrubbed his face with his hands, forking them through his hair. He'd done it again. Other than the fact that she had red hair—and he could attest to the fact that it was natural—he had no idea what she looked like. Wouldn't recognize her if he saw her again.

Which he definitely did not plan to do.

Dropping the used condom in the trash, he thanked god he at least hadn't been too far gone to remember the condom when he looked at the filthy mess of her bathroom. He glared at his bleary reflection in the dirty mirror and stepped into his jeans. No doubt about it, he'd sunk about as low as he was going to go.

It was way past time for a serious attitude and lifestyle adjustment.

He took a cautious glance over his shoulder, ten minutes later, at the darkened house and eased onto the leather seat of his pickup.

Where the hell was he? His stomach clenched. It took a minute to remember and get his bearings. Damn, he hated when that happened. And it happened too often of late.

The powerful engine of his Silverado roared to life. With a pop of the clutch, he headed for the southbound highway, towing all his worldly possessions: a leather satchel of clothing, his newest horse trailer, and his only friend in the whole world, Jim, his palomino quarter-horse stallion.

The pink glow of dawn feathered the horizon by the time he spotted his exit. Paradise Beach, Population 1312.

"Now thirteen hundred and thirteen," he muttered, "and I sure as hell hope it's my lucky number."

The road to his grandmother's place looked different. More new buildings and homes than he remembered. He took the back approach, coming to a stop behind the stables.

After lowering the ramp, he slapped the horse's flank and gave a short whistle. "C'mon, Jim, we're here."

The horse did not budge.

"Jim! Yah! Back it up, bud." He gave a short yank on Jim's tail.

The horse crowded closer to the front of the trailer.

"Damnit, Jim! I'm tired. I need some sleep." He wedged between horse and wall and walked to stare face-to-face. "Don't do this to me again. Do you understand what I'm saying?"

The horse snickered and turned its head.

He grasped Jim's ears and forced the animal to face him. "Back. Up."

Tyler threw his weight against the horse's shoulder and pushed, but Jim had him on weight.

Working up a sweat, he finally convinced Jim it was in his best interest to get out of the trailer and into the stable. After feeding the horse and making sure he was comfortable in the stall, Tyler headed toward the house and the welcoming light from his grandmother's kitchen window.

It took a minute to locate his key to the back door. The second he stepped in, inhaling the familiar scents, he knew everything would be all right.

"Sonny?" His grandmother's chirpy voice echoed down the hall. "That you?"

"Yeah, Gram," he answered, already bent in front of her double-door refrigerator to look for leftovers.

Steps sounded in the hall, but he had his eye on a triple-layer chocolate cake and was now looking for milk.

"Shut that door, you heathen, and come give your granny some sugar!"

He immediately complied, hugging her close to his heart and bending to place a smacking kiss on her soft, powdery smelling cheek.

Loosening his embrace, he stepped back and looked at the woman who'd been like a second mother to him. "Gram!" He made a big deal of perusing her, not entirely sure he was comfortable with the feminine peignoir set. "Lookin' sexy, there! Got a new beau?" He loved teasing her and waited for her playful swat.

Instead, she chewed her lip.

"As a matter of fact, I have more than that." She motioned toward the hall door, where a tall, distinguished-looking man with salt-and-pepper hair stood in a robe.

"This is Mason," Gram said. "My, ah, husband."

Tyler paused and then set the carton of milk on the granite counter. "Stop clowning around, Gram."

The man—Mason—stepped forward, hand outstretched.

Tyler looked at it. With hands like that, he doubted the guy had ever done a day of hard labor in his life. Probably didn't even know how to ride.

He took the hand and held on. Best to establish his territory from the get-go. "Tyler Last."

Mason gripped his hand and didn't break eye contact. "Mason Edwards."

Tyler tightened his grasp.

Mason reciprocated.

The old guy had balls, he would give him that.

"Oh, for pity's sake," Gram groused, "would you two stop your pissing contest?"

Tyler dropped the older man's hand and stepped back to the counter to pour a big glass of milk. "Soon as I polish off a hunk of cake and drink this, I'll be heading upstairs to bed. I need at least a few hours of sleep."

"That's a good idea," Gram said, walking to rise and kiss his cheek. "We're going to do the same thing. Our flight leaves this afternoon."

"Flight?" he asked around a mouthful of cake.

Gram nodded, blue eyes bright. "Yes. We're going on a deepwater diving trip for our honeymoon."

"Since when do you dive?" Could Mason be trying to kill off his grandmother to get her money and property?

"We took lessons," Mason piped in. "We're both certified deepwater divers."

"I thought you were into parasailing these days," Tyler said to Gram. Parasailing she could do right there in Paradise Cove.

"Nah—got bored with that." Gram batted her eyelashes at Mason, and Tyler's recently ingested cake threatened to reappear. "Let's go back to bed, Pookey."

Pookey?

By the time Tyler put his dishes in the dishwasher, he heard a suspicious sound and walked to the hall.

"Please, Lord, don't let that be what I think it is," he muttered.

He stood there and listened. Damn. Looked like he was sleeping out in the stable with Jim.

His grandmother was having sex.

2

Things were definitely heating up. Pushing wakefulness aside, Tyler reached for his elusive lover. She licked his face. All over. Then whinnied. Whinnied?

He jerked awake and found himself eye to eye with Jim. He shoved away the horse and stood, adjusting his jeans.

"Shut up," he said, pointing at Jim, and then headed for the house. Celibacy was more difficult than he'd imagined.

Banging on the bathroom door greeted Tyler, half an hour later, when he turned off the shower.

"Sonny! Get out here and kiss me good-bye. And I have something I need to tell you before I leave."

Maybe she and good old Mason weren't really married. That would be good. One less thing to worry about.

"Be right out." After a cursory drying, he stepped into boxers and a clean pair of jeans. Still buttoning the fly, he opened the door. "What is it?"

"Oh, my Lord! What happened? You look like you've had the snot kicked out of you!" Gram tugged on his arm and turned him to look at his back. "Have you seen a doctor?"

"Yes. I'm fine." He glanced over his shoulder, able to see the tops of the welts the redheaded she-cat had made on his back, on top of the bruises he already sported from his last rodeo performance. "That's one of the reasons I'm retiring." He bent to scoop a T-shirt from his duffel bag and slipped it on. "What did you want to tell me?"

"Well, there's no other way but to come right out with it." She paused. "I'm a businesswoman, as of last month."

"Care to explain?" He sat down on the hall bench, pulling his grandmother down with him. He sensed there was more and wished she would just spit it out.

"I went into a partnership with Roger Ferris. You remember him, don't you, Betsy Ferris's boy?" She took a deep breath. "Anyway, he's become quite the real-estate tycoon around Paradise Beach. In exchange for selling him some of my beachfront property, he made me his partner! Isn't that wonderful?" She smiled up at him, not looking like it was all that wonderful.

"Gram, what are you not telling me? I know you have a plane to catch, and I have some serious beach time scheduled, so I—"

"That's what I'm trying to tell you, damnit!" Gram's hand flew to her mouth as though she was shocked at what it had just said. "I mean, I know you've always loved the peace and quiet of Paradise Cove, and, well, it may not be, ah, as quiet or peaceful as you remember.

"Roger and I are building a luxury beach community on the cove. Beginning almost next door and running along most of the beach. My house will ultimately be used as the clubhouse." She peeked through her eyelashes and shrugged. "Unless any of my heirs want it. And, well, since my house is sort of part of everything now, I have to abide by the deed restrictions of the community." Her shoulders slumped. "What I'm trying to tell you is livestock is forbidden."

"Meaning?" Although he had a sneaking suspicion of where she was headed.

"No horses."

"Too late. Jim's already in your stable."

She nodded. "I assumed as much. What I'm trying to tell you is you're going to have to keep him hidden during your visit."

"Hannah!" Mason's voice boomed down the hall. "We need to hit the road if we want to get lunch before we check in."

Gram stood and gripped Tyler in a fierce hug. "I hope you find the answers you need while you're here," she whispered, her peppermint-scented breath calming him as much as it had as a child.

His grandmother had underestimated the potential volume of the construction noise, Tyler decided a few minutes later when he stepped onto the beach. With the hammering, sawing, and tractor and backhoes in operation, he could scarcely hear himself think. And what was that awful squawking?

He walked down to the edge of the water and looked at the flurry of activities. In front of it all, at the edge of the beach, a scrawny, black-garbed character paced, yelling into a bullhorn. He squinted. What in the hell was she wearing?

Damn. A smile crept across his face, despite the irritation of all the noise. She was dressed as the grim reaper.

Meg Holder gripped the bullhorn in her sweating hand and did her best to disguise her voice. "Stop the construction! Now! Paradise Beach is for everyone to enjoy, not just the privileged few! Stop the construction or face the consequences of your sins!" She tried for a maniacal laugh, but inhaled spit and went into a coughing spasm instead.

Wiping her palms on her costume, she caught a glimpse of her watch. Yikes! It was past time to head home for a quick shower if she ever hoped to get to work.

Her Miata was beyond hot in its hidden parking place. After a quick glance around, she shed her grim-reaper attire, stuffed it in the trunk, and hopped in the car. The skin on her back and thighs, exposed by her white halter top and denim shorts, immediately protested the feel of hot leather. Even her teeth were hot.

Thirty minutes later she took a turn on two wheels and screeched to a stop in her allotted parking space. A glance at her watch confirmed she'd just made it on time. Again.

"Morning, Mr. Ferris!" she called as she breezed through the front door, baring her teeth in a smile.

"Meg." He nodded and made a big deal of looking at the clock. "Perhaps you should try setting your alarm for an earlier time."

And perhaps you should stick this job where the sun doesn't shine. Of course, she couldn't say that. She needed the job. But if the lottery ticket in her purse was a winner, she was so out of there. The first thing she would do would be to buy up all the property along Paradise Cove and then tear down the high-priced tenement her boss was building.

She sighed. Unfortunately, for now she was stuck in a thankless job, barely making her bills and working for a boss that made Attila the Hun look attractive.

Attila—rather, Roger—cleared his throat, drawing her attention.

"Didn't we forget something, Megan?" He glanced pointedly at the empty coffeemaker. "Coffee?"

"No, thanks," Meg replied, dropping her purse into the drawer of her desk. "Too much coffee makes you jittery, you know."

He made a sound like a growl. Coffee also made you irritable, she thought as she got up to make the stupid coffee.

Terra, Roger's personal—and she took the position to an all-new level—assistant, shot Meg a condescending, from-the-teeth-out smile.

Meg glared at her. Everyone knew Terra only got the job because she let Roger know she had no problems with a little slap and tickle behind closed doors.

Meg shuddered. No job on Earth would be worth having sex with Roger Ferris. Yuck.

An eternity later, it was finally quitting time. She turned off her computer and switched the phones to the answering service. Bent beneath her desk to retrieve her purse, she heard *Attila* call her name.

"We're taking off now," Roger said to Meg, while at the same time smiling at his bimbo next to him. "Can I trust you to remember to lock up this time, after you dump all the trash?"

"Sure." *But I'll need a bigger bag for Terra.* "No problem."

Without a backward glance, the two of them left.

"You're welcome. Thanks so much!" she said to the empty doorway. "You have a fabulous evening, too."

After her daily trip to the dumpster, she locked the office and headed for Paradise Cove.

Everyone on the construction site left early on Friday, so there was no need to don the sweltering costume.

The sun was setting by the time she finished her dinner and a quick shower. Clad in a tropical-print, gauze wrap skirt and halter top, she padded barefoot onto the sand of Paradise Cove, blanket draped over her arm.

Tonight, as always, she wondered how many nights she would have before access was closed to her and so many others.

Pushing the gloomy thought from her mind, she sat on her blanket and reached into her thermal bag for a wine cooler. She twisted off the top and took a drink, watching the brilliant colors of the sunset.

Was it wrong to pray for a winning lottery ticket? Anxiety

gripped her chest, thundered through her entire body. Wait. What she felt was more than anxiety.

She blinked twice, sure she was imagining. That couldn't be a cowboy on a golden horse riding down the beach, glowing in the waning sunset.

Could it?

3

Tyler didn't want to think about how happy he was to see another human being. Gram and Mason hadn't even been gone twenty-four hours, and he was already desperate for conversation.

He pulled back on Jim's reins, slowing to a trot, and appreciated the view.

A woman with dark, shiny hair sat alone on a blanket on the beach. In the shadows it was difficult to see her face, but he knew without a doubt she was pretty.

Jim chose that moment to do his show step, prancing sideways down the beach. He leaned close to the horse's ear. "Cut it out. I'm fine. I know how to talk to women. Just get me over there."

In response, Jim reared up on his hind legs. It was a pose they'd done many times, but tonight it embarrassed Tyler. He pushed down on the pommel. "Damnit, Jim! Now just walk," he said when the horse returned all four hooves to the sand.

The sight of the horse and rider, silhouetted by the sunset, took Meg's breath away. They were magnificent—so picturesque they could've been a movie poster.

She hurried to close her mouth and appear nonchalant as they approached.

"Howdy." The cowboy tipped his white hat.

Did he really say "howdy"? Before she could respond, the horse executed what looked remarkably like a bow.

"Did your horse just bow?" It had to be a dream. Real cowboys and horses didn't do things like that.

Teeth glinted. "Yes, ma'am, he did." The man stroked the horse's pale mane and then patted its golden neck.

Leather creaked. The cowboy dismounted, his expression unreadable, and stood by the horse's head,

Meg struggled to regulate her breathing. Before her stood the living, breathing embodiment of her every fantasy.

The horse nuzzled the man's shoulder and pushed his back with enough force to make him stumble.

"Cut it out, Jim!" He swatted at the horse.

"You named your horse Jim?"

He jammed his hands into the front pockets of his jeans and rocked back on his heels to peer up at her from beneath his hat brim. "What would you have named him?"

She thought for a moment. "I don't know." She shrugged. "Silver?"

He grinned, teeth again flashing in the emerging moonlight. "But he's a golden palomino, not silver. I think Goldie would sound sort of sissy for a stallion."

She laughed and he joined in. He had a nice laugh.

Without invitation he sat on the blanket and placed his hat on his bent knee.

"Hi," he said, his voice warm and intimate.

"I don't remember seeing you here before." She shifted an inch or two toward the edge of the blanket and concentrated on her breathing. Dang, he smelled good. She swallowed in an effort to prevent drooling.

"That makes two of us." He reclined on one elbow, like he was posing for a calendar. "My grandmother owns the place on the bluff, up yonder." He pointed toward Hannah Gardner-Edwards's house. "I used to spend every summer here. If I'd met you, I'd have spent even more time here." He closed the gap between them. "I'm Tyler."

Her breath fisted in her chest. Shoot, shoot, shoot. *He* was the grandson Hannah talked about fixing her up with? If only she'd known. Hard on that thought came another more depressing one. Now, with her grim-reaper persona, getting to know him could be risky. A glance at his tan, handsome face sent a shot of yearning through her.

It might work. Thoughts of her *Powers of Seduction* book came to mind. *Don't give too much away on the first meeting. Make him work for it.* She mustered a weak smile at his introduction and said, "I'm not."

She held her breath, relaxing only when he widened his smile, as opposed to getting up and running into the night from the weirdo on the beach.

"You're going to tell me your name, aren't you?" He leaned closer. His minty breath bathed her heated lips. "Or am I going to have to kiss it out of you?"

Was he for real? Did lines like that actually work? Then again, this was a ships-passing-in-the-night kind of thing. Did it really matter?

Running her tongue over her dry lips was purely instinctual, but Tyler growled deep in his throat as though she'd done something erotic. So, she did it again.

"Better men than you have tried and failed," she lied when she found her voice.

He smiled against her mouth. "I doubt that," he said, his

words vibrating her mouth an instant before his lips took possession.

She doubted it, too.

She would like to think she opened her mouth to stop him, but she knew better. He deepened the kiss, the warm smoothness of his tongue tangoing with hers as he lowered her to the blanket.

Good thing she was laying down or else she would have collapsed in a boneless pile of need. She closed her eyes tighter. If he was a dream, she didn't want to wake up before the good part.

His calloused hands slid up her rib cage, grazing the sides of her breasts—making them heavy and aching—to settle beneath her hair. His knuckles bumped against the back of her neck while he worked the tie of her halter top.

Her heart began beating double-time, her breathing shallow. What they were doing was so not her style. But what had being herself gotten her? Her lack of a love life was what demanded she buy the seduction book in the first place. If she didn't use the tips, what was the point?

Within seconds she was bare to the waist. Cool Gulf breeze caressed her breasts, tightening her nipples.

She should protest, she knew. And she might if she could form a coherent sentence. Which was really hard to do with his hot mouth devouring her right breast while his calloused hand kneaded the left one. Dang, it felt good.

Tingling started at her toes and worked its way up, surging moisture between her legs. It would be so embarrassing to climax from just a kiss. But it had been so long since she'd felt any kind of arousal. She gripped his firm buttocks through the worn denim and squeezed, attempting to pull him over for more intimate contact.

The horse whinnied and stomped, vibrating the sand.

Tyler stopped midsuckle, his back stiffening.

"I have to go." In one movement he tugged her top into place and hopped to his feet. He tipped his hat. "It's been a pleasure meeting you."

"But—" Was it something she did?

He took a few running steps to vault into the saddle.

And he would have vaulted into the saddle, had the horse not taken a side step at the last second. Instead, jean-clad rear met hard-packed sand with a thud.

Until that moment, she'd never heard a horse laugh. She bit back a smile and picked up her wine cooler.

Cheeks burning, Tyler stood and dusted himself off. Jerking Jim's reins, he concentrated on putting one foot in front of the other. Jim, damn him, lagged back until Tyler thought he would rip out the horse's teeth if he tugged any harder. After a few more steps Jim followed docilely back to the stables.

"You made me look stupid out there, you know," he told Jim, back in his stall, as he pulled off the saddle. In reply, the horse snuffled. "Yeah, I know, but old habits die hard. One kiss and I went into autopilot. Thanks for reining me in. I meant what I said. I'm turning over a new leaf."

The horse snorted.

Tyler returned to the empty house, took a quick shower, and then stretched out naked on the cool sheets.

His first day as a new man, and what did he accomplish? He almost scored another one-night stand—the very thing he had vowed to stop. No more anonymous sex.

And he'd been made a fool of by his horse. That wasn't new. It was one of the reasons he'd decided to retire. Jim was smarter than him; he began refusing to go into the arena quite a while before Tyler's decision to retire. They both knew it was time to move on.

His thoughts swung back to his mystery woman; memory

of her sweetly scented soft skin had him hard in record time. He shifted on the sheets and then did something he hadn't done in years. He took matters into his own hand.

Every inch of skin on his body was on fire. Her heady scent again filled his nostrils. Would she have touched him like this? He cupped his balls, rubbing the pad of his thumb across the sensitive skin while his other hand gripped his iron-hard cock. At first the strokes were slow. He increased the pressure and speed, his breath coming harder and faster, his strokes emulating his mystery lover's responsive body.

One thought of her, poised above him, took him to the brink.

Muscles tightened from his feet up the backs of his legs to his butt. His back arched. His release slammed into him. He shuddered and drifted off to sleep only to awaken a little while later, tangled in the wet sheets, hard and needy again.

He looked at the mess he'd made earlier and groaned. There was only one thing left to do.

Laundry.

Don't be a tease by withholding sex. Don't be shy. It's a safe bet your target is more turned on than you by the prospect of physical gratification.

Meg's cheeks heated. Her guilty glance swept the office as she shut the *Powers of Seduction* book and tucked it safely into her tote.

She'd been bold—as least, she thought she had. What made Tyler run?

The chime on the door sounded. Tyler walked in in bold, magnificent, living flesh and blood.

If she were the fainting type, she was sure she'd be on the floor.

Mortified he would reveal that they had met, she slumped lower in her desk chair and hid behind the computer monitor. How on earth had he found her?

Tyler glanced her way, then zeroed in on tacky Terra. It wasn't a stretch to imagine what drew his attention.

Terra shoved her boobs together with her upper arms and leaned over her desk. Probably on the off-chance he hadn't seen all her assets. "May I help you?" she purred in her imitation sex-kitten voice.

To his credit, Tyler didn't seem to be struck mute by Terra's obvious flirting. He removed his hat and nodded in greeting. "Roger Ferris in?"

"Did you have an appointment, Mr. . . . ?"

"Last. Tyler Last. I'm Hannah Gardner-Edwards's grandson." He looked past her to the door of Roger's office. "I really do need to speak with Mr. Ferris. On my grandmother's behalf."

Terra slumped back in her chair, her collagen-enhanced lips in a pout she no doubt practiced in the mirror. "Sure. Go on in."

As soon as the door clicked shut, Meg shot out of her chair. "I just remembered I need to, ah, pick up some doughnuts and, um, go to the post office." She grabbed her tote and fished for her keys as she walked to the entrance, one eye on Roger's door. "I'll be back in a while."

"But who will answer the phone? Take messages? Make appointments? Meg, what if—"

"Don't worry! You'll be fine." She had to get out of there.

Tyler frowned at the sound of a familiar voice coming from the outer office, then looked down at the model of the beach community. What had he just noticed before he started listening to the voices? Oh, yeah. "There's no public beach access."

Roger Ferris nodded and leaned back in his executive chair, fingers tented. "It's a gated community. Don't you think public beach access would negate that?"

Tyler regarded the weasel for a moment before responding. "In Texas it's illegal to have a private beach."

"Who said anything about a private beach?"

"In effect, that's what you're doing by not having public beach access."

"The public can always access the beach," Roger assured him with a smirk. "By water." At Tyler's look, he went on. "The law states no private beach, which means it has to be accessible. It *is* accessible."

The snake in the grass had a point. Damn him.

Without a word, Tyler nodded, put on his hat, and walked out of the office. Maybe he should talk to the grim reaper.

The blonde bimbo tried to waylay him again, but he kept walking. The dark-haired girl was gone. He could escape.

Outside he shook his head and resettled his Stetson. There was a time, not long ago, when he would have taken what the blonde offered.

Images of the mystery woman on the beach again drifted through his mind.

He didn't even know her name. Why did he feel so connected?

The blonde was more the type he'd always been attracted to, yet she left him cold. Hell, he hadn't even noticed the other one, except that she had dark hair and, for an instant, his heart had tripped at the thought of running into the one woman who had captured his interest.

No doubt about it, in his mind he'd already cut a filly from the herd.

4

"Hell, no! We won't go! Hell, no! We won't go!" Sweat trickled beneath the black grim reaper's garb, sticking Meg's T-shirt to her heated skin. "Public beach means public access! Save the beach!" she yelled into the bullhorn.

The Texas sun beat down as hot as it had since her arrival two hours ago. Weren't the construction workers ever going to pack up for the day, so she could leave?

A movement caught her peripheral vision. Tyler! And he was headed straight for her. For a moment she stood, admiring the sure stride, the long gait, and the lean hips, while he steadily closed the distance between them.

She turned to run, but he was quicker. A hard hand clamped around her arm and held fast.

"Who are you and why are you so determined to stop construction?" he asked, peering down into the eye holes in her mask as though he could see right to her soul. "We need to talk."

Hot and tired, not to mention sexually frustrated, thanks to him, she made a growling sound and tugged to free her arm. He held on.

She really hated to do it, but if he found out who she was, he could jeopardize everything. Thoughts of her embarrassment on the beach Friday night gave her strength.

With a mighty swing she whacked him in the head with her bullhorn.

He fell to his knees but was obviously unhurt.

Hefting her tunic, she grabbed her sign and sprinted for the safety of her car, relieved that no footsteps followed.

Tyler got to his feet, rubbing the spot where the edge of the bullhorn hit. Lucky for him, he had a hard head.

Behind him construction noise dwindled as the workers put away their tools for the day. He glanced at the setting sun, anticipation making him forget the grim reaper.

Tonight he would discover the name of the future mother of his children. Or have a hell of a good time trying.

Meg dabbed perfume in her cleavage—well, what cleavage she had, anyway. Compared to tacky Terra, she was practically flat.

Excitement sizzled through her veins. She patted the seduction book and said a little prayer. It'd been so long since she'd had sex, she was almost giddy. She picked up the giant economy-sized bottle of chilled wine, two glasses, and headed for the beach.

The double handful of condoms she'd tucked into her bra gave her bustline an interesting, though lumpy, appearance and scratched with each step.

Finally she reached her destination. She set the bottle and glasses aside and spread her blanket on the sand, then sat down to wait. Moonlight gilded the water. Tonight the beauty escaped her; the waves did not work their soothing magic. Each lap on the shore was another minute she waited alone.

She felt the vibration before she saw them. Rider and horse moved as one entity, coming ever closer with each powerful beat.

Moonlight bronzed Tyler's bare chest, his powerful muscles rippling the awesome expanse of smooth skin. Atop his golden head was the ever-present hat. As he drew closer, she saw he wore cutoff jeans and . . . boots?

The horse stopped. Tyler alighted in one graceful movement to stand before her in all his magnificent glory. Wow. She hoped she didn't blow her chance.

Her gaze traveled hungrily over his incredible body, causing her to worry about her physical shortcomings. Even his legs were beautiful.

"Nice boots," she said and then winced. *Smooth, Meg, smooth.*

Tyler appeared not to notice. His grin flashed white. "You like 'em? They're my beach boots."

"Beach boots?" Was he kidding?

"Yep. Had 'em made special just to wear here." He hefted one leg, the boot close to her face. "Eel."

She could only nod, having a direct view up the leg of his cutoffs. It thrilled her to see he was commando beneath his shorts. She took that as a good sign.

While he settled on the blanket, she reached for the wine and glasses.

"I missed you this weekend," Tyler said close to her ear.

Her stomach flip-flopped at the thought. He'd actually noticed she wasn't around. Imagine that.

"I, um, had stuff to do."

He tucked a strand of her hair behind her ear, leaving a burning trail of need. "I thought maybe you were avoiding me."

Lordy, he had a smooth voice. Deep and rich, with just a

hint of the Texas drawl that always made her hot. She shifted on the blanket, wishing she hadn't worn the thong panties that were trying to escape the hard way.

"No. I was busy. Really."

"Kind of lonely," he murmured against the shell of her ear, causing the fine hairs on the back of her neck to stand at attention.

"You had Jim; you weren't totally alone," she said in a weak, breathy voice, then tilted her head for easier access.

His low laugh rumbled where his chest touched her ribs, setting off vibrations deep within her. "I'd never do this with Jim," he said, then ran the tip of his tongue along the outer rim of her ear. "I'd get hairs in my teeth."

She hoped her giggle didn't spoil the mood, but the mental image of him dragging his tongue along the horse's ear was just too hilarious.

In the gathering darkness, he grinned down at her. "I knew I could get a laugh out of you." His lips brushed the tip of her nose. "Are you going to tell me your name tonight, darlin'?"

The intimate smoothness of his voice, combined with him calling her "*darlin'*", almost broke her resolve. Almost.

She shoved the chilled wine bottle between them, gaining some distance. "Why don't you pour the wine while I think about it?"

Wine splashed into the goblets, the surf and Jim's occasional snorts the perfect counterpoint.

Tyler dug a little hole next to the blanket and sunk the bottle to keep it upright and then turned back to her, his glass raised. "What are we drinking to?"

His light eyes reflected the moonlight. She swallowed and racked her mind for an answer. Finally she said, "You decide."

He looked out at the water for a while, hat tugged low on his forehead. Then he smiled and removed his hat.

She didn't trust that smile, but she definitely felt its heat clear to her bones. Whatever he was thinking, she instantly knew she wanted to be a part of it.

"Wagers."

"Wagers." She took a sip of wine. "What kind of wagers?"

"You never played strip betting?" He touched his bare chest with his spread fingers in a gesture of mock surprise.

"I don't think you have either." She took another sip. "I think it's something you just made up."

"Careful, you'll hurt my tender feelings." He finished his wine in one gulp and countersunk the stem in the sand. "Let me explain the rules, darlin'." He held up his hat. "I'll bet you I can throw my hat to hang on my saddle. If I make it, you have to take something off."

"And if you don't?"

He grinned. "That's the beauty of this game. It's a win-win proposition. If I lose, I take something off, and so on, until we're both nekkid."

Pressing her lips together to keep from smiling, she asked, "But what's the purpose of the game?"

His teeth flashed in the darkness. "To get nekkid."

She laughed. "Gee, what a surprise." Since she had every intention of getting naked with him, she had no objections. "Go ahead. Try."

Without looking in the horse's direction, he let out a short, shrill whistle and threw his hat like a giant Frisbee back over his shoulder.

Jim shuffled to the side. The hat landed gracefully on the pommel.

"You cheated," she pointed out, pouring more wine into both glasses.

"No rule says you can't use props." Glass rims clinked together. "Take it off," he ordered in a raspy voice, then took a sip of wine.

"What should I take off first?" She finished her wine, hoping to muster courage.

"Lady's choice." He leaned back on his elbows and crossed his ankles, drawing her attention to his beach boots.

Meeting his gaze, she stood and reached beneath her skirt. With a little shimmy, the thong slid down her legs, after which she neatly stepped out of it and tossed it to the far side of the blanket.

The way Tyler looked at her was enough to make her spontaneously combust.

Sitting back on the blanket, she arranged her skirt for maximum coverage and picked up her glass. "Your turn."

"What's the bet?" His voice sounded choked. That was a good thing, in her opinion.

"I bet I can say the alphabet before you can finish off that glass of wine." Before he got the glass to his mouth, she took a deep breath and began, finishing with a triumphant "... X, Y, Z!"

Tyler swallowed the last of his wine on Z. "Damn, you talk fast!" He wiped his mouth on the back of his hand. "Did I make it?"

"Nope."

Rising, he unzipped his cutoffs, one metal tooth at a time. When he stopped, she raised an eyebrow. "If I take them off," he said, "the game is over."

A smile tilted her mouth; the wine was definitely giving her a buzz. Blaming the wine was preferable to the idea of Tyler causing her heart to race and the feeling of light-headedness. "No, you'd still have on your beach boots."

"Believe me, darlin', the boots would be no hindrance. Maybe you should take something else off . . . just to make it fair."

A ripple of awareness flushed her from head to toe.

With deliberate, slow movements, she unlaced the front of

her knit tank top. The front popped open, revealing her lace-covered breasts.

In a flash, Tyler had her in his arms, tugging the top down her arms and tossing it aside.

"Maybe we should kiss a while, to cool down," he said against her lips.

Although kissing Tyler made her anything but cool, she was game. She slid her arms around his neck and pulled his mouth down the last millimeter to initiate the kiss.

Laying her back on the blanket, he covered her with his hard body, taking command of the kiss. His hand snaked into her bra cup and held up a condom package.

"My own personal condom dispenser. How did you know I needed one?" He grinned, wiggled his eyebrows, and said, "I like it."

His boot heel clicked against her ankle, causing her to wince. Breaking the kiss, she dared, "I bet you can't take off your boots without using your hands."

He leaned back and smiled. "Nope. And neither can you take off your skirt that way." He sat up and tugged off both boots in record time and then looked pointedly at her. "Game over. Skirt. Off."

Knees wobbling, she stood and tucked her thumbs under the elastic waistband of her pink gauze skirt. Ever so slowly, she lowered the skirt. Cool sea breeze caressed her hips and navel. The skirt inched lower.

Gaze locked with his, she let the skirt drop to her feet. A fine mist from the Gulf glazed her skin, whispered across her exfoliated folds.

The next instant, Jim whinnied and knocked into Tyler, pitching him forward. His head hit Meg's abdomen, knocking her flat on the blanket.

Tyler did a face plant between Meg's thighs, up close and personal.

5

Meg looked at the back of Tyler's head, too stunned to react. Too mortified to move.

Behind Tyler, Jim pranced backward on the beach as though he were very pleased with what he'd just done.

Tyler smiled against her tender flesh. At least, it felt like he smiled.

She jerked. Was that his tongue?

He caressed her thighs, relaxing her muscles, hands moving higher until he coaxed her to spread her legs.

His warm, velvety tongue stroked her labia, pausing at the front to swirl around her distended nub.

He placed a tender kiss where all her nerve endings centered, screaming for more.

Their gazes locked.

"Tell me your name." His hot breath bathed her weeping flesh.

Resisting an insane urge to clamp her legs together, she managed a shaky, whispered, "No."

He reached for the wine bottle. The aroma registered at the

same time the cool liquid trickled between her legs. His eager tongue lapped every last drop, and then he sucked the nub until she arched off the blanket, leaving her weak and needy. And so close to the verge of what could very well be her first genuine climax her teeth ached.

"More," she finally said in a choked voice.

He stood and shucked his shorts while she watched in rapt fascination.

His skin was almost blinding white from midthigh to waist. Although she tried to avoid staring, her gaze kept coming back to his impressive . . . assets. Said assets were in fine form, jutting from a nest of sandy curls.

"That's it," he said, obviously following her line of vision. "Dispenser." He held out his hand. When she just looked at the tip of his fingers, he wiggled them and said, "Condom! Give me a damn condom!"

In her mind she'd pictured a grand seduction, with her rolling on the condom on in a slow, torturous path.

Reality was quite different.

With a strangled sound, he yanked a condom out of her bra, the weather-proof edge of the wrapper scraping her sensitive skin. He ripped it open with his teeth and, in the blink of an eye, was sheathed and ready for action.

It was all very impressive, and she would have told him so, but before she could draw a breath, he hooked his hands on her shoulders, spreading her legs wider with his knees.

In one powerful thrust, he entered her. Immediately, he began plunging. Deeper. Harder.

Her breath hitched. Before she realized it, her orgasm rushed up to meet her, nearly drowning her in a tidal wave of release.

In the moonlight she caught a glimpse of Tyler's smile and rallied her strength.

He wasn't going to get away that easy. Gone were the days

of sexual submission. *I am woman, hear me roar.* She was going to be in charge of her own destiny—and it started with controlling her climax.

Hooking her heels behind his back, she neatly flipped him over and sat astride him. Unhooking the front clasp of her bra, she dropped her pile of condoms onto his chest. "Dispense your own condoms, cowboy." She did an experimental wiggle that elicited a groan from both of them.

She dropped the bra to the blanket and leaned forward for him to take her nipple into his hot mouth.

His suckling caused wetness to gush around their joined bodies. Of their own accord, her hips began moving, picking up the cadence of Tyler's, adding little circles when the thought struck her.

Tyler licked his lips and watched moonlight glisten on the wet nipples of the woman who rode him with such enthusiasm. He'd never considered himself a breast man, but the delicious, wicked taste of her had him wanting to howl at the moon.

He reached to nip lightly at the tips, his ab muscles vibrating with the prolonged effort, and was rewarded with the hitch in her breath and faster thrusts of her hips.

The woman was a goddess. Bathed in moonlight, head thrown back in hedonistic enjoyment, she took his breath away.

Mentally going through every statistic he could think of to prolong the agony of his ecstasy, he was almost out of control when he felt her inner contractions.

Her back arched, nipples jutting toward the inky sky, throat corded. Her breath hitched, her knees clenching his hips.

He followed her lead, coming with a force flat-out alien to him until that moment.

Weak. He was too weak to move, much less speak. But as soon as he rallied, he would tell her how special it was—how special *she* was. Surely that would cause her to at least tell him her name. What transpired between them could not have been one-sided.

Cool. Cool air bathed him. Why was she getting up? He smiled to himself. *Bet she's getting another condom, the little hottie.*

Rustling on the other side of the blanket drew his attention, but his eyelids were still too heavy.

His hat plopped over his cock.

Startled, he opened his eyes to find her dressed, smiling down at him, her face in shadow.

"Thanks for the ride, cowboy." She bent to pick up her belongings. "I needed that. Bring the blanket tomorrow night for a repeat performance." With that, she turned to walk away and then glanced back. "Good job. You actually stayed in the saddle for more than eight seconds!"

6

Tyler lay there with his hat protecting what little modesty he had left while he struggled to gather enough strength to respond and go after her. Or open both eyes or move his arms.

Good thing he'd retired. He was getting old; the thought goaded him. Then he thought of her unbridled response and breathless enthusiasm and grinned. He may not be as good as he once was, but he was as good once as he ever was.

His smile faltered.

She still hadn't told him her name. Damn! It had happened again! Anonymous sex. And here he'd thought he'd succeeded in turning over a new leaf. He'd thought she was different.

Hard on that thought, another more disturbing one occurred.

Was this what his *love 'em and leave 'em* attitude felt like to his many faceless women? Worse, would he be just another hitch on her bedpost, a faceless victim?

Maybe she didn't want him to know her name because she never planned to have anything more than meaningless sex with him.

With slow movements, he managed to drag his carcass off the blanket and get dressed. He picked up the remaining condoms and stuffed them in the pocket of his shorts then sat to pull on his boots.

Damn. Being a sex object was hell. He felt cheap. And used. He didn't like it.

He reached for Jim's reins, avoiding eye contact.

Jim snuffled and sidestepped when Tyler placed his foot in the stirrup, dragging Tyler by one foot in a circle.

"Cut it out!" He swung into the saddle. The horse shook its head. "Just shut up," he told Jim, "and take me home."

Meg stood beneath the pulsing shower and attempted to wash away the humiliation. She'd always despised the *slam, bam, thank you, ma'am* type of sex, yet she'd been guilty of it tonight.

Wrenching off the water, she grabbed her towel and stepped from the tiny shower stall. The terrycloth of her towel irritated her abraded flesh, still tender from Tyler's five-o'clock shadow. The very thought of him brought back instant recall, causing her to squirm with need.

What possessed her to get up and leave when what she really wanted to do was ride him and have her wicked way with him until the sun came up? And stay in his arms while she slept?

Her lotion did little to cool her heated skin. Even her lightest nightgown weighed heavily on her.

Restless, she wandered around the tiny cottage she'd called home for the last two years.

Originally a beach house for summer and holiday use, the owners had moved away a decade before, deeding it back to the original owners, who chose to lease it instead of sell it outright. Meg always dreamed of persuading them to sell it to her. Now that wouldn't happen.

Mrs. Edwards owned the entire cove. Now that she'd gone

into partnership with Attila, any hope Meg had of persuading her otherwise was squashed flatter than the seagull under the tractor she'd seen yesterday.

She trailed a finger along the intricately carved molding of the chair rail in the miniscule kitchen. Opened a Cup-o-Soup and drank it cold. It was time to get used to not having conveniences like microwaves and electricity.

If Roger found out the identity of the grim reaper, she would need to find a good, sturdy cardboard box and a dry underpass.

At her desk the next morning, Meg looked up to see Tyler strolling through the door. Just the sight of him caused moisture to surge in places that had no business surging. Not here, anyway. And certainly not now.

Slumping behind her monitor, she fought the desire to peek at his gorgeous backside while he spoke to tacky Terra.

A moment later he stepped through Attila's door and shut it with a final click.

"He's gay, you know," Terra said when Meg sat back up.

Memories of their own brand of "*sex on the beach*" had Meg biting back a smile. "Really? What makes you think so?"

Terra smirked and leaned back in her chair, thrusting forward her augmented chest provocatively. "No straight man fails to notice these babies."

Well, you paid good money for them, isn't that what you wanted? "Uh, maybe he just isn't interested."

The other woman snorted.

"Maybe he has a girlfriend." Her thoughts that morning were definitely focused on a committed relationship.

"That wouldn't stop him," Terra said with a confidence that really began to grate on Meg.

It certainly hadn't stopped Roger, that was for sure. Would Tyler be any different? Miserable at the thought, she grabbed her bag and said, "I'm going to take an early lunch," and left.

* * *

Tyler walked out of Roger's office, determined to introduce himself to the dark-haired receptionist and ask her to lunch. So what if she reminded him of his mystery lover? Maybe he'd just developed a thing for brunettes. Besides, he needed to get on with his plan for turning over a new leaf.

Last night had been a mistake. Hell, his whole relation-ship—if that's what you could call it—with the mystery woman had been a mistake, as far as he could tell.

He needed some damage control.

Her desk was empty.

"Where is she?" he asked the blonde.

"Gone to lunch." She leaned over so far her overinflated boobs threatened to escape the dangerously low neck of her sweater.

A mental image of them floating toward the ceiling like he-lium balloons had him biting back a smile.

The blonde batted her equally fake eyelashes, obviously misunderstanding his facial expression. "Anything I can do for you, sugar?"

Been there, done that. "No, thanks." He donned his Stetson and stepped into the sunshine.

The brunette had to be close by. He would just find her and strike up a conversation.

Meg saw Tyler squinting through the plate glass of the sand-wich shop and choked on the last bite of her turkey sandwich. Jumping up, she ran for the ladies' room. When she ventured back out a few minutes later, he was gone.

Refilled Coke in her hand, she paid her bill and peered up and down Main Street before venturing back to the office.

Facing Tyler by light of day and introducing herself was in-evitable.

Just not today.

* * *

Tyler shifted in his saddle, the creaking leather failing to relax muscles strung tight with apprehension.

Weak. When it came to his beach babe, it was a condition to fit every situation.

Thoughts of her made him weak, throwing right out the window any resolve he'd made to avoid another anonymous sexual encounter. Kissing her made him weak. Hell, sex with her not only made him weak, it damn near put him in a coma.

And he craved that weakness again. And again. And again.

He may not believe in love at first sight, but he knew damn straight about lust at first sight. And he had the near-constant hard-on to prove it.

The waves washed to the shore, bathed in the glow of the moonlight.

He shifted in the saddle, disgusted for even thinking the sound of waves made him horny. It was his overactive imagination that did it. He could just picture the two of them frolicking, naked, in the surf. Taste the salt of the waves on her tits. He would lift her, her legs going around his waist, her hot, wet center teasing his cock . . .

"Shit! Where the hell is she?" He flexed his thigh and leaned to turn Jim for one more ride down the beach.

Jim had other ideas.

With a snort the horse trotted backward a few steps, shaking his head.

Tyler clicked his tongue.

Jim looked back over his shoulder as if to say, "Are you kidding me?"

"I know, boy, I'm tired, too. Just once more down the beach. Then we'll call it a night."

That's when he looked up and saw her.

Partially hidden in the shadow of a swaying palm tree, she stood, bare feet braced apart on the sand, the Gulf breeze ruffling the thin, pale fabric of her sundress.

He and Jim sauntered closer.

"I thought you weren't coming."

Her lips tilted in a faint smile. At least, he thought it was a smile; could have been a shadow.

"Tyler," she said in a low, suggestive voice that started his blood to boiling, "you know where you're concerned, I always come."

His cock jumped to attention at the double entendre.

He slid from the horse and into her waiting arms. Home. It felt like home to be held close to her again.

A flex of his hips bumped his erection against her. Arms firmly around her, he brushed kisses across her cheeks and the tip of her nose before he settled into a properly efficient welcome kiss.

Dragging his lips down the side of her neck, he said, "Let's go for a ride on the beach."

She sighed. "I was thinking about a different kind of ride," she said, dragging her hand down his side to cup the bulging fly of his jeans.

"We can do that, too." He went for the land speed record in shucking his jeans. It took some work to get them off over his boots, but finally he stood before her in nothing but his hat and boots.

Hands on hips, she gave him a thorough once-over that practically had him falling to his knees begging for more.

"You do realize how ridiculous you look, don't you?"

"Oh, yeah?" He took a step closer, grabbing the hem of her dress before she could get away. In one movement it was up and over her head. He tossed it to land like a giant white parachute skidding across the sand.

Now it was his turn to stare. His heart squeezed. If this wasn't love, it was the damnedest case of lust he'd ever encountered. But he didn't want to scare her, so he simply said, "Nice panties. Lose them."

"B—but then I'll be naked." Her hands fluttered as though she were thinking about shielding her breasts from his hungry eyes. "And the saddle . . ."

Granted, not everyone was as comfortable in the saddle as he was, so he dragged the blanket from their other encounter from the saddlebag and folded it to cover his big Western saddle. "How's that?" Before she could answer, he had relieved her of her panties and grasped her beneath the arms, hefting her onto the saddle. Excited to be sharing a moonlit ride on the beach, he swung up behind her.

It was important to share interests. She needed to learn to ride so they could enjoy their retirement.

He clicked his tongue and Jim set off at a sedate walk. Tyler took advantage of their leisurely pace to run his hands appreciatively over the woman nestled against his rock-hard erection.

But when he cupped her breasts, flicking the pebbled nipples with the tips of his thumbs, she stiffened and swatted his hands away.

"Don't you think you should keep your hands on the wheel . . . or whatever it is you hang on to on a horse?"

Chuckling, he leaned down to nuzzle her neck. "I'm a professional." His words were muffled against the sweet, soft skin. "So is Jim. I don't have to hold on to anything I'm not inclined to hold."

"Oh."

"Relax." His left hand squeezed and massaged her breast while he snaked his other arm around to slide his fingers along her seam and fondle the hidden nub. After a few more steps, her stiffness subsided.

His didn't.

"Uh, Tyler?"

"Hmmm?" Damn, he loved the little shimmy she did in response to him dragging his tongue along the side of her neck.

"Maybe we should stop and, um, put the blanket to, ah, better use?"

He released her breast to cup her cheek, turning her head for his kiss. "Trust me," he whispered against her lips.

Once again cupping her breast, he leaned her forward, his eager cock straining for the warm wetness of her pussy.

He knew he should be wearing a rubber. It didn't matter.

He knew they were taking a chance. It didn't matter.

He knew there was a very real possibility of making a baby with a woman who wouldn't even tell him her name. It didn't matter.

All that mattered was pushing into the silky wetness he craved.

One flex of his hips had him buried to the hilt. Already her greedy opening was sucking his cock deeper, her inner contractions making it difficult not to allow his dick to do a little, happy dance.

He must've squeezed his thighs with his next thrust, because Jim began to trot.

His lover gave a surprised shriek, grasping the pommel in a white-knuckled death grip.

Just as he was about to rein Jim in, they got into the rhythm of the trot with each thrust. It felt interesting. The trot picked up speed. It felt stimulating. Jim trotted faster. Excitement built. The woman wiggled her ass against him, initiating deeper penetration. Tyler couldn't help it. He flexed his thighs with his final thrust as they shouted their climax.

Jim broke into a canter, disconnecting their bodies, and then lurched into a full gallop.

7

She screamed and shot up out of the saddle like she was thinking about jumping off. At this speed, she would do some real damage.

He clamped his arm around her midsection and hugged her back against him while he groped for the reins. "Lean down and hold on!"

"No, sir!" Her voice carried back to him on the wind rushing past them. "That's what got us into this mess in the first place!"

He squeezed Jim's sides with his knees and leaned, guiding the runaway horse into the shallow water.

The cooler water of the Gulf must've brought Jim to his senses, because he came to an abrupt halt, tossing them headfirst into the deeper water.

They broke the surface at the same time, gasping for air.

She shoved her sopping hair from her face, coughing.

"Are you all right?" Tyler tried not to kick her with his boots while he treaded water.

She nodded. "Now what?" she finally said.

His boot touched sand and he stood, drawing her to him, pulling her close between his spread legs. "The water doesn't seem as cold as it did at first. Why don't we just relax for a minute?"

Beneath the water, his cock was making a rapid recovery.

"Ever made love in the ocean?" He trailed nibbling kisses along her neck.

"N—no." The waves bumped her gently against his aroused torso. She looked up, her eyes wide in the moonlight. "Again?"

He shrugged and nodded.

She shrieked and jumped up, her legs wrapped around his waist. "Something's in the water!"

He laughed, knowing deep inside he would protect her with his life if she was right. "Probably lots of 'somethings,' darlin'."

He felt her relax, her body gliding with his in the rhythm of the surf. Soon she returned his kisses with building enthusiasm, squirming against his sex, practically climbing on top of him.

It was only natural that he grab her waist to lift her and then bring her down on his cock. Just as it was only natural for her to cling tighter and sigh as he slid in and out of her with the lazy cadence of the waves.

Their orgasm took them both by surprise. One minute they were smoothly copulating, letting the water do its magic. The next, a tidal wave of release washed over them, threatening to drown them in sensation and possibly even saltwater.

Weak, they staggered toward the shore, where Jim now waited.

She looked around. "I should go home. It's late."

"Tomorrow's Saturday. You don't have to work or anything, do you?" Suddenly her leaving was the last thing in the world he wanted. "Let's dry off and look for the blanket." Despite his best intentions, he ran his hands from her shoulders to knees and back up, sluicing water from her smooth skin.

"It'll turn up, sooner or later."

"What about your dress and panties?" While the idea of her walking down the beach in her birthday suit held infinite appeal for him, he knew he would want to gouge out the eyes of anyone who witnessed her trek.

She came closer, the tips of her breasts poking his chest, and brushed her lips over his. "I'll get it tomorrow."

"You know, we really should shower all the saltwater off. You could wash my back."

She grinned and lightly punched his shoulder. "What a guy." She leaned in to kiss him again and whispered, "I'd much rather wash your front." Her hand sought—and found—him ready for her again.

At her surprised look, he assured her, "We don't have to make love again. We could talk." Yeah, right. He wasn't sure he could "just talk" to her even if someone threatened to cut off his left nut.

"Tyler," she said in a singsong voice, "You lie." She laughed. "And we don't make love. We have sex. Just sex."

Okay, he would let that one slide. For now. "Tell me your name."

Trailing one finger along his flagpole erection in an idle caress, she said, "What difference does it make? Why can't we just enjoy what we have for as long as we have it?"

How many times had he said those very words? Now he wondered if he'd sounded as condescending. Damn, he hated being a sex object.

But if that's all she wanted . . . that was what she would get.

He hauled her close to his excited sex. "Want to relive your misspent youth?"

"Excuse me?"

He tweaked her nipple, causing her to squirm in his arms. She may be new territory to explore, but he had the road map hardwired into his DNA.

Sweeping her into his arms, he strode to a beach shower and pulled the chain, dousing them both in tepid water.

Yanking it again, he rubbed against her wet torso, his erection bumping against her.

Satisfied that the sand and saltwater were reasonably washed away, he swung her up into his arms again and whistled for Jim to follow their progress up the beach to his grandmother's house.

By the time they'd gotten their clothes and reached the stables and had put Jim up for the night, the muscles in his legs and arms were beginning to vibrate. No doubt about it, he was getting old. There was a time he would have done what they did all night and gone back for more. Now he would like a nap.

Of course, he couldn't tell the sexy little number by the door how much she sapped his energy. He had promised her a walk down memory lane. He snatched a can of cocoa butter and a can of spray cheese from the shelf and led her toward his truck.

One red-hot memory coming up.

Meg let Tyler pull her out of the warmth of the stable, allegedly to relive a teenage memory. By the look in his eye, she would say his memories were a lot more interesting than hers.

While he'd curried Jim, she'd eyed the hay and conjured up a few fantasies of her own. Since she and Tyler were temporary, she wanted to create as many memories as she could.

Heck, if Tyler thought she'd been a wild bad girl as a teenager, who was she to argue?

At the truck, he threw open the passenger's side front and back doors and patted the backseat, his grin white in the moonlight. "Hop in, sweet thing."

She hesitated. How did one go about climbing into a leather backseat while naked? Not for the first time, she wished she weren't vertically challenged.

Hard hands bracketed her waist, hoisting her to sit on the warm leather. It felt kind of . . . interesting.

Tyler grabbed a towel from the front seat and brushed the dirt and leaves from the bottoms of her feet. Sitting next to her, he took off his soaked boots and dried his feet, letting the boots drop to the ground. "Don't want to get my truck muddy."

She scooted back to allow him more room. He would have none of that.

Grasping her ankles, he said, "Okay, darlin', let's see if we can burn up a few of those old memories." He turned her and placed one foot on the backseat back and one on the front-seat back, exposing her in the most intimate way possible. "Relax," he said, patting her between her spread legs. "I won't do anything you haven't done before."

Wanna bet? Embarrassment at her position and her renewed wetness warred with curiosity as to what he would do. Curiosity won.

He *tsk*ed and shook his head. "Such dry skin. Probably from too much saltwater. Lucky for you I have just the thing to help." He held up a tan jar and dipped in his fingers. He plopped a large glob of whatever it was on her abdomen and began to thoroughly massage it into her stomach and breasts, paying particular attention to her nipples.

When she tried to squirm, he grabbed her foot and slabbed on another dollop of the thick cream. "Such rough heels. Good thing I found this cocoa butter." After working in the butter on both feet and up her inner thighs, he thoroughly massaged the remaining ointment into her folds. As wet as she was, it was a miracle the butter didn't slide right off.

She whimpered when he stopped, but she shouldn't have worried.

He produced a can and wiggled his eyebrows. "I don't have any whipped cream. Guess spray cheese will have to do." He designed little rosettes on each nipple and then licked and suck-led off the warm cheese.

Blowing on each recently cleaned nipple, he paused. "Hot damn, you're gorgeous, woman." His smile looked almost ten-der. "Thank you for letting me keep the door open so the dome light could stay on."

Strangling on her arousal, she could only nod and wait to see what he would do next.

It wasn't a long wait.

Warm cheese filled each fold, then Tyler made a big produc-tion of licking off every eager cell of skin weeping for his atten-tion.

So close to an earth-shattering orgasm, she bucked her hips against his mouth, silently begging for release. But he wasn't finished yet.

Against the ever-present background of the surf, the squirt-ing cheese was loud. Tyler circled his erection with a halo of yellow processed-cheese spread and then proceeded to totally encase his penis.

By the time he'd finished his masterpiece, her mouth was watering. She'd always felt oral sex with other partners less than appealing. But since meeting Tyler, she'd had a definite change of heart.

When he knelt by her head, one finger leisurely stroking her breast and commanded in a hoarse whisper, "Eat me." She found she was more than ready, willing, and oh-so-able.

8

Tyler gritted his teeth and focused on moving air in and out of his deprived lungs while his beach babe threatened to suck his cock dry. He would have been fine had she not decided to play with his balls while she sucked and licked and . . . well, you get the idea.

In an effort to prevent embarrassing himself—damn, it felt good!—he reached between her still spread legs and drew patterns in the swollen wet folds, occasionally foraying to her engorged nub or dipping into her wetness just to hear her moan.

Wait. That was him moaning.

He got between her legs and nudged her feet back up onto the seats for greater access, positioned himself, and, with one powerful thrust, was home.

Afterward he lay there, sprawled on top of her, too weak to move. What was it about this woman? He should move. It was the gentlemanly thing to do. But his body wasn't obeying his mental signals.

Propped on shaking elbows, body still joined with hers, he brushed away a strand of hair that clung to her damp forehead.

Unable to resist, he kissed her, then rested his own damp forehead against hers. "Bring back any high school memories?" Stupid, it was the first thing he thought to say, and as soon as it was out of his mouth, he regretted it. He didn't want to be compared and found lacking to any of her past lovers.

She wiggled, and he promptly reversed their positions so he could take their weight.

Damn, I could stay right here forever, he thought, loving the way her fingertip drew little circles over his heart, the warmth of her breath caressing his skin.

"I don't think I had the same experiences in high school that you had," she finally said and then sighed. "I was actually pretty shy."

He snickered, and she pulled one of his few chest hairs.

"Ouch!" He rubbed his chest, capturing her hand before it could do any more damage. Their gazes met. "What's your name?"

Instead of answering him, she scooted out of the truck and started walking away.

"Wait!" He scrambled off the seat and looked around for his boots. "Wait! I'll take you home."

"That's okay," she called back over her shoulder as she bent to retrieve her dress. "It's not far."

"How 'bout I walk you home?" He hopped to get his foot in his waterlogged boot.

"No, thanks!" she called from farther down the beach.

Standing there at dawn, buck naked, with one boot on, it hit him.

He loved her.

9

Meg watched Tyler ride up and down the beach the next night from the safety of her cottage. Yes, she was a chicken. Yes, she would love nothing better than to go meet him and replay their beach-blanket boinking. And any and every subsequent boinking. But it wasn't going to happen.

She had to protect her heart.

It would be too easy to fall in love with Tyler Last. Too easy to crawl into bed with him and forget the future of the beach without her support. And that wouldn't be fair to anyone who loved the beach as she did.

A tear trickled down her cheek when Tyler finally turned Jim and headed back down the beach.

Alone in her bed, sleep eluded her. She tossed and turned, flipped and flopped. The covers were heavy, her nightgown oppressive, her body empty.

She threw back the covers and hopped out of bed. Before she could talk herself out of it or remember all the reasons why it was a bad idea, she found herself standing in Miss Hannah's kitchen, the spare key the older woman had given her for emergencies clutched in her fist.

Around her, the big old house was quiet. The ticking of the grandfather clock in the entryway made a soft counterpoint to the beating of her heart. The wood risers of the stairs cooled the bottoms of her bare feet. The air clicked on, making her glad she'd left her nightgown in the kitchen, as she felt the cool air swirling over her heated skin, pebbling her nipples.

She knew instinctively which room was Tyler's, even without the leather bag with the Stetson on top next to the door.

Wrong. It was a bathroom. A big bathroom. Almost as large as her bedroom at the cottage.

A sound at the door had her gasping and spinning to face the intruder.

Tyler leaned against the doorway, one arm braced above his head, his white boxers riding low on his lean hips. "Lord, if this is a dream, I don't want to wake up." He took a step into the room. "Where were you tonight?" He stretched his arm to flip on the light.

"Don't!" Embarrassment heated her cheeks. Her seduction plan would be so much easier to carry out in the darkness. "I, um, couldn't make it tonight." Her gaze drank in the sight of his gorgeous body, her womb aching for his touch. "But I had to see you." She walked until her bare breasts touched his firm pectorals. "Touch you." She ran her fingertip up the side of his ribs to swirl around his flat nipple. On tiptoe, she brushed her lips across his. "Kiss you," she whispered against his mouth.

His arms locked around her, lifting her from her feet, aligning her with his aroused body. His mouth clamped onto hers, demanding entrance, withholding nothing.

His hands were everywhere.

Cool wall tile touched her back. He tore his lips from hers and drew her breast into his hot mouth, suckling so hard she felt it all the way to the soles of her feet.

She whimpered with need when he released her breast, cool air on her wet nipple amplifying the loss as he placed her legs around his waist.

His mouth took hers in another bone-melting kiss, spinning her senses out of control.

His iron-hard erection shoved its way into her eager body. Immediately he began to move, each thrust pounding into her, bumping her hips against the cold hardness of the tile in a delicious counterpoint to his passion.

Climbing his body, she went wild with need. Her womb clamped like it was attempting to suck him into her very core.

Wave after wave of pure pleasure washed over her. So powerful it brought tears to her eyes.

A millisecond later, Tyler's hard body became impossibly harder as every muscle clenched with the power of his release. With a roar he slammed into her one last time and then shuddered.

Weak in the aftermath, Meg hung there, impaled against the wall, grateful for the support.

Before she could recover, Tyler leaned, still deeply embedded, and turned on the shower.

Still joined, he kicked away his boxers and stepped with her into the rapidly filling, plugged tub. Water sluiced over her, wetting her hair, blurring her vision, while he resumed his feast on her mouth.

His hard hands clamped beneath her arms and lifted her until her nipples were level with his mouth.

Meg's senses began to reassert themselves, frustration building due to her position.

Before she could speak, he reclaimed her lips and turned off the shower.

Kissing, they lowered into the water, where he began a very thorough bathing.

"I could definitely get used to this," Meg murmured, head

lolled against the back of the old-fashioned tub, eyes closed while Tyler soaped her breasts with talented hands.

He rinsed the soap and licked her nipples. "How about this?" he asked, his breath hot against her skin.

"Mmm-hmmm," She tried not to squirm with her new-found lust.

Something hard and slippery entered her, causing her to sit straighter.

"Relax," he crooned.

She opened her eyes. It was difficult to see in the darkness, but she could've sworn his eyes blazed into hers.

His hand held a long, slippery object. It appeared to be an elongated bar of soap. He slid it around her folds, paying special attention to her now aching nub. Her hips bucked a couple of times.

He petted her, quieted her movements. "Easy, baby, easy." He guided her hand to his jutting penis. "Here. Hold on to this while we get you rinsed off, okay?"

In reply she gave a little squeeze that had him groaning.

He splashed water over her nether regions, judiciously sliding one finger, then two, then three into her in his effort to rid her of every trace of soap.

She would have kept what dignity she had left intact, had he not chosen that moment to wiggle his deeply embedded fingers. She screamed—actually screamed—as her climax washed over, threatening to drag her under the water with its ferocity.

Before she caught her breath, he flipped the tub stopper and arranged her limp legs on either side of the lip of the tub. The action brought her hips up to the exact level of his mouth.

What a happy coincidence.

Her fingers dug into the lip of the tub while Tyler's mouth and tongue took her up and over the threshold two more times.

Spent, and so sexually sated she could purr, it was an effort to open her eyes when he lifted her out of the tub. Tyler's version of drying was more caressing by terry cloth, but her muscles were now so weak she was just grateful to be still standing.

He sat on the closed lid of the commode, his monster erection still obvious, and reality hit her, along with a tiny niggle of excitement.

Payback time.

She dropped to her knees on the plush contour rug and reached for the part of his anatomy literally leaping to attention.

His hands clamped down on her shoulders, halting her short of her intended target. "Stop."

Stop? Didn't her want her to pleasure him? "Why?"

"Because I'm about near to shooting my load." He grinned and tugged her to her feet. "I don't want to waste it."

She gestured to her nudity. "I didn't bring anything, did you?" Though their passion had precluded protection before. She didn't want to risk it again.

His shoulders slumped. It would've been comical, had she not felt so needy.

"The only thing I have is a hard-on." He smirked. "The condoms are in my room."

She made a move for the door, but he stopped her by grabbing her hand.

"I kind of like it here," he said, pulling her toward him.

"I do, too, but if we don't have a condom, we can't have sex." She hadn't lived to be twenty-six without learning anything.

"How about if we improvise?" He reached beneath the counter and rummaged around, finally bringing out a roll of plastic wrap.

"Why does your grandmother have plastic wrap in the bathroom?"

"She wraps it around her hair when she conditions it, as I recall." He ripped off a generous portion. "Let's give it a try."

Her *Powers of Seduction* book advised being adventurous. Why not?

Meg took the length of wrap from him and stood straddling his legs. Which, coincidently, gave him easy access to play with her while she sheathed him. He grinned and licked his lips. A definite win-win situation.

He noted that her hands shook a bit as she carefully wrapped his throbbing cock in the plastic. The heat multiplied tenfold. Beneath his questing fingers, she was slick, wet, and obviously ready.

He growled, low in his throat, when she slid her hands up and down his length.

Their gazes met.

"I'm just making sure it's sealed," she assured him, although he thought her lips twitched.

He grabbed her hips and aligned her opening.

"Ride me," he demanded with a fierceness that surprised him.

10

She lowered herself, inch by agonizing inch, until she'd taken all of him.

With a frustrated growl he flattened her breasts against his chest and did his damnedest to remove her tonsils the hard way. Lordy, he couldn't get deep enough.

He grasped her tiny waist and raised her until she almost left his cock and then slammed her down again. The combined friction of her and the wrap made him feel as if he might burst into flames. He increased the pace of their combined thrusts. Faster. Harder. Again and again.

His need was a living, breathing thing. He wanted to bury himself so she didn't know where he ended and she began.

Frantic to touch and taste every inch of her, he was aware on some level of a difference. No matter what she claimed, this was not just sex. It was more.

So much more.

He had to make her understand.

And admit it.

Her thighs clamped his, her slender back arched. Her scream when she came echoed from the tiles of the bathroom walls.

The sound, the feel, the smell, the taste all conspired to wrench his climax from him.

Weak. God, he was so weak. What did sex with this woman do to him? He couldn't remember ever being so wrung out.

On his lap, she stirred and began to rise. He wanted to tell her to stop. Wanted to tell her how special she was to him. Wanted to tell her to wait for him to catch his breath, that he was just out of shape.

Instead cool air bathed his sweating skin.

"Tyler?" Her voice didn't sound as winded as he felt. "Tyler!" Damn. She sounded odd.

He cracked open one eye. "Huh?"

"Where's the plastic wrap?"

11

_____

Both gazes flew to his penis, which looked sort of bare and vulnerable, just hanging there, exposed.

Shit. His first thought fell out of his mouth. "You had it last."

"Are you kidding?" She motioned toward something, but he was too distracted by the bobbing of her breasts. "Do something!"

Do something. Right.

"Now, don't get all riled up." He stood and walked toward her. "Let me help you." He dropped to the floor, the tile grinding into his kneecaps. He petted her thighs apart. "That's it, baby, relax. Don't move."

He inserted a finger, ignoring the hot, slick moisture, and tentatively moved his fingertip.

She gasped but did not move.

"I think I feel the edge. Move your foot a little that way." He nudged her leg, and she obeyed. Inserting the index finger of his other hand, he was able to grasp the edge.

By the time he dragged the mess from her delectable body,

his hand was drenched, and they were both experiencing altered breathing.

He loved her. It didn't matter if he didn't know her name. It didn't matter if she loved him back. It didn't matter if they didn't make love again. He loved her.

And nothing would ever be the same.

He watched her breasts rise and fall with her shallow panted breathing, the hard, puckered tips of her nipples. The unmistakable flush of sexual arousal colored her pale skin.

He flipped on the light.

Yep, her eyes were unfocused. She licked her lips, a pained expression on her face.

She was hurting, needy. He could help her. He twisted the faucets.

Lifting her into the refilled tub, he gently bathed her heated skin, smoothing body wash until she was restless and panting, shifting against the slick surface of the tub.

Beneath the water he petted her, calmed her, then, ever so slowly, inserted his finger, worrying the pad of his thumb over her distended nub.

She arched, her nipples protruding from the water. "Please," she said in a scratchy voice. Her hand came up to cup her breast, offering it to him.

He leaned closer to swipe his tongue over her nipple. They both groaned. He nipped the tip with his teeth, eliciting a gasp from her, although her eyes stayed closed.

Watching her face while he pleasured her, he knew if he lived to be one hundred, he would always remember her like this.

Gulping in air, she arched again, sloshing water from the tub, and then quieted.

He reached for a bath sheet and lifted her from the tub, leaning her against his side while he dried her.

After laying her on the sheets of his bed, he went to get the bottle of pear body lotion. Determined to deny his own gratification, he thoroughly massaged the lotion into her skin.

She barely roused when he climbed in beside her and pulled the sheet over them.

With a sigh she snuggled close to his heart.

Just as he was drifting off to sleep, he heard her whisper, "Meg. My name is Meg."

12

Sunshine streaming through the open window woke him after the best night of his life. He couldn't stop smiling. Meg. The future mother of his children was named Meg. He stretched and reached for *Meg*, only to encounter cold sheets. Other than a faint indention on the other pillow and a lingering scent of pear, it was like she had never been there.

He tugged on his boxer briefs and slippers and headed toward the kitchen. As he suspected, it, too, was empty.

A key sounded in the lock, and Meg let herself into the kitchen, a grocery bag in her hand.

For a moment they stood, smiling at each other.

Tyler rallied first and reached for the bag. Her continued stare caused a telltale lump in his boxers. Then he followed her gaze and wiggled his toes.

She met his eyes and grinned. "Now, what do you call those things?"

"They're my house boots." He stuck out his foot. "Like 'em? Gram had them made for me for Christmas a few years ago."

"Well, they're unique." She studied the brown felt. "I don't think I've ever seen slippers that looked like cowboy boots."

"Yeah, cool, huh?" He peeked into the bag. "What did you get for breakfast? What's this?" He pulled out a big green bottle. "Champagne? For breakfast?"

She yanked the bottle out of his hand and placed it in the refrigerator. "I already made breakfast. It's in the warming oven. I thought it might be nice to have mimosas." She chewed her lower lips. "But if you don't want any, I can always—"

"No, darlin' *Meg*, don't be getting all bristly on me." He nuzzled her neck, arousal slamming through him when she tilted her head for better access. "What've you got planned for today?"

She went still.

He stopped nuzzling and looked at the distress on her face. "What? You got a date or something? 'Cause if you do, break it. You're officially out of circulation."

"Excuse me? What do you mean by that?"

"I mean I'm putting my brand on you." There. He'd officially declared his intentions. Only problem, she didn't seem too taken with the idea. Not like he'd thought she would be, anyway.

"Your—your brand! Have you totally lost your mind, cowboy? I'm not livestock!" She started to stalk past him, but he was faster. She shot him a withering look.

Used to be a time when fast was a good thing.

Damage control was needed. He stepped back and raked a hand through his hair then flashed a smile he knew had an effect on women.

Evidently, not this woman.

He huffed out a breath. "Could we start over?" He bent his knees to stare into her stormy blue eyes. "Please?"

She visibly wilted. "I'm sorry. I shouldn't have yelled at you."

"True." He smiled down at her. "Guess we need to get you over your fear of branding irons."

"Let's just have breakfast and discuss instruments of torture later."

"Ahhh, I love the beach. No doubt about it, I could definitely get used to this." Tyler tilted down his hat to shade his eyes and rested his mimosa on his tan belly.

Meg glanced over at him and chewed the inside of her cheek. Should she mention the potential problems with his grandmother's project?

Tyler had been so sweet and helpful during breakfast. Floating in the pontoon lounge chairs while tethered to his grandmother's dock was also his idea. And mimosas had never tasted so sweet.

Despite self-preservation warnings, she was more than halfway in love with Tyler. She had to share her passion about the beach just as surely as she'd shown her passion for the man floating next to her.

"I love it, too." It was easier to talk with her eyes closed, face up to the sun. "That's why I was so saddened by your grandmother's decision to hook up with Roger Ferris."

"Oh? Why's that?" Despite his lazy tone, he had an alertness to his voice that gave her courage to continue.

"I grew up in Paradise Beach. My parents still live here. Every summer we rented a cottage here on the cove. My sister and I practically lived on the beach right up through college." She took a sip of her drink. "It's always been a safe haven. A family beach. But now . . ."

"Now?" he encouraged.

"Well, now, once the new gated community is built, the beach won't be a family beach anymore. Access will be closed off."

He was silent for so long she thought he may have fallen asleep. Her eyes were definitely getting heavy from the combination of the relaxing rocking of the waves, her drink, and the sun. Not to mention her sexual escapades from last night.

"Have you talked to anyone about this?"

"I tried to talk to your grandmother when she first decided to go into business with Ferris Properties. I didn't get far."

"Any idea who the grim reaper is?"

Jerking at the mention of her alter ego, she lost her drink to the Gulf, and only some fast strategic moves prevented her from capsizing.

"Grim reaper?" she asked when she regained her balance, trying to sound casual.

He nodded, hat still pulled low over his eyes. "Yeah, surely you've seen her. Or heard her god-awful squawking through her bullhorn. She's out here almost every morning and afternoon, protesting the building." He snorted. "For all the good it's done her."

"Do you agree with her?" She held her breath.

"I dunno." He shrugged. "Who am I to judge anything or anybody? I'm sure she thinks she's right. But so does Roger Ferris."

"Roger Ferris is a slimeball!" She grasped the pontoon chair until she regained her balance again. "I mean, I've heard he isn't the most reputable builder."

"Oh?" Tyler tipped his hat and looked over at her, causing her stomach to somersault again. "Why's that?"

She couldn't tell him she worked for Roger and knew firsthand of his shady dealings. And she certainly couldn't tell him she was the grim reaper. At least, not right now.

So instead she strove for nonchalance and shrugged. "I think anyone who blocks public access to Paradise Cove is a jerk, plain and simple. The beach needs it. The people need it."

"I went and talked to Roger," he said, once more sliding his hat low on his face. "He claims there is access—by water. Guess, legally, that's all he has to have."

If she told him about the fences she had seen the purchase order for last week, he would want to know how she knew. Darn.

"Not everyone has a way to get there by water," she pointed out instead.

"True."

They floated in silence for a while.

"Meg?"

"Hmmm?" Despite the sun charbroiling her, she was loathe to move, lethargic from the soothing tide, the champagne, and the contentment of being with the man next to her.

"I'm feeling like I could stay on for more than eight seconds now."

She opened one eye and regarded his smiling face. If by some miracle they ended up together, she knew she would never live down that flippant remark. Her gaze swept him. She could live with that.

"What did you have in mind, cowboy?"

"I'm thinking maybe you could lose that little string you call a bathing suit and climb on over here and help me relieve some of my frustration."

His smooth drawl stroked her senses as surely as his calloused hands had stroked her skin all through the night.

"I think we would capsize and both drown." But what a way to go.

"Then let's try something else," he said right next to her ear. She jerked and would have fallen had he not gripped her chair. For a big guy, he sure moved fast. And quietly. She hadn't even heard him slip into the water.

He slid the tips of his index fingers under the edges of her bikini top and skimmed the edges of her nipples. Her breath lodged. Her nipples immediately puckered, begging for more.

"You have the fastest hands of anyone I've ever known," she said in a breathless voice, watching her top float out to sea.

"I hope so, darlin', I surely hope so." He closed his hands around each breast and lightly squeezed before taking one into his mouth and sucking deeply. "Damn, I love your tits," he said, his breath hot against her nipple.

Experiencing altered breathing, she forgot to be offended by his word choice.

His talented hands slid down her sides and untied the strings holding her bikini bottom together.

She meant to protest—after all, they were in public. But instead she lifted her hips, allowing him to remove the offending fabric and toss it aside.

The warmth of the sun, combined with the warmth of the water resting at the juncture of her thighs, made her want to spread her legs for increased stimulation.

Tyler's hand did it for her.

"Tyler—" She gripped the armrests and stiffened.

"Shhh, darlin', you're fine. I got you. Relax."

And indeed he did have her. She was anchored firmly to the chair by his mouth on her right breast and his fingers buried deeply within her.

The sun, the water, the man and his talented mouth and hands . . . all conspired to bring her to a lightning-fast climax that left her weak and panting.

Through heavy eyelids she noticed a blob of fabric floating toward her suit that looked suspiciously like Tyler's trunks.

The next instant, the chaise rocked crazily, then righted itself, with Tyler stretched out on top of her, his erection prodding her. His big hands on either side of her face steadied her for his bone-melting kiss.

"Hi," he said when they broke for air, the tip of his nose touching hers.

Up close she realized his eyes were really more turquoise than blue, with little flecks of gold in them.

"Hi, yourself." She carefully spread her legs as wide as possible to accommodate him without unseating them both. Every inch of skin pressed to Tyler's skin burned with the contact. She wanted him. She needed him.

She loved him?

The very thought struck terror in her heart. What good was it to read the *Powers of Seduction* book if you fell in love with your first victim? Dang, she couldn't do anything right.

But she couldn't let Tyler know. She'd been the one to insist they keep it casual. There was only one thing to do. Cringing at what she was about to say, she looked him in the eye and said, "Shut up and fuck me, cowboy."

13

Something flared in Tyler's eyes but was quickly gone. Gaze locked with hers, he replied, "Yes, ma'am," and plunged into her with enough force to set the chair rocking in the waves.

With a squeak she grabbed his warm shoulders and held on. Within seconds the rhythm caught her up. Desperate for him and the pleasure he gave her, she gave in to her passion.

Against its tether, the chair groaned and bucked with their movements. The rope grew slack and then taut, snapping with each thrust.

Rushing to meet their climax, it hit them just as the rope gave its last hurrah, along with the chair. The resulting action plunged them deep into the boat channel beside the dock.

Saltwater burned a path down her throat through her nose. Her vision was nothing but dark green water. Popping to the surface, coughing, she saw Tyler treading water a few feet away.

He grinned, teeth white against his tanned face. "Woo-wee! Hot damn, what a ride!"

Although she agreed, it was like a slap in the face to hear him say it. But what did she expect? It was what she'd wanted. Casual, no-strings-attached sex.

Sometimes you had to be careful what you wished for.

Back onshore she wrapped a towel around her nudity, avoiding Tyler's lascivious glances. "I really should be going." She slipped her feet into the flip-flops she'd left by the dock. "Tomorrow is a workday, and I have a ton of laundry to do for the week."

He looked at her so long she had to force herself to stand still and not squirm beneath his rapt gaze. Finally he nodded.

"Yeah, I have some stuff to do today, too. See you tonight?" he called as she turned to walk away.

She pretended not to hear.

Tyler sat on the porch watching the sunset and took a draw from his beer. Beside him the coals of the grill had turned to white dust. The steaks he'd planned for dinner were now inedible.

Where was Meg? Why the hell hadn't he thought to get her phone number?

Maybe a miscommunication. Yeah, that had to be it. She was probably waiting for him on the beach, all that smooth, perfumed skin hot and ready for him.

Practically tripping in his rush to get to her, he went to the stable and saddled a reluctant Jim in record time.

The wind off the Gulf, the solid sound of hooves meeting packed sand, and the waves rushing to shore didn't work their usual magic on him tonight.

Tonight, he would not, could not be soothed by anything less than holding Meg in his arms again.

He tipped his head to allow the breeze to caress his face and breathed in the sea air.

He'd done it. And it was easier than he'd thought it would be.

Not only had he made some calls and pulled strings to hopefully stop Roger Ferris from destroying the public beach, he'd sold his grandmother on the idea when she called.

But his biggest and best accomplishment, in his opinion, was that he'd succeeded in turning over a new leaf. Not only that, he'd fallen in love. And with Meg at his side, he could do anything.

After three or four passes up and down the cove, Jim's steps slowed. By the tenth turn he headed back to the stables, and no amount of cussing or discussing could change his mind.

The night was long and lonely, but Tyler used it to plan his strategy.

First on the agenda was convincing the grim reaper to talk to him. He already had what he needed to force Roger to include a beach access road, but after talking to Meg about it, he would rather halt the project altogether. According to Tyler's attorney, his grandmother would lose nothing, and the property would revert to her if the project folded at its current phase of completion. Maybe the grim reaper had some information he didn't.

Next, depending on what he found out, he would head for Ferris's office. If he could stop the development, he would. If not, he could at least get Ferris to do the access road.

Which left him free to pursue Meg and convince her to marry him. His grandmother had already given her enthusiastic blessing. He tried not to worry about the fact that he'd had a hell of a time convincing Meg to even tell him her name. She was warming up to him. He could tell.

The morning sunshine hit his sleep-deprived brain square between the eyes. Pulling his hat low to allow his eyes to adjust, he stepped out onto the beach.

Yep, there she was, pacing back and forth in front of the oblivious construction crew, yelling into her bullhorn.

He walked a circuitous path and came up behind her.

"Stop the rape of the beach!" she yelled.

He grasped her shoulder and spun her around, ripping her mask off in one fluid movement.

"Son of a fucking bitch! Meg! What the hell are you doing in that garb?" Reality hit him. "You're the grim reaper."

"Quick, aren't you, cowboy?" She gave a tight smile and ducked her head.

In the blink of an eye he stood holding nothing but the insubstantial black garb. "Wait! Meg!" He took off at a run, but the sand sucked down his boots with each step.

By the time he reached the parking lot, she was gone.

Muttering every cuss word he had ever heard, he stomped back to the house.

A quick shower cooled him off somewhat. He needed to keep his head when he dealt with Ferris. Long-ago mental training from his rodeo days served a new purpose. It allowed him to put Meg at the back of his mind and focus on what had to be done. For now.

The street parking was light, so he was able to pull in his truck practically in front of Ferris Properties.

The front office was empty, but the door to Ferris's office was ajar, and it looked like a light was on.

Tyler strode straight toward the door, sort of relieved no one else was in yet. Gripping the cool knob and pushing open the door, he had his other hand raised for a courtesy knock when he saw them.

The blonde was stretched out, nude, with her eyes tightly shut, on the top of Ferris's desk, her grapefruit-with-nipples breasts jiggling with her movements. Between her fake-tan, spread legs, Ferris enthusiastically licked her bleached-blond pussy.

Embarrassed on Ferris's behalf, Tyler knocked and discreetly cleared his throat.

Ferris shot out of his chair, his pants falling to his shoes, his pitiful pecker just hanging out for people to laugh at and point.

Of course, Tyler was too much of a gentleman to do that—well, these days, anyway—so he turned to look at the blonde while Ferris adjusted his clothing.

Not long ago he would have enjoyed the view of her slow movements. She sat up and actually had the balls to shoot him a sex-kitten look, skimming her hand over her more than ample boobs to pinch her own nipples. Next she dragged her hand down to pet her pussy, legs still spread wide, before she got up.

There was a time when his jeans would've immediately shrunk at the sight. Today, though, he could only think how abused that part of her anatomy looked. And disgusting.

Whatever Ferris had at home, it had to be better than what was spread on his desk.

Finally—finally!—the blonde stood and picked up her clothes. With slow steps she walked past him, brushing her dampness against the back of his hand as she passed.

It took great effort not to recoil and wipe his hand.

Ferris walked to shut the door and motioned Tyler to a chair. "I had a call from your attorney this morning, Last," he said when he was once more behind the big mahogany desk. He leaned forward, his hands on the smooth surface. "You have me by the short hairs." He glanced at the closed door. "Especially now. Tell me what you want."

"Well, you know, right up until today I would have said a public access road." Tyler stretched out the moment by adjusting the brim of his hat. "But now I think I want it all." Their eyes met. "Stop the construction and sign my grandmother's property back to her."

"I can't do that!"

"Sure you can." He stood, adjusted his hat, and turned toward the door. "I think Mrs. Ferris would probably agree." He opened the door and said over his shoulder, "You have twenty-four hours."

The front-office phones were ringing. The blonde, now

dressed and pouting, answered it as the dark-haired girl hurried through the front door.

"Meg?" Tyler willed his heart to stop beating. He didn't want to know what she was doing here and what part she played in the whole mess.

She just stood there, looking at him with that deer-in-the-headlights look.

Had she said something, anything, he would have forgiven her. But she said not word one in her defense.

He lost it.

"I guess we really don't know each other at all." Anger simmered just below the surface. If he didn't get out of there soon, he didn't want to think about what might happen.

Despite his best intentions, he advanced on her. It sent a surge of satisfaction to see her take a step back.

"No wonder you didn't want to tell me your name." Another step. "Here I thought you couldn't help yourself; you were so taken with my charm you just had to fuck my brains out."

Behind him he heard a gasp.

"And I was so pathetic! I was actually touched—touched!—when you finally told me your name. Hey, I just noticed something. You never did tell me your last name. It isn't Ferris, is it? 'cause I would think it would be a conflict of interest to have your lying mouth on my cock. And who knows where else it's been!"

Tears glazed Meg's eyes, but he was on a roll.

"Then to top it all off, I find out you're the damned grim reaper who's been causing all that noise pollution at the beach construction site. When I think how hard I got whenever I thought of you, and now I know all I had to do was walk out on the beach and flip up your skirt—"

"Grim reaper?" Ferris's voice boomed from the cinder-block walls of the office. "Meg, is that true?"

She nodded, a tear trickling down her flushed cheek. Had he not been so outraged, Tyler would've felt sorry for her. Maybe.

"You're fired," Ferris said. "Get your things and get out. I'll mail your last check." He stalked to the door of his private office. "And don't be surprised if you hear from my attorney." *Slam.*

When Tyler turned back, Meg was running out the door. Damn, that woman was fast!

But he was faster.

He caught her arm just as she reached a tiny red car in the parking lot. She tried to jerk away, but he held tight.

"Why?" he demanded, doing his damnedest not to be affected by the sparkle of tears in her deep blue eyes.

She raised her chin. "Why not? I saw an opportunity and took it. Isn't that what you want to hear?"

"No! I want to hear that you were in this thing we had every bit as much as I was! I want to hear you say you had nothing to do with Ferris or his shady dealings. I want to hear you say you need me—need my help, I mean."

"Sorry. The job for knight in shining armor is antiquated. Probably been outsourced. Besides, I don't need your help. Your help is what got me fired." She got into the car, started the pitiful-sounding engine, and took off.

She was wrong. She did need his help. He would prove it.

But, most of all, she needed his love.

And he sure as hell couldn't live without hers.

14

Meg sat on the beach drinking a flat wine cooler and wishing she could turn back time.

Tonight she sat alone. Sure, she'd done it thousands of times. But that was B.T.—before Tyler. She missed him with an ache that bordered on unbearable.

She swiped at the lone tear trickling down her cheek and tried to rouse her indignation by recalling his harsh words. But, deep down, she understood and couldn't blame him. The facts were damning.

Roger had withdrawn his beach project, and for the last week any construction sounds were from tearing down. For some reason she suspected Tyler was to thank for that. And she would thank him.

Assuming she ever saw him again.

For over a week Miss Hannah's house had been dark. There were no midnight rides on the beach. Both Tyler's truck and horse trailer were gone.

Dang. She wiped at her eyes again. Why did she have to do something stupid like fall in love with the jerk?

Vibration on the sand drew her attention. As the white speck drew closer, she held her breath, afraid to trust her eyes. Besides, they kept leaking.

Horse and rider pranced up, jingling all the way. Good thing the sun had set, she thought, or all the white, silver, and sequins would blind her.

Jim's mane was braided with jingle bells. Jingle bells surrounded each of his ankles . . . Well, they would if horses had ankles. Then there was Tyler. . . .

She'd never seen such a beautiful sight. Her heart swelled just looking at him.

He reached up, moonlight sparkling from the sequined fringe on his elbow-length gloves, and held his hat high in the air while Jim stood on his hind legs.

As soon as Jim had all fours on the hard sand, Tyler jumped down and walked toward her with a dazzling smile.

She hoped the smile meant he'd forgiven her.

He stopped at the edge of the blanket and removed his hat. "Hi," he said, his voice low. He motioned toward the blanket. "Mind if I sit down?"

"It's never stopped you before." She took a swig of wine cooler and wiped her mouth with the back of her hand. "I'm sorry. That was rude. Forget I said it."

He sat next to her but kept his distance. Darn.

"Are you drunk?"

"Nope, not yet."

"Then I guess we should talk fast." Removing his gloves, he tossed them into his hat at the edge of the blanket and then reached for her hand.

Through fresh tears she looked at their joined hands and prayed he wasn't about to dump her again. She couldn't stand it.

"Meg." Tyler swallowed and started again. "Meg, I know I

said some awful things to you at Ferris's office. It was shock—and hurt—talking. I didn't mean any of it."

"You didn't?" She sniffed and wished she had a tissue.

He shook his head. "And about that job as white knight? Would one slightly tarnished cowboy who happens to love you with all his heart and soul do?"

"Would you repeat that? Please?"

"I said would one slightly—"

"No! The last part."

He scooted closer. "You mean the part about loving you with all my heart and soul?"

She nodded.

"I love you," he said, close to her ear. "I think I have from the first time I laid eyes on you." The horse snorted. "Jim loves you, too. Will you marry us?" He leaned down. "Are you laughing or crying?"

"Both." She sniffed again and threw her arms around his neck to pull him down for a kiss. "Yes, of course I'll marry you!"

He crushed her to him, his mouth taking hers in a carnal preview of what was to come. "Say it," he demanded when they came up for air.

"I'll marry you."

He growled.

"Oh, you want to know if I love you?" She giggled, sure her happiness would make her float away at any second, had she not been anchored securely within Tyler's embrace.

Smiling, she put her arms around his neck and played with the hair brushing his sequined collar. "Yes, I love you. I thought you would have been smart enough to figure it out by now."

"Hey, you give me too much credit. I didn't figure out the grim reaper. I tell you, woman, I'm pathetic." He stood and tugged her to her feet. "Let's go for a ride and then make love in a bed like an old married couple."

She checked out his costume, head to sparkling toe.

"I like your boots."

"You do?" He grinned down at her.

She nodded.

He pulled her into his embrace and nuzzled her neck and then whispered in her ear, "They're my hero boots."

Saddle Sore

Nelissa Donovan

1

"Goddamn it, Jake, if you walk out that door, don't think you'll walk back through it without—"

"Your fist in my face?" Jake smiled sadly. "Yeah, I figured."

Dean brushed a hand through his shoulder-length hair. "That's not what I was going to say." As they locked gazes, Dean worked to control his temper. "It's the wrong thing to do, Jake."

He shrugged. "Maybe. But it's my decision to make, not yours. Not anymore." Jake's keys were already in his hand as he walked onto the front porch. "You taught me to stand up for what I think is right, and I think this is right. They belong here, Dean."

Dean was silent, his thoughts churning like a monsoon moving in fast from the south. "And we don't? What about the horses, Jake? Would you feel the same if it had been one of our mares or studs?"

The sandy-haired twenty-year-old scrubbed a hand across his clean-shaven face. "We don't know for sure that the wolves are the ones doing the killing. They deserve a shot here. It's what Mom would have wanted."

Jake's words rattled through Dean's bones. "Look, come back inside, and we'll talk about it." He tried to keep the heat from his words and from his eyes. Eyes that had a tendency to send people scurrying.

"You mean come back inside and let you convince me why you're right, and I'm wrong? No, thanks." The lanky cowboy turned and walked down the limestone steps toward the trucks parked in the drive nearby.

As Dean moved outside, a strange ache filled his chest. "Jake! Damnit. Get back in here!"

His brother ignored him and kept walking. When was the last time the boy had done that?

He's not a boy. Not anymore, Dean.

His mother's voice whispered through his mind as it had many times in past years. Reminding him of what it was like to be ten or sixteen or now twenty. Reminding him to try to see things from Jake's perspective and not just from the position of the responsible older brother who wanted to keep him safe.

Dean watched as Jake threw himself inside his truck and slammed the door. The headlights came on as the motor rumbled to life. Dean stayed put as the ache in his chest slipped into his gut with a sickening lurch. He watched until the taillights of the old Ford disappeared around the curve of the granite drive.

"Damn," Dean said. "Friggin' goddamn."

The encroaching night seemed to close in on him, the aroma of pine and evening primrose leaving him restless instead of calmed. Dean tensed. He knew it was coming. His hand gripped the alder door. Only one wolf—at first, but as the sun began to sink farther behind the granite peaks to the west, another and then another.

Funny, but Dean felt like howling right along with them.

* * *

"No, Jesse, I can't ' just look' at the GPS. I told you, it's not working."

Cassandra Darling jabbed at the frozen digital display, her eyes flicking from it to the empty stretch of highway in front of her.

She heard a pointed sigh through her headset. "Right." Cassie bit her tongue to keep from letting Jesse know what she really thought about his comment and said instead, "Jesse, are you going to help me or not?"

"Yeah, yeah, keep your pants on."

The clickety-clack of fingers on a keyboard told Cassie he'd been helping all along. She smiled. Jesse could be exasperating, but he *was* efficient.

"All right, you're going to take the next right at . . . . oh, let's call it Nowhere Lane Number One. You'll travel approximately ten more miles, and then turn left on Nowhere Lane Number Two. That should lead you directly through the center of . . . what did you call it?" Cassie heard a snort. "Oh, yes, the rip-roarin' town of Granite Hollow. Try to keep your powder dry, sweetheart."

Cassie laughed as she turned onto the nearly invisible side road—lane—and was still grinning when she said, "Will do. Same goes for you."

She could almost see Jesse's dimpled smirk. "Don't count on it. I deserve a little fun. So do you, actually, which is why I still don't understand why you jumped at this assignment. You know it's going to be nothing but angry hotheads and bleeding-heart toadies. Just what you need after your breakup with Mr. Rocking Climber Cheat and Run."

Cassie grimaced. "I'm not here to make friends, Jesse, or to prospect for a more reliable boyfriend. This release was supposed to be as smooth as butter. The perfect setting—the perfect opportunity for the pack."

"Nothing's ever perfect, Sunshine. Not even you. Remember

that, and don't get too down on yourself when you can't craft a solution that pleases everyone. Someone, or something, always ends up on the losing end."

A knot of tension hardened in Cassie's stomach. "I don't buy that. There *can* be a win-win."

Jesse's chuckle was affectionate but edged with concern. "You keep telling yourself that, Cass, and it just might come true."

Cassie flicked on her headlights as the twisted road began to darken. "I'd better go. Don't want to miss this next turn— wherever it is."

"Right. We wouldn't want you ending up in Vail, doing anything so foolish as relaxing."

Smiling, Cassie touched the headset. "Ranger One, signing off."

Another sigh. "How many times have I told you? You're number two. *I'm* number one."

"Good-bye, Jesse. Have a great night."

"Night, Cass. Be a bad girl whenever the opportunity presents itself."

Cassie punched off her phone and freed it from behind her ear. She hadn't expected it to get dark so soon or for the drive to take so long. It had been a very strange thing to leave the crazy big-city bustle of Phoenix and begin the snaking drive east. Only an hour up the Beeline Highway, and the landscape had morphed from majestic saguaros, mesquite, and pale paloverde to leafy cottonwoods and vast grasslands surrounded by juniper and towering ponderosas.

Once she'd turned off the main highway and began winding her way down the cracked and patched back roads, it was plain to see why the government, in conjunction with the Wilderness Preservation Coalition, had chosen this spot for the wolf release. Cassie's eyes drifted to the rim of granite spears that rose to the north like an imposing citadel. All rights to the thirty thousand acres had been given to the coalition by a foreign investor, and when the coalition had approached Fish and Wildlife about possibly using the area for a release, they'd jumped at the opportunity.

It was near perfect. Or so everyone had thought. Simon Alistair, the coalition's chairman, had volunteered to oversee the project himself, which had surprised Cassie. She'd met the man on a few different occasions and never figured him for a field controller. He struck her as more of a big-bash fund-raiser and PR events type of guy.

The pack had been ensconced in their new home for nearly five months now, and from the reports she'd read, the small community of Granite Hollow hadn't raised much opposition to the release until recently. Cassie needed to find out what their concerns were, investigate both sides, and hopefully make a recommendation that would ease tension. It didn't help any that the agent assigned had quit a month ago without giving notice. Her bosses hadn't even realized he was gone until one of the coalition members had called to ask if Peter was coming back.

Peter had never been a reliable guy, in Cassie's opinion, but her opinion hadn't been asked when Peter was assigned.

"Holy shit!" Cassie slammed on her brakes and the T-Bird screeched to a halt. She squinted to see past the glare on her windshield. Something big. In the middle of the road. Thank god she hadn't been the one to hit it.

The car door creaked as she stepped out into the night, and then silence washed over her as if she had dove into the deep end of a pool. She could hear the strange echo of her own labored breath and imagined her heartbeat was nearly as loud.

"Oh," Cassie said as she drew closer and knelt. It was a deer. The metallic tang of blood hit her at the same time she spotted the deer's belly. Entrails were splattered across the asphalt, along with other parts and chunks.

A tingle vibrated up from the base of her spine to the top of her head, and Cassie's gaze snapped to the inky darkness that lined the roadway to her left. The silvery reflection of several pairs of eyes blinked back at her from the dense foliage. Cassie's jaw tightened, and beads of sweat broke out across her chest and back.

"No problem, Cass," she whispered to herself. Wolves didn't attack people, and they weren't about to fight her for rights to the roadkill. She scanned the dead animal with a practiced eye. Taking advantage of roadkill was a dangerous and lethal habit for the wolves to have established, and as Cassie backed up confidently to her car and slipped inside, she was certain this roadway wasn't part of the preserve. The one thing the government and wildlife conservationists had had to concede to citizens in each release area was boundaries. Invisible lines the animals were not allowed to cross, or they risked capture, relocation, or worse.

A low rumble reached Cassie's ears through her open window, and she leaned out to look up and down the dark road. Nothing. She could have sworn it had sounded like a car engine. Actually, like an old Jeep. Her father had owned one for twenty-five years, and Cassie would never forget that telltale rumble. In her mind it always signaled that trouble was on its way.

She looked at the corpse again and tried to relax the death grip she had on the steering wheel. "Bet you never figured I would be doing this, Dad."

2

Cassie bumped her front tire into the cracked curb as she parked. She squinted up at the badly faded marker, lit only by a weak garden up-light. "Flanagan's Place," she said aloud. Looking down at her Blackberry, she used the stylus to scroll forward and sighed in relief. "This is it."

Finally. It might have taken her an extra hour, but hopefully it wasn't so late she couldn't grab a bite to eat before bed. She'd taken about fifteen minutes on the side of the road by the downed deer to write a quick account and to take pictures. She would have to report the incident to the sheriff and the ranger assigned to this district in the morning.

Slinging her briefcase over her shoulder, Cassie exited the car and closed the door behind her. She breathed in deeply. The air was crisp, clean, so different from the LA smog she was used to. And was that—yes—she could smell flowers of some sort, and pine, and other earthy aromas that reminded her of Wisconsin, where she grew up.

"No time for old memories, Cass," she said aloud to herself, smoothing a hand down her A-line skirt and then tugging her form-fitting jacket into a more professional position.

It was too dark to get a solid impression of the small town, but Cassie was certain she'd not passed more than six or seven businesses lining the main street, with maybe a home or two sprinkled in between, their lights burning softly through faded curtains.

If not for the faded sign, the two-story farm-style home in front of her—the only registered hotel/bed-and-breakfast within fifty miles—would be indistinguishable from the other homes scattered around. In fact, there weren't even any lights on inside. She checked her watch again: 8:05 PM. Surely they wouldn't have turned in *this* early. She had said she wouldn't be in until around seven.

After several knocks and phone calls with no answer, Cassie rubbed tired eyes and conceded that they must be out. "Okay . . . guess I'll go find something to eat and come back."

"They're at the meeting."

Cassie cried out and spun around. A broad figure filled the space at the bottom of the porch steps, arms crossed, face in shadow.

"I didn't hear you," Cassie stammered, working to compose herself. She swallowed and walked forward. "Do you know what time they'll return?"

"Depends."

Cassie's feet slowed as the man's deep tone set off alarm bells. She stopped at the top of the stairs. If she were to walk down, she would end up directly in the man's face, and he looked about as intent on moving as a mountain might. "Depends on?"

"On whether or not the result of the meeting sends them to Callahan's for a stiff drink."

Cassie's heart thrummed, and her mouth went dry. "And you are?"

His head came up, and he pushed his hat back on his forehead. "Just a concerned citizen, ma'am."

The dim porch light left much of the man's face and body in shadow, but there was no shadowing his eyes. They glowed like golden torches, and Cassie had to force herself not to step backward. *Golden eyes.* She'd only seen eyes like that on one other creature—

"They were concerned you would show up late without any clue where to go."

Cassie couldn't stop staring. The man was huge, six-four or maybe -five, with powerful arms and dressed like he'd stepped straight out the screen of *Hondo* or *Deadwood*—literally. Leather boots, a gnarled and dusty Stetson, and—*was that a gun on his hip?*

"Something wrong?"

Her gaze snapped up from her perusal back to his face. He stepped forward. The light from the porch illuminated a weather-toughened face grounded by an authoritative jaw and, again, those eyes.

And something else.

It wasn't until he tilted his head a fraction that Cassie noticed the scar. It ran from the middle of his ear down his cheek to nearly his chin. It looked old, the skin softly ridged and tanned a shade lighter than the brown skin on the rest of his face.

"What hap—?" Horrified at what she'd almost asked, Cassie cleared her throat and tried to find something neutral to look at. Like the stinkbug that was scuttling across her Milani pumps. "Uh, where did you say the proprietors are?"

He didn't answer right away. Cassie looked up to find his eyes narrowed, his gaze resting intently on her face. "My gun makes you nervous?"

His words were soft, and Cassie couldn't control the shiver

that ratcheted down her spine. She couldn't decide if he was hitting on her or ridiculing her. "Not really. Should it?"

He smiled, and a powerful wave of desire hit Cassie. She felt the tips of her breasts tingle and her clit tighten. *What is wrong with me?*

"It is loaded, but so are a lot of things in life. Like thinking our government always works in its citizens' best interests."

Cassie ignored the strange sensations that pulsed through her and forced herself down the flight of stairs to stand directly in front of the rugged cowboy. She stopped on the bottom step, and, even elevated six inches, she was dwarfed by the man's bulk. She thrust out a hand. "Cassandra Darling. You should know I work for that very government." She smiled, hoping to put him at ease. Hoping to erase the inexplicable curl of desire that had somehow harnessed itself to her at the cowboy's arrival.

He didn't take her hand. Silence stretched between them, and Cassie dropped her arm to her side, her stomach churning. Only inches apart, Cassie could sense the tension in his shoulders, and the twitch of a rather prodigious muscle in his neck confirmed it. Even so, she kept her cool. She was all about cool. Offend no one, and reserve judgment until you have all the facts. It was the mantra she'd lived by in her job, and it had served her well.

"Do you have something you would like to say to me?" Cassie looked him directly in the eyes, which was hard to do, as her gaze wanted to stray to his fine pecs or to the chiseled outline of his broad chest through his denim shirt. "I'll listen if you do, and if not, I'll kindly ask you to step aside so I can go find something to eat."

His golden eyes never flinched, nor did he look away. Cassie found herself breaking eye contact first, as staring into their warm amber depths left her a little light-headed and her mouth

so dry she doubted she could say another word without chok-
ing.

"They'll be back in an hour."

Cassie looked up, her mouth open and ready to reply—but
the cowboy had already started walking down the street.
"Wait!" she called, wondering if she'd lost her mind to be yelling at an angry mountain man with a gun. "You didn't tell me
your name!"

Without turning, she heard, "Dean McCabe. Might be good
to remember it."

A cupie doll. They'd sent a goddamn cupie doll.

Dean yanked off his hat and pounded it against his jeans before running a hand through his dark hair and shoving the hat
back onto his head. When Carla and Floyd had told him they
were expecting a boarder—the new agent sent to mediate—he
was sure it would be the typical park-ranger-turned-bean-counter
like they'd had before. Dean had never received a straight answer as to why the agent had left abruptly or who was supposed to be replacing him. And his recent calls to Washington
hadn't gotten him anything other than the message that things
were "being handled."

He'd planned on giving the new agent the lowdown before
the coalition whack jobs got their hooks in him—and then he'd
spotted *her*.

Silhouetted on the shadowed porch, she looked a hell of a
lot like Jessica Rabbit, minus the furry sidekick. For some
reason, as soon as he'd set eyes on her, Dean was angry all
over again. Furious, actually. While he'd intended to engage
whoever they'd sent in an open discussion of the issues they'd
been facing and the government's total lack of response, all he
could think of when faced with the petite, knockout blond

was how kissable her soft, pink lips looked and how her tits would feel in the palms of his hands. She looked more like a high-powered mortgage broker than a US Fish and Wildlife agent, and she smelled a hell of a lot better than Peter had, too.

Dean closed his eyes as her scent came back to him—honeysuckle. Sunshine and toasted sugar. "Damn," he murmured, his thoughts now shifting from her scent to her curvaceous body, pixie face, and wide blue eyes. He'd gotten an instant hard-on when she had sashayed down the steps to stand directly in front of him, her tits pointing at his chest like an open invitation to see if they tasted as good as they looked.

And even though he'd been a total asshole, she'd been as cool as a six-pack stashed in the creek in January. For some reason, that knowledge filled Dean with a flush of hot pleasure and then, just as quickly, foreboding. Maybe it meant she would have enough common sense to see through the coalition's slipshod excuses, or it meant she'd already been paid off and was just biding her time to tell the good folks of Granite Hollow to go fuck themselves.

Dean ground his teeth and tried to shake off the play-by-play of their encounter as he walked toward the double doors of the meeting room. The heavy oak smacked the back of the wall as Dean entered. Twenty-something heads turned, and the yelling died down.

"They're saying it's not the wolves that're doing it, Dean!"

Dean stared at the red, shiny face of his closest neighbor, Ted Cochran, before his gaze cut to the dais where four people sat. "Mayor? You believe that?"

The mayor stood, his jowls jiggling with the force of his shifting bulk. "Take a seat, Dean. We were just discussing what the experts have told us regarding the latest attack."

"I can listen standing up," Dean said, his gaze arrowing to the profusely sweating grad student sitting on the mayor's right side. Their qualified "expert."

Mayor Grimble raised caterpillar-sized eyebrows. "Well, say it again, Calvin."

Calvin swallowed, his Adam's apple bobbing like a cork in a storm-driven sea. "Well, uh, like I was saying . . . the attacks aren't consistent with the pack's normal behavior."

"Was Cochran's sheep killed by a wild animal?" Dean asked.

"It appears as though—" His head came up as Dean moved to stand directly in front of him. "Yes. Yes, it was definitely killed by some animal, but it could have been a wildcat or a cougar or even a badger—"

"A sheep-killing badger?" Dean said, eyebrows arched. Snickers broke out through the room.

Calvin flushed crimson and looked to the mayor for help. If they actually *had* a qualified animal behaviorist monitoring the incidents, Dean wouldn't feel the need to torment the coalition so mercilessly—maybe—but how they were running things was a joke. A slap in the face to the citizens of Granite Hollow, who had at first been, if not supportive, at least tolerant of the release. His gaze rested on the coalition's leader, Simon Alistair. The rumpled, finger-tapping businessman always seemed distracted, and it was obvious the man was way out of his depth. Dean had tried to discuss the issues with Simon, but somehow he always seemed to slip just beyond Dean's reach.

"Listen," the mayor said as he cleared his throat and sat back down. "The coalition is doing what they can to track the pack's movements. So far they've seen no indication that they've been in town at all."

Ted stood up again. "Then what in the hell's been after our livestock and pets, Mayor? Explain that!"

The mayor lumbered back up, rattling the entire table. "We don't know, Ted. If we did, we would already have taken care of the problem."

"What about the prints, Mayor? Anyone with half a damn brain could see they were canine, not a goddamn mountain lion or badger." Ted slammed his hat against the seat in front of him and then leveled a finger at the coalition leader. "No more games, Alistair. If your people won't do something about it, then we will."

Shouts of assent filled the room as the faces of the coalition members paled, which was when Dean spotted Jake. He was all the way to the side of the dais, his face creased with worry, his mouth pressed into a thin line.

Dean held up a hand and silence fell. "Simon, why the hell aren't you tracking the wolves? We know they're collared."

Simon cleared his throat and shook his head. "We are. But we don't know where they are every second. We don't have that kind of man power or equipment."

Jake stepped forward. "We've never seen any of the pack below Rustler's Ridge. And think about it, Dean, if it were wolves they would be eating what they killed. You wouldn't have found *any* parts of the Flanagans' cat—" He tipped his head to the older redhead in the front row and said, "Sorry, Carla," before his gaze came back to rest on Dean—"let alone the body. Same with Cochran's sheep. It's got to be something else."

Dean wondered at the narrow gaze Simon threw his little brother's way. As though he didn't want Jake to divulge even that small of a detail, which was one of the reasons Dean had been so pissed off about Jake siding with the coalition. Something just wasn't right about the entire operation.

After Jake had walked out earlier that night, Dean had thought long and hard about what this might mean for them.

For the ranch. But so help him, if the kid was sure enough to stand opposite him on this issue, he'd better be prepared to defend his position. "So, are you the new expert on the pack's behavior, Jake?"

"He might not be, but I am."

All heads shifted toward the doorway and the strong, unfamiliar female voice.

3

Cassie forced her pulse back to a reasonable level as she scanned the room. Dean McCabe was squaring off with a younger, lighter, and definitely smoother version of the hulking cowboy. The young man was nearly as handsome as the intimidating Mr. McCabe. Even so, Cassie found her herself wanting to examine every inch of her gun-toting cowboy, now that she had him in a well-lit room, but there wasn't time for that.

She strode forward. "Good evening." She moved past Dean, her arm brushing his as she passed. A thread of electricity pulsed through her at the contact, and Cassie suppressed another shiver as she stopped at the front of the room and turned. "My name is Cassandra Darling, and I'm with the US Fish and Wildlife Service."

Her eyes lighted on Simon, and Cassie nodded almost imperceptibly. It wouldn't be prudent for her to seem too friendly with anyone involved with the coalition. He nodded back, his expression neutral. Cassie turned back to the twenty-some people who were crammed into the small room. "I look forward to meeting each of you individually to discuss your concerns—"

"What took you so long?" came a booming voice, and Cassie shifted to view a good-looking, dark-haired woman, her face painfully flushed. "We were told all this would be monitored and controlled! It's been nearly a month, and the only 'experts' available have been the coalition members, and nothing's been done!"

Cassie forced her expression and voice to stay neutral. "I'm sorry. That's something I'm here to determine as well. We will get to bottom of the situation and figure out what needs to be done. You have my word."

The woman's gaze never wavered, but Cassie detected a hint of curiosity and maybe hope. "And how do you intend to do that?" the woman asked.

"I need to get input from those who have experienced the depredations," Cassie said loudly. Voices rose in unison, and Cassie raised a hand. "Individually. Once I've had a chance to speak to the sheriff and look at reports, I'll be contacting the parties involved so we can—"

"So you're saying more time can go by, and more mutilations can happen, while you chat up the locals?"

Cassie faced Dean McCabe, her stomach forming a new knot at the ringing timbre of his voice. "Mr. McCabe, I understand this is an urgent matter. I also understand the correct way to assess this situation so that a decision can be made expediently. It's what I do."

Dean moved in closer, but Cassie stayed put. She was forced to bend her head back to meet his brilliant amber gaze. "I suggest that whatever you 'do,' sugar, you do it fast, or the consequences won't be healthy for anyone here in Granite Hollow."

"That's Ms. Darling to you, not 'sugar,'" Cassie said, matching Dean's low voice. Blood rushed to her face, and she cursed herself for being affected either way by the rough cowboy's presence or his inflammatory words. "And thank you for that, Mr. McCabe. I'll take that into consideration."

She turned, nodded again to those present, and walked out, her entire body burning with irritation and something else. Something Cassie didn't want to think about. Couldn't think about. Not now. Not here. And definitely not with Dean McCabe.

Sunday had been a bad day all around, and the following week hadn't gotten much better. Dean had done his damnedest to stay out of town and away from Miss Cassandra Darling and from Jake. Damn, but the woman had looked just as good under the bad fluorescent lighting in the meeting hall as she had half in shadow on the Flanagans' porch.

Dean slammed the door behind him, not bothering to lock it before he strode across the lawn toward the stables.

Christ. That was all he needed, to get cross-eyed horny over a government bombshell sent to decide the future of Granite Hollow and possibly even his ranch. Without Jake around, things had been tougher, the days longer, and the nights bone-deep quiet.

Except for the howls.

The yips and long-winded yowls weaved into the encroaching darkness each night like the whispers of the trees, the hoots of the owls, and the rush of the stream nearby. *Part and parcel.* Jake's exact words. The wolves were part and parcel of Granite Hollow. They belonged to the land, and the land belonged to them.

Dean grunted and tried to push his thoughts in another direction, but it was no good. The smell of fresh hay and honey-suckle filled the air around him, and Dean remembered that Agent Darling had smelled pretty damn good, too. Carla and Floyd and his neighbor Ted had kept Dean in the loop about

Cassie's agenda in town. So far she seemed pretty fair-minded, but Dean would reserve judgment until she actually concluded her findings and made a recommendation. At least there had been no more killings. Dean knew people were set on taking their own measures against the wolves, and while Dean had every intention of protecting his livestock, he wasn't bent on hunting down the wolves. The media would have a field day if someone actually managed to take one out, which was the last thing Granite Hollow—and his ranch—needed.

The Rocking T's reputation was everything. If word got around that wolves were a threat, it could be just the wild card to make certain people decide to take their prized mares elsewhere. Even so, he was less worried about his spread than he was about his neighbors', whose operations were considerably smaller. It would take only one bad season for some of them to pack it in.

Trying to spin his thoughts in a different direction, Dean saddled Romulus and headed out to locate the herd of rescued mustangs that roamed the Rocking T. It was time to round them up for culling and branding, and he needed to get a head count.

As the hours ticked by, Dean's thoughts kept wandering back to the cool blonde and then on to his brother Jake. Normally his younger brother would be riding next to him on a day like today, yakking up a storm about this idea or that opportunity until Dean wanted to shove a rag in his mouth. Funny, but now the silence stretched like the icy grip of January—cold and seemingly never-ending in its gray dullness.

"Whoa," Dean said softly, pulling back on the stallion's reins and looking skyward. The lake-blue skies were bisected by only a few passing clouds—and something else. Dean watched the dark, lazy circles of the turkey vultures for a few minutes, judging direction and distance before urging Romulus into a gallop.

Ten minutes later, Dean slowed the stallion to a trot and

then to a walk as they drew closer. He noted recent signs of the mustang herd in the grassy meadow, and his stomach churned. As he crested the ridge, the meadow rolled out below him, and in the center of the field the vultures fed.

"Yah!" Dean spurred Romulus down the small hill toward the horde of black, sending them lumbering and careening skyward at his approach.

He reined the stallion to a halt, swung his leg over Romulus's wide flanks, and dismounted. The grassy ground had been flattened and torn up by the struggle, and the flies had already descended on the bloody kill. "Shit," Dean said, recognizing the old paint mare—a mustang his father had purchased nearly thirteen years ago at auction. She was one of the oldest in the herd. He knelt, placing his bandanna over his mouth as he leaned in for a closer look. The belly had been ripped open and the legs gnawed on, but the majority of the flank, shoulders, and head was still intact. An experienced tracker, Dean began to scan the surrounding field until he found what he'd been looking for—tracks. Several of them. And they weren't mountain lion, bear, or badger.

"Goddamn," he growled as he stared into the ponderosas that lined the clearing and then up at the granite peaks that speared the achy blue skies behind them.

4

"The evidence strongly suggests that the wolves *have* been involved in these depredations, Mr. Alistair."

"Simon, please, Cassandra. We're all on first-name terms here."

Cassie didn't return the coalition field-operations manager's tight smile. "What I don't understand, Simon, is why you haven't been able to track the wolves involved?" Cassie looked pointedly at the six members of the coalition staff that crowded the living room of the five-bedroom cabin they'd rented for the duration of their study.

Most gazes slipped away from Cassie's, except for Simon's. He was quiet for a moment and then said, "How much time have you spent in the field, Cassandra?"

Cassie sat back in the chair and forced her irritation into the background, ignoring his challenge. "You do realize that if we can't distinguish which ones are doing the depredations, they will all be removed?"

Simon Alistair leaned forward on the desk, his expression

unreadable. "Is that going to be your official finding? Will you be recommending relocation?"

Cassie's gaze didn't waver, but she did wait before answering. She didn't want to tell him it probably would be her official finding as she still had evidence to comb through and more people to interview, and there was something disconcerting about Simon's emotionless attitude. But she supposed a calm leader was better than a half-crazed one.

"I can't answer that now, Simon," Cassie finally said. "I have more research to do, which includes spending a day with your field ops to observe the pack and their habits. I would like to do that tomorrow."

A scrape of a chair pulled Cassie's attention to the back of the room, where a young man stood. "I can take you out, ma'am."

Cassie realized it was the handsome sandy-blond young man who had faced off with Dean McCabe earlier in the week. "And you are Mr. . . . ?"

"Just Jake, ma'am."

"All right, Just Jake." She grinned. "But only if you stop calling me 'ma'am.' Makes me feel like my grandmother."

His face reddened, but he smiled, and Cassie's breath caught at the stunning quality it brought to his serious but handsome features. Jake took off his hat. "We'll go out early on horseback. You should know we haven't been getting signals near town, which is why these killings don't make sense. I can't figure why they would be killing for sport. There's plenty of natural game on the mountain."

Cassie returned his smile, admiring Jake's passion, and remembering that same fire in herself when she had first started working closely with the release programs three years ago. While her passion for the majestic animals had never faded, the reality of what it took to try to reintroduce a native predatory species into the now "civilized" world quickly tempered that blind ardor. "It's not unheard of. Sometimes an animal will develop a lust for the killing. And as far as not having picked up signals near town, it could be that one or more of the collars are defective or giving off weak signals. It's something that needs to be checked."

Cassie steadied her gaze back at Simon Alistair. "We have to do everything we can to get this situation under control. It's vital to *all* the release programs that we maintain impeccable relations with the communities and that they follow the letter of the law exactly. If we cut corners or err on the side of the wolves at the expense of the community, we put *all* of the current programs and future programs at risk."

Simon's iron expression never wavered. "Of course, we understand that, Miss Darling."

Cassie smiled. "Do you, Mr. Alistair?"

He didn't answer, and Cassie stood, knowing she'd outworn her welcome. She almost felt sorry for the man, but stubborn ignorance in something as important as this wasn't acceptable. There were lives at stake, those of the wolves and those of the domesticated animals and the livelihoods of the people in this town.

She turned back to Jake. "It was nice to meet you, Jake. The coalition is lucky to have someone with your dedication and passion assisting them."

The young cowboy moved to the door with her, his boots clunking on the hardwood floor. "I would like to walk you out, if that's okay."

"Certainly," Cassie said, curious despite her vow to remain as detached from the coalition members as she could prior to her official determination. But this young man intrigued her.

Once the door closed behind her, Cassie felt the tension lift from her shoulders, and she walked with ease to her car, with

Jake mirroring her steps. "Was there something you wanted to say to me in private, Jake?"

"Actually, yes."

Cassie studied his handsome face and was again struck with the knowledge that he looked familiar. His green eyes were shadowed with concern and something else—maybe a little trepidation.

"I don't suppose I should be asking you this, but you seem like the type of person who might be able to talk sense into someone."

Cassie's curiosity flared even greater. "Whatever you say to me in confidence, Jake, will stay confidential."

He ran a hand through his collar-length hair before looking up, his gaze somber. "There's talk that certain people are taking things into their own hands and hunting the wolves. They intend to shoot on sight, and I know them all well enough to tell you they mean it." He held up a hand before she could respond. "They're good folks. I've known them my whole life, but they're scared, Miss Darling. Scared for their animals, their livelihood, and even for their children's safety. I've tried to talk to them, but they won't listen." He glanced over his shoulder at the coalition headquarters. "Not anymore. But there's someone they *will* listen to, if he would speak up."

"What makes you think this person will be influenced by me?"

The corners of Jake's eyes crinkled, and he smiled. "Because he respects tough, knowledgeable people, and that's exactly what you are, Cassie."

Cassie started at the familiar use of her name, but she didn't take offense by it. Quite the opposite. She felt comfortable with this man. As if she'd known him forever. It was a strange feeling. "All right. Who is this person?"

"Dean McCabe. My older brother and owner of the Rocking T."

* * *

As Cassie checked her hair in the car visor mirror, she thought back on the day's events, particularly her conversation with Jake McCabe. Against her better judgment, Cassie had accepted Jake's invitation for an early dinner, and over fried chicken and mashed potatoes, she had ended up telling him things about herself she probably shouldn't have. And Jake had been more than willing to disgorge his own history. She learned that Dean had raised Jake from the time of their mother's death, when Jake was nine and Dean twenty. Apparently their father had been scarce before their mother died, and afterward stopped coming around altogether. Or, Dean had convinced him *not* to come around. . . . Jake didn't sound too sure which way it had played out.

Cassie couldn't help but think Jake might have been the lucky one by not having his father around. Too bad she couldn't say the same.

He'd also told Cassie that Dean had been running the ranch pretty much on his own since that time, and Cassie couldn't help a grudging amount of respect begin to color her initial opinion of Dean McCabe. It was a pretty amazing accomplishment for a twenty-year-old to raise his younger brother by himself *and* manage a successful horse ranch.

Cassie smiled and flipped the visor back up. She looked out the window at the quiet, one-story, sprawling ranch home and took a deep breath. "Well, it's not going to get any easier five minutes from now."

When she'd agreed to speak to Dean, Cassie had thought it wouldn't be such a difficult thing, but now it was all she could do not to run in the opposite direction and pretend she and Jake had never had that discussion. Late afternoon was already winding down, and Cassie wanted to get it over with and get back into town before the pitch black of Granite Hollow settled in like velvet drapes.

"Quit being such a wuss, Cass," she said under her breath as she walked toward the front steps. Jake had assured her that Dean would be a perfect gentleman, if a little brash, and that he wasn't prone to shooting people.

Cassie wiped sweaty palms on her skirt before she knocked. As her fist connected, the dark wood eased inward, throwing Cassie off balance. She caught the edge of the door and steadied herself, her eyes blinking to adjust to the change in light. "Uh, hello? Mr. McCabe?"

No answer. Cassie backed out and rapped loudly on the wood, clearing her throat at the same time. "Mr. McCabe?"

Nothing.

Cassie frowned. She imagined people probably left their doors unlocked in Granite Hollow, but it seemed odd that they would leave them wide open as well. As a niggling of concern filled her abdomen, Cassie stepped inside.

A brass table lamp shone brightly on a side table, and Cassie couldn't help but glance at the photos scattered around the large but comfortable-looking great room. A large pine-framed photo caught her eye near the door, and she picked it up for a closer look. A petite black-haired woman with an enormous smile filled the picture. She was holding a baby in one arm, her other wrapped around a tall, thin boy of about ten or eleven. Even at that young age, Cassie was struck by the brilliant amber gaze and warm, slightly devilish smile.

Dean. He looked so happy, so comfortable with his mother and baby brother. So proud.

"What in the hell do you think you're doing?"

Cassie shrieked and nearly dropped the picture as she spun around. "Dean?"

"Who in the hell else would it be? Last time I checked, this was my house."

Every line in Dean's granite-hard body was stretched tight, and his golden eyes seemed to flicker with barely controlled rage as he filled the doorway. Cassie was quick to set the photo back down and face him squarely, her heart thrumming in her throat. "I came to see you, and the door was open—"

"So that gives you the right to come inside and snoop?" He stepped closer, and Cassie was forced to step back.

Heat filled her face, but Cassie refused to look down. "Of course not. It's not like that."

Another step and Cassie found her back touching the wall and Dean blocking everything in front of her. Heat from his body filled the narrow space between them, and Cassie felt a sliver of desire curl inside her abdomen.

A sun-browned hand slapped the wall on one side of her head, followed by the other, and Cassie stared up in shock as Dean's head lowered until their faces were only inches apart. "What *is* it like, then, Cassandra?"

Cassie focused on Dean's full lips and tried to remember why she was there. The entire situation was ludicrous, surreal, and she was certain she must be dreaming.

His breath blew warm across her cheek as he settled in closer. "Well?" he growled.

Cassie pressed her fingers into her palms, her head floaty. "I—I thought you might be home and . . . are you going to kiss me?"

Dean smiled, and Cassandra's nipples tightened under his smoldering gaze.

"What would you do if I did?"

Cassie shivered and forced her gaze off his lips and back to his eyes. "Depends."

Dean raised dark brows. "On?"

"How hot the kiss makes me. I'm not known for my self-control when it comes to men who can kiss like gods and fuck like stallions. Are you one of those men, Dean McCabe?"

Cassie couldn't believe what she'd just said, but it was too late to take it back. Too late to try to salvage her professional image—at least with Dean McCabe, and, Cassie realized as she stared into the rugged cowboy's blazing eyes, she didn't care.

5

Goddamn, but it was all Dean could do to keep his hands on either side of Cassandra's head and not on her beautiful tits or cupping her hot mound.

He still couldn't believe what she'd just said, but the fact that she'd said it made his cock rock hard.

Cassie's gloss-pink lips trembled slightly under his gaze, and Dean let her sugary scent fill his senses. His mind reeled with visions of what he wanted to do to her, right now, right there.

And what was one kiss? He would just have to make certain his hands stayed on the wall. Her face was already raised as Dean's mouth descended. He captured her lips in a crushing kiss and then lightened the pressure as her mouth yielded to his. Their tongues met, and Dean breathed in her essence. *Goddamn*, she tasted as good as she looked. Dean shifted, his hands sliding down the wall.

He growled deep in his throat as he palmed the curves of her hips and drew her tight against his aching cock. Dean felt her gasp against his mouth as their bodies came together.

He heard Cassie's pumps clunk to the floor, and it was at that point that Dean realized he was actually holding Cassie off the ground. His hands had moved to cup her ass; he'd lifted her up a good six inches. "Perfect," he murmured. "A perfect handful."

He had also lifted her skirt to her waist, and Cassie's exposed, tanned thighs caught his attention; his heart skipped a beat as he thought of those gorgeous legs wrapped around his waist. "Sugar, I want to bury myself between those gorgeous thighs."

Cassandra groaned, her blue eyes easing closed, and Dean nuzzled her neck, her skin silky against his rough chin. "What do you have to say about that, Cassandra Darling?"

Dean heard her sharp intake of breath and waited to be told to go to hell, but instead, he heard a throaty chuckle and pulled away to look at the blond bombshell who had somehow managed to make him forget everything except for how badly he wanted—no, needed—to fuck her.

Her smile was sinful, and Dean's entire body thrilled at what her expression broadcast loud and clear. "I know I'll regret this, but—" Dean felt fingers brush across his abdomen, and every muscle in his body contracted at her touch. "I want you, Dean McCabe. I want to wrap my legs around your neck and feel you deep inside me."

Dean hissed between his teeth as her hand eased between their bodies to rub across the front of his jeans. His cock bucked in response, and with one hand he pulled off his shirt. She kept rubbing, and Dean kissed her forehead, her eyelids, each cheek. Nothing else mattered at that moment but how she tasted and felt beneath his hands. He eased her back against the wall, his body trembling in anticipation.

Like a goddamn schoolboy, Dean thought, but didn't care.

There was no other thought but *her*. Her golden hair, silky skin, and knockout curves. Dean's mouth stopped at the swell of her breast beneath her silk top.

"I want you to take this off," Dean said, his voice nearly unrecognizably thick with desire, and heat flooded Cassie's pussy.

He cupped both of her ass cheeks again, freeing her hand from between them. *Ohmygod . . .* thought Cassie as she stared at Dean's bare chest. The deep brown skin told her his shirt was off nearly as much as it was on, and the ripple of chiseled muscles from shoulders to abs reminded her that this was a *real* man. Not a gym-ripped stockbroker or mortgage banker looking for a three-month nooky partner and someone to pose with at parties.

Her fingers shook as she reached down and pulled her top over her head, tossing it aside. Every nerve in her body pinged with electricity. She leaned back slightly, her back touching the wall, allowing Dean a better view.

"Damn," Dean muttered.

Cassie smiled, her heart thudding so hard she thought surely he could hear it. Her hands went to the tiny clasp at the front of the black lace bra.

"Wait," Dean growled, and Cassie's hands froze as Dean lifted her until her breasts were even with his face. "Now, sugar."

She couldn't believe she was doing this. While she wasn't known for her good judgment with men, this had to take the cake. Even so, Dean's hot breath brushing the sensitive tops of her breasts and the thought of what this man could—would—do to her blocked any other doubts she might have.

Dean leaned in and lapped at her lace-covered nipples. First one and then the other. Cassie gasped as bolts of pure pleasure arrowed into her pussy.

"Still want to tease me, sugar?"

Taking a deep breath, Cassie unhooked the snap and let the bra fall open. Cool air caressed her beaded nipples, and Dean whispered, "Goddamn beautiful."

Cassie watched as Dean kissed the top of each breast. "I'm going to taste you."

"Yes," Cassie said, her own voice thick. "Please. . . ."

She almost shouted as Dean's mouth captured her entire nipple, pulling it into his warm mouth. His hands squeezed her ass as he kept her lifted, his tongue wrapping around her areola and pulling the diamond-hard tip in and out of his mouth.

"Jesus Christ," Cassie gasped, her head falling forward to rest against the top of Dean's head. His thick raven hair smelled like sun and wind and pine. Cassie squirmed as his tongue continued to flick and suck in a rhythmic pattern matched by his hips against the thin sheaf of her panties.

"Hmmm," Dean said, his voice coarse with desire. "You taste as good as you look and feel. Makes we wonder how you taste in other places."

An image of Dean's head between her legs, his shoulder-length hair brushing the inside of her thighs, filled Cassie's mind, and she groaned. "Now who's teasing?"

Dean lowered her until they were face-to-face. His strong-jawed visage, along with the intimidating scar and those wild, wolf eyes, left Cassie speechless. That was what Dean reminded her of, something wild—untamed—exactly like the animals he had pitted himself against.

"Sugar, there's something you should know about me." His gaze burned into hers, and Cassie could only stare. "I never tease."

Before Cassie could respond, she was upended and she found herself hanging over Dean's shoulder, her face nearly

even with his perfect butt. She heard the door slam closed behind them as a result of Dean's quick kick. They were striding
across the great room and through an adjoining doorway before Cassie could protest.

Not that she wanted to.

Her entire body was on fire, her panties soaked in anticipation, her heart hammering like a conga drum. "Dean McCabe,
what are you—"

Cassie gasped in shock as she felt a calloused hand on her
upturned ass. He'd stopped walking, and even from her
topsy-turvy position, Cassie knew they were in a bedroom.
His hand slipped under the thin silk of her panties and caressed her bare ass cheek, his thumb trailing ever closer to her
throbbing lips.

"I have a mirror above my headboard, sugar, and I can see
my hand on your firm ass."

His hand moved up and down, sending chills throughout
Cassie's entire body. "Dean, please," Cassie whispered, hating
the desperate tone of her voice, but knowing that if he didn't
touch her *there* she would explode.

"I can see the outline of your swollen pussy beneath your
panties, Cassie," Dean said softly, and Cassie groaned louder.
He drew his thumb down the edge of her panties, barely brushing the skin just beyond her pussy lips. "Hmmm . . . and I can
feel how wet you are."

"Dean!" Cassie said, her body shaking. "Please!"

"Please what, Cassandra?"

Cassie knotted her hands into fists and smacked them both on
Dean's hard ass. "Please touch me! Please use those long fi—"

A scream tore loose from Cassie's throat as Dean's finger
slipped under her panties and plunged into her creamy hole.
And he didn't stop there. His finger slipped in and out of her

pussy with the same mesmerizing rhythm he'd used to attend to her breasts earlier, and Cassie bit her lower lip to keep from shouting Dean's name with each magnificent thrust.

As the heat from her juices filled the room with the smell of sex, Cassie felt herself spiraling toward climax.

"That's it, sugar, let me see your beautiful pussy come."

Dean's rough voice and gently twisting finger was all it took. The orgasm shook Cassie from head to toe, and she couldn't help her scream or the sweet contractions around Dean's still plunging finger. Her head spun as the waves crashed over her again and again.

"Ohmygod," Cassie moaned against the muscled indentation at the small of Dean's back. Gently she felt his hands move to either side of her hips and pull her over his shoulder and down in front of him. The room was still spinning as Dean laid her on the bed, her skirt still up around her waist and her panties askew.

"That's what I want to see," Dean said softly, and Cassie looked up. He smiled wolfishly, and Cassie couldn't believe it, but her desire was as sharp as it had been two seconds ago before she had started orgasming all over the place. "Your eyes go smoky green, darlin', when you orgasm *and* when you're angry."

Cassie blinked up at him. How had he noticed that? No one had ever noticed that before but her, and half the time Cassie thought it was a figment of her imagination. "I don't think so," Cassie said, feeling like his observation was too personal. Which almost made her giggle. *Too personal . . . after what he just did to me? Am I crazy?*

To her surprise Dean laughed and put his hands on his hips. Which was when Cassie got her first visual of the bulge in Dean's pants. Cassie licked her lips unconsciously and almost brought her own finger back to her throbbing pussy. She came up to her knees, fighting not to act like a complete bubble-headed tramp at the thought Dean's cock in her hand and in her mouth.

"That was incredible," Cassie said. She moved closer to where Dean stood at the edge of the bed. She placed a hand on the flat of his stomach and drew her finger down the ridges of his abs. A myriad of scars bisected the otherwise perfect flesh, but Cassie didn't care about them. In fact, they intrigued her. She was certain they were born by a dozen interesting stories surrounding Dean's rough-and-tumble life, and she would be thrilled to hear every one of them—at some later time.

But now, now all Cassie wanted to hear was the sound of her own lips touching his skin, tasting every inch of it. As she tenderly kissed each muscled ridge, her hands slid down the sides of Dean's waist to hook into belt loops at the front of his jeans. She nuzzled her cheek against the bulge of his cock as her other hand cupped his balls through his pants, and she was rewarded with a sharp intake of breath.

With her other hand Cassie began to unbutton his fly, her mind so focused on her task she failed to notice that Dean's own hands had moved forward to cup her swinging breasts. She hissed in pleasure as his fingers found her nipples and squeezed.

"God, woman, you're going to make me come before my cock is even out of my pants."

Cassie smiled against his bulge. "Oh, no, cowboy, we're not having any of that. The only place you're allowed to come is in my mouth or in my pussy."

A growl reached her ears a fraction before Cassie felt hands lifting her up and bearing her back onto the bed. With one hand, Dean ripped down his jeans and his cock sprang free. Cassie's eyes widened, and her mouth watered as she stared.

God, he was huge and beautifully proportioned. His cock

rocked with the force of his erection, and Cassie reached out to caress the pearly bead that had formed at its tip.

"Darlin', I need to feel myself inside you."

Cassie lifted herself onto her elbows and raised up to kiss Dean's neck, her tits pressing against his chest. "Then do it, cowboy."

6

Dean could barely see straight as he stared at the nearly naked woman lying in front of him. Sure he'd had great sex before, but this was different. He was a schoolboy all over again. All Dean could think of was pleasuring *her*, making *her* come around his finger again, watching *her* eyes darken and change color with passion.

What in the hell was wrong with him?

He grabbed her around her waist and spun her around, facing away from him, exposing her beautiful ass once again to his perusal. With a quick yank he pulled her skirt past her knees and then all the way off, along with what was left of her lace panties, leaving her completely bare, her golden skin gleaming with beads of moisture. Now up on her knees, her ass pressed into the air and her hands flat on the bed in front of her, Dean couldn't imagine anything or anyone more intoxicating, more fucking *sexy*.

Dean palmed his erection with one hand and ripped open a condom he'd grabbed off the bureau with other, sliding it onto his cock. He kissed her above the line of her ass and breathed in her musk, his heart hammering with anticipation, his cock so rigid it was almost painful. "Are you ready, Cassandra?"

Cassie tossed a glance over her shoulder, and Dean almost lost it right there as she smiled, her pink lips full and moist. "Fuck me, Dean."

With one hand pressed against the small of her back and the other parting her damp, swollen lips, Dean placed the head of his cock at her entrance and slid in only a fraction. He felt Cassie press back, but he held her still with his hand. "In my own time," Dean said between clenched teeth as he reveled in the sensations of Cassie's hot, tight channel stretching to accommodate him. He slipped in a little farther, and Dean couldn't believe how unbelievably tight she was.

He heard Cassie panting softly, her hands clutching the quilt. "I'm coming in all the way, darlin'," Dean said with a growl.

Before she could respond, Dean gripped her hips and pulled back on her at the same time he lunged forward.

They shouted in unison, and Dean paused, letting the sensations of Cassie's pussy gripping his entire length pulse through him. He pulled back slowly and then thrust forward, reveling in the feel of her sliding around his cock. Cassie absorbed his thrusts and met them by pushing back until their bodies were smacking together, and Dean's balls were bouncing against her soaked pussy lips.

"Oh, god!" Cassie cried out, and Dean swore, sweat beading over his entire body as his cock pumped in and out in a manic rhythm.

He heard Cassie call out again, and Dean knew he couldn't hold back. He roared as his own climax tore through him, shattering any thoughts and raising goose bumps on every inch of his skin.

He pumped until the spasms eased and then held himself slightly above Cassandra, one hand wrapped around her waist.

Un-fucking-believable.

Dean didn't know any other way to describe what he'd just experienced.

After another deep breath, he pulled out and checked the condom, relieved when he saw that it had held. Deftly he pulled it off and tossed it into the trash by the bed before rolling over and taking Cassandra with him. Dean was pleased to find that Cassie fit perfectly into the curve of his body, her firm ass pressed up against his groin, her fragrant hair nestled just beneath his chin.

Words felt out of place, but Dean knew one of them would have to say something. He just hoped it wouldn't have to be him, as he knew he would likely screw things up the moment he opened his mouth.

As Dean caressed Cassie's side, his thoughts replayed their incredible sex. *Christ*, Dean swore silently, *I wouldn't mind screwing her all over again. Right now.* His cock started to harden at just the thought, and Dean smiled grimly. *I've been possessed, bewitched by a five-foot-something, blond bombshell with eyes bluer than a sapphire lake and a smile wider than the Arizona sky.*

He nuzzled her diminutive ear and then nipped the lobe and was rewarded by Cassie squirming her rear end tighter against him. Dean's hand migrated to the flat of her belly. "Sugar, that was incredible."

Cassie rolled over to face him, and her flushed features and open, honest gaze mesmerized Dean. "That was, hands down, the best sex I have ever had, Dean McCabe." They studied each other for a moment, and Cassie reached up to stroke the fine ridge of scar tissue that ran from his left ear almost to his chin. "How did this happen?"

Dean took her hand and kissed her fingers, his gaze never leaving hers. "You don't want to know."

She smiled, and Dean's heart almost stopped. "I do," she said.

For the first time that Dean could remember, he wanted to talk about it. "It's not a pretty story."

Cassie snuggled closer and kissed the scar before leaning back. "But it's part of *your* story, and I want to hear it."

The memory slid into Dean's mind like it was yesterday, and only the sensation of Cassie in his arms kept his anger on simmer. "When I was seventeen my mom started getting sick. It was so bad one night I knew we had to get her to the hospital, but she wouldn't go without . . ." He paused, fury burning in his throat at the memory. "She wouldn't go without our dad. So I went to town to collect him."

Dean rolled onto his back, and Cassie continued to gently stroke the side of his face and neck. "He was deep in a game of poker at the bar, as usual. Problem was, the asshole playing with him was convinced my dad was cheating and decided he couldn't leave until he gave back all the money he'd won."

"And did he?" Cassie asked.

"Fuck, no. It was more important to teach the asshole a lesson than just to give him his money and get the hell out of there to be with his wife."

"What happened?"

"They fought," Dean grunted. "But instead of gutting my father, the prick sliced me instead."

"Jesus, Dean," Cassie whispered. "What did your dad do?"

"He beat the guy to a pulp and then pulled me out of there, screaming that any normal dumbshit would have had enough sense to stay out of the way."

Cassie gasped, her hand finding his and squeezing. "He was a complete jerk-off!"

Dean chuckled, the sting of the memory fading in light of Cassie's heated words. Her tits pressed up against him didn't hurt to distract him either. "Yeah. He was. At least one good thing came out of it. After that my mom refused to let him back into the house."

"And your mom?" Cassie asked tentatively. "Did she get to the hospital?"

"Yeah," Dean said softly. "She did."

"Was . . . was she okay?"

Dean lifted Cassie's silky hair and breathed in its fresh scent. "That's not a good story either, sugar. Can we save it for another time?"

Cassie snuggled closer, and Dean groaned as her hand cupped his balls. "Yes. I'm sorry, Dean, I shouldn't have asked. It's just . . . I feel like I know you, but there's so much I really don't know—"

Before she could say anything else, Dean slid Cassie beneath him and found her lips with his own in an intoxicating kiss that left them both breathless. "I can think of better things to do than talk," Dean growled.

Cassie took his lower lip between her teeth and then released it, her tongue snaking out to trace its contours. The feel of her tongue arrowed straight to Dean's cock, and it bucked in response. Cassie reached up and pushed on his chest until he rolled over onto his back.

Dean watched as she flipped around, her ass in his face, her tan legs straddling his chest, and her mouth near other critical areas. "Now let me have a taste of you, Mr. McCabe, and if I remember correctly, you—"

Before she could finish her sentence, Dean pulled Cassie's hips low and drew his tongue across her beautiful, pink pussy lips. He flicked his tongue across her clit, eliciting more mews of pleasure, before drawing back slightly. "You were saying, Miss Darling?"

"Nothing," Cassie choked out, "nothing at all, cowboy." Without another word, Cassie wrapped her warm mouth around the head of Dean's cock. She dipped her head in a steady rhythm of hand meeting mouth, and Dean clenched his teeth to keep from groaning aloud like a sixteen-year-old. Forcing himself to refocus on the beautiful, creamy flower in front of him, Dean teased, flicked, and thrust with his tongue, reveling in her sweet taste and the muted moans of pleasure vibrating against his cock. They both increased their tempo, and Dean did groan aloud against Cassie's glistening pussy lips as she drew his cock to back of her throat.

"Come for me, Dean," he heard her whisper, and Dean couldn't help but oblige as she sucked him deep once again. The orgasm exploded throughout his body and mind, rendering him completely helpless. He waited until the waves eased, and he could hear his own heartbeat once more, before flipping Cassie over to stare at her flushed and sated face.

"Let me return the favor, sugar."

Dean thrust first one and then two fingers inside Cassie's pussy, bringing her steadily to the brink and then easing back until she shouted for release.

He captured a nipple in his mouth and flicked the crystal-hard bead as he twisted his fingers across her clit. Cassie screamed as she came, and Dean smiled against her nipple, sucking it until her contractions eased and her body collapsed beneath him.

Dean lowered himself and then rolled onto his back, keeping Cassie on top of him. He waited until his breathing eased and then pressed his lips against the top of Cassie's head. "So, what's the verdict, sugar? Am I 'one of those men'?"

Cassie raised her head, and she nodded with all seriousness. "Damn straight, but with one difference."

Dean raised a brow.

"You're more than a stallion. You are a god, Dean McCabe."

Smiling, Dean tucked Cassie back under his chin, his hands cupping her rear. "And you, Cassandra Darling, are one hell of a goddess."

7

Insanity. Total, utter insanity. Cassie knew she'd lost her mind. Potentially she would lose more than that if word of what she and Dean had just done got back to the wrong people. Even so, as she lay wrapped in his arms as he drifted off to sleep, Cassie realized she wouldn't change it for the world. Not one luscious moment. Just the thought of what they'd shared made Cassie moan silently and her clit dampen.

She'd had no idea she could have *that* many orgasms, or even that much sex, and not be sore or completely worn out. She felt like she could do it again if Dean was to suddenly wake up and touch her just about anywhere.

"God help me," Cassie whispered, her mind reeling. Which was when she remembered why she'd come out to see Dean in the first place. How could she now bring up what Jake had asked her to do? And what would she tell Jake if she didn't? *"Oh, by the way, instead of convincing your brother to speak to the townsfolk and convince them not to shoot the wolves, I fucked his brains out for three hours and then made myself right at home."*

"You're thinking."

Cassie jerked in response to Dean's deep voice near her ear. "You're all tense, like a cat ready to pounce on a mouse."

Cassie sighed, detangled herself from Dean's embrace, and sat up. She brushed hair away from her face and looked around the now darkened room. "I should go."

"You don't sound like you really want to do that."

Pinching her bottom lip between her teeth, Cassie slipped out of bed, her feet hitting the cool pine floor. "Dean, I—I didn't come here to, well, to do what we did."

She heard rustling behind her, and Cassie almost turned and jumped back into Dean's arms. God, but she wanted his hands on her body and to feel his warm breath on her neck.

"I don't imagine you did," he said.

Cassie began searching for her clothes in the dim light.

"Looking for these?"

Cassie turned to see Dean holding up her underwear with one finger, his lips quirked in a wicked grin. She reached for them, only to have Dean grab her hand and pull her to him. Cassie hissed as her bare body met his. "Dean. . . ."

Dean trailed a hand over the side of her face. "Listen, sugar, I'm not about to announce our time together to anyone. I may be a hard-ass, but I'm not a prick. I understand you have a job to do." Cassie heard Dean breathe in deeply and then let it out with a whoosh. "And so do I."

With that he pressed her panties into her hand and released her. Cassie felt bereft without Dean's arms around her. She found her skirt by the end of the bed and hurried to dress while he was off in the corner of the room doing the same. He left and came back with her blouse, bra, and shoes, his face a study of stony neutrality, and Cassie felt a niggling of unease work its way through her abdomen. By this time she was used to the angry Dean or the sweet and sexy Dean, but not this calm and unruffled Dean. It didn't feel right.

"Come on. I've got something to show you," he said the moment she finished dressing.

Silent, Cassie followed, her thoughts twisting around her emotions until she was a knot of anxiety. She trailed Dean out of the house, across the dark yard, and down a slight hill to a well-lit shed detached from the sizable stable and barn to their right. Dean unlocked the door and ushered her inside. He walked across what looked like a medical workroom to a sealed steel door and opened it. Cassie realized it was a large walk-in cooler. She stepped around Dean as he flicked on the fluorescent overhead lights. A horse lay on the floor on top of a large tarp.

Cassie moved closer, her trained eyes taking it all in as her pulse raced and her stomach soured. "Do you have gloves?" she asked without turning her head. A pair found their way into her hands, and Cassie slipped them on. "Where?"

Dean crouched beside her, his face grim. "In my north pasture, about two miles out. She's from one of the wild mustang herds."

"Did you take pictures?" Cassie asked as she began to probe the animal's mouth.

"Yes."

"She's an older mare." Cassie continued her inspection, her thoughts focused, her mind taking in each detail. When she reached the areas that had been depredated, she examined the torn edges with extra care. "The eyes, and the ears; this was done by—"

"Scavengers," Dean muttered. "Yeah. I know."

Cassie rocked back on her heels and clasped her hands, her lips pressed into a thin line. "These other areas definitely look like a big predator." She gazed up at Dean. "Did you see them?"

His amber eyes glowed with a simmering fury as he shook his head. "Just the tracks, and I can guarantee you they were not from a cat or badger."

Cassie took off the gloves, her stomach burning with disappointment. "I'll need to see those pictures and take a closer look at your mare." Cassie couldn't look Dean in the eye. Her body flushed with heat despite the chill of the cooler. "I'm sorry, Dean. You will be compensated for—"

"Keep it. It's not about the money."

Cassie looked Dean in the eye, her heart aching for him and for the wolves that would certainly suffer over what was happening in Granite Hollow. "I will make my recommendation as soon as possible, Dean."

The fire in Dean's eyes didn't fade, but Cassie detected that it was no longer directed at her. Thank god. Cassie didn't think she could deal with that. Not now. Not after what had happened tonight.

Dean turned off the lights and then plunked his hat back onto his head before ushering her out through the freezer's door and to the front courtyard. Cassie stayed by the car while Dean went into the house for the keys she'd left on the entry table.

Cassie realized she had completely breached her own ethics, not to mention her profession's code of conduct, by sleeping with Dean, but it was too late to regret her decision now. Her dad would have said it was just further proof that she was a nogood slut just like her mother. Fuck first and think later.

She shivered, forcing away the memory and refocusing on Dean as he walked back toward her. This was his livelihood at stake, and that of his neighbors. She needed him to know she wasn't just blowing hot air. That she knew how imperative it was to help protect this town *and* the wolves under the agency's protection. "I'll be going out tomorrow to track and observe the pack. We'll be looking for broken collars, disruptive behavior, and things of that sort. We need to get a handle on which animal is responsible."

The silence stretched between them as they walked toward Cassie's T-Bird.

"I don't hate them."

She stopped and faced Dean. "What?"

"The wolves." Dean gently tucked a strand of hair behind her ear. "My mother used to tell Jake and I stories her grandfather told her, about how his tribe interacted and honored the wolves before they were killed off."

"Your mother was Native American?"

Dean nodded sharply. "Half. I thought the reintroduction could be a good thing. We've had disease these past few years among the deer herds, and the rabbit population is out of control. I knew there would be some occasional livestock loss . . . but not this. They aren't even eating their kills. This is a bad situation, Cassie."

Cassie's heart ached for Dean. Unable to stop herself, she took Dean's hand and turned it palm up, kissing the calluses that creased it. "I'm sorry, Dean. It wasn't supposed to be this way."

Silence stretched between them, but Cassie didn't mind. She knew that once she got into that car, her time with Dean was at its end. They couldn't be seen together in town, and the likelihood of them continuing any type of relationship seemed impossible. Even so, Cassie felt a connection to Dean that she couldn't explain away as just an appreciation of mind-blowing sex. It was deeper than that. At least for her.

"I should go," Cassie whispered.

"Yeah," Dean said, his voice gruff.

He walked her to her car, and Cassie got inside, her throat tight with all the things she still wanted to say, questions she wanted to ask. Which was when she remembered Jake's request. "Dean," Cassie started.

He pushed her door closed and leaned close to her open window. "Cassandra," he returned, his gaze steady.

Ignoring the charismatic pull of his amber eyes, Cassie said in a rush, "I heard a rumor that some people are planning on tracking and killing the wolves. Can you tell them . . . tell them I'll move as quickly as I can. Tell them to be careful. It's a federal offense, and there's a hefty fine."

Dean smiled. "I can do that, Miss Darling."

"Good," Cassie said briskly as she started her car with a shaking hand. "Good night, Dean."

Hooking his fingers in his belt loops, Dean stepped away from the T-Bird. " 'Night, sugar."

Cassie stared at Dean a long moment longer before thumbing the window closed and forcing herself to drive away. Away from the best damn sex of her life. Away from a man she wanted to know everything about. Away from a possibility she wasn't looking for and didn't want. Not now. Not here. Not that it mattered now. Cassandra Darling was snagged, hook, line, and sinker.

"It's beautiful, Jake."

Cassie turned in her saddle for what felt like the hundredth time to take in the view of the valley behind them and the mountain around them. Bordered by thick stands of ponderosas and junipers, meadows rolled out in front of them like green and gold carpet runners. Again Cassie felt like she was in a movie. The panoramic views were incredible.

"It's always been special land. Dean and I spent lots of summer weekends up here camping and finding ways to torture each other." Jake grinned, and Cassie walked her mare closer, her interest piqued.

"Torture, huh? That was your idea of fun as kids?"

Jake pulled up on his Appaloosa, and Cassie's pinto mare stopped alongside. "Well, Dean and I really were never kids at the same time. It was more like father-son, but since he wasn't my dad, I was more inclined to find ways to make my brother near crazy. Mostly by yapping my fool head off and picking up every snake, tarantula, or centipede I saw."

Cassie laughed as she pictured Dean trying to rein in Jake's wonder of the natural world. "I don't imagine any of those friendly woodland creatures ended up in Dean's sleeping bag, did they?"

Jake rested his arms on the pommel of the saddle and grinned slyly. "I'll take the fifth on that."

They'd gone out together two of the last four days to observe the pack, and Cassie never tired of Jake's stories. Especially the ones about Dean. The jerk. He hadn't returned any of her calls the past few days, and Cassie knew she had certainly blown any chance she might have had with the volatile cowboy. He probably thought she was some city slut who screwed anyone that posed an invitation. The sudden ache in her chest brought her back to reality, and she looked up as Jake tapped her leg and pointed.

Cassie followed his finger and gasped. Not more than fifty yards away she saw flashes through the trees . . . white . . . black . . . gray . . . and then, with a swiftness that took her breath away, a deer broke cover and crashed out of trees onto the meadow. It was running full-out, and, even so, close on its heels came the pack. Jake and she patted their horses to keep them quiet and leaned low in their saddles, hoping they would stay hidden in the trees on the opposite side. It was still early, only five P.M., and she and Jake hadn't expected to see any activity from the wolves until much later in the evening after they'd set up in one of the blinds near the pack's lair.

With well-orchestrated teamwork they brought the deer down, and Cassie watched in awe as the entire scene played out before them. Just as it should. The alpha and beta ate first, then the nursing mothers, and finally the omega. There was no mutilating, no shred and run, and each member seemed to know its place and rank without question.

"God, Jake, they are so beautiful," Cassie whispered, her eyes still glued on the organized chaos of the feed.

Jake nodded, his hands shaking as he fiddled with equipment he'd yanked from his saddlebags. "All their signals are strong. I can account for each member. That's the whole pack, Cass, except for the new pups, which they haven't collared yet. There are no weak signals."

Cassie recognized the bewilderment in Jake's eyes and was sure hers reflected the same.

"Could it be coyotes? Is that possible?" he asked.

Cassie shook her head. "Unlikely. I've never seen coyotes attempt something as big as your mare. Not unless it was sick, and your mare didn't look sick." She looked back to the wolves. "But *they* are an efficient killing machine. For them to have adapted so well, so quickly, is a testament to the keepers that prepared them for this. I—I don't want this to be the end of the road for them, Jake."

Their gazes met. "Neither do I. What can we do, Cass?"

Cassie gently pulled on the reins, backing her mare farther into the brush and away from the canines whose futures she was forced to decide upon. Jake followed, and they stayed silent for almost a half mile. "I don't know what the answer is right now, but I know I need to make a decision soon. Before there's another killing. It's not fair to anyone, the wolves or the ranchers, to just hang in limbo, hoping for the best."

Jake nodded but stayed silent, his young face tight. "Do you still want to head up to the blind?"

"If you don't mind I'd rather go back into town. I have a lot of thinking to do and reports to review. Better to start on that now, I think."

As they crested a low rise Cassie blinked through the gloom, shocked to see a flash of light on the mountain. It was gone as quickly as it had appeared. "Did you see that?"

"What?"

Cassie pulled her mare in and stood in her stirrups. "There. About a half mile west. I thought I saw, well, it looked like headlights from a car."

"There aren't any roads up here, Cass. Except for the fire road, but that's about ten miles east of here." Jake nodded in the direction Cassie had indicated. "That area is nothing but granite crags, shale slides, and tailings from an old copper mine. Mountain lion territory. Not a place suited for the wolves or for most people." He grinned. "The only people who go there are mountain climbers from Phoenix in early spring. They like the challenge of the granite face on the south rim."

"I've known a few of those crazy rock climbers. Dated one, in fact."

Jake reached over and brushed a strand of hair out of Cassie's face. It reminded her so much of Dean she nearly grabbed his hand and held it against her cheek. "No mountain climbers here, Cass. Just lonely cowboys with hot heads and strong passions."

She smiled at the sandy-haired cowboy. "Yeah. I think I've met a few."

"Cut him out, Frank, and get him in with Massey's group in the south pasture!"

Dean wiped his face with his bandanna before putting his hat back on and surveying the organized chaos of the corrals and pens spread out before him. Stocky brown and black pinto mares and foals milled in corners, while their stallion rolled his eyes and snorted warnings whenever the men got too close.

He took a deep breath, tasting dust and the tangy resin of pine, and he played with the idea that tonight might be the right time to do some heavy thinking. Dean hadn't had a moment to himself the entire week. Each night the house had been full of hired hands, and from sunup to sundown they'd been out on the range. Which, Dean reasoned, was probably a good thing. Otherwise he would have been inclined to spend every waking moment with Miss Darling, even if it was just to make certain she didn't do something so foolish as to find interest in someone else.

No matter how hard he tried, he couldn't get thoughts of the petite blonde out of his head. And not just of how she felt in his arms or how she felt beneath him. Dean found himself longing just to hear her voice, her laugh, and to see her smile.

It was goddamn disgusting how much he longed for it. In his thirty-one years Dean had never felt this way, never knew he *could* feel this way. When he'd gotten her messages the other day, he'd had to physically restrain himself from driving into town, breaking into her room, and convincing her in as many ways as he could think of to come back to the ranch.

But nothing good could come out of him panting over Cassandra Darling. Once she was done with her investigation she would go back to her world of sun, smog, and high-rise buildings and forget all about Granite Hollow. Forget all about the crazy-ass, scarred cowboy with horseshit on his shoes and a wild look in his eye.

Dean figured the best thing he could do was stay busy until the insanity passed. And since he hadn't heard that a decision had been made regarding the wolves, a part of Dean questioned whether or not Cassie was doing anything at all to get the situation resolved. It wasn't as if he actually *knew* Cassie. Not really. Not deep down.

"We're about done here, Dean," Frank said as he walked over to Dean. "You want me to ask Cliff and Jack to hang on for a few more days to help keep an eye on things?"

Dean forced his thoughts away from Cassandra and back to his friend and foreman, Frank Buchanan. "No, thanks, Frank. Jake's coming home tonight, and he can help out. Plus, we still have Terry and Carl on full time." As Dean shook Frank's hand, the thought that things could meander back to a more reasonable pace almost made him smile. "I appreciate you bringing in your boys this week."

"Anytime. You know those damn kids need work just to keep them out of trouble." Frank smiled and then waved to his crew. "Day's done, boys!"

The past week had also reminded Dean how important his family and the ranch were to him. He missed having Jake around, and just because they'd had a difference in opinion, it didn't mean they couldn't still work together and live under the same roof. Hell, the kid had guts to do what he was doing, following his belief. Their mother would have been proud of him.

As the crew packed up, Dean leaned on the fence to watch the mustangs. They were a good-looking bunch this year, fat and healthy, their coats shiny. The foals looked promising, too. A small light-coated mustang with a white patch down her forehead caught his eye. Even with the sudden change to her world, the filly was playful and her body language comfortable. She nipped at the other foals and then skittered sideways, egging them on. Dean smiled, his shoulders relaxing for the first time in weeks.

"You're a keeper, darlin'," Dean said as his eyes trailed the filly's antics.

Just like someone else.

His mother's voice sounded so clear sometimes it was almost as if she were standing beside him. "It's none of your concern, Mom," Dean muttered, his eyes still following the filly's romp, but inside he smiled. She might be right. Hell, when was she *not* right?

The thought left a sinking feeling in Dean's gut, and he

ground his teeth. Damn it. He'd told himself he wouldn't do this. Wouldn't pine for a woman he couldn't have.

Can't say she doesn't want you if you haven't had the guts to go find out, Dean. . . .

Dean slapped his hat against his thigh and eyed his truck. "Guess it can't hurt to find out."

9

"No! Next week isn't good enough. It needs to get to someone who can make a decision today, Richard."

Cassie paced the narrow room, the cell phone so tight against the side of her face she was certain her ear was redder than the magenta quilt on the double bed of her room in the B and B. "I realize decisions aren't made overnight, but the situation here is critical. We're past the point of taking our time with this. . . . I don't care if you have to wake up the President! Get them to read my report and either agree with my recommendation, or make one of their own. It's been a week already, and that's a week too long!"

Cassie flipped the cell phone closed with a snap, her blood boiling and her chest rising and falling rapidly with the force of her breath.

"Stupid political bullshit!" Cassie said, throwing the phone onto the bed. A week. A fucking week, and they still hadn't made a decision. It hadn't happened yet, but it was only a matter of time before a wolf or more livestock was killed. Either could be disastrous for Granite Hollow.

"Shit, shit, shit," Cassie muttered as she ran her hand through her hair and checked the clock. Nearly one o'clock. Half the day gone already.

It didn't help any that Dean hadn't returned her phone calls, hadn't shown up to the town-hall meeting, hadn't indicated in any way that he was interested in Cassie. She was beginning to wonder if she'd imagined their whole encounter. Old, dirty thoughts began to creep into her head. Thoughts about what a useless whore she was. How she screwed up everything she touched. How there was no way for a man to really want her. Love her.

A knock on the door shut out the memories of her dad's brainwashing, and Cassie almost sobbed, pressing a fist to her mouth. *Get it together, girl. . . .*

"Carla?" Cassie called.

"It's Jake, Cassie."

Jake. Cassie pinched the bridge of her nose and took a deep breath. She opened the door, her smile tight.

The cowboy smiled in return before his gaze turned somber. "What's wrong?"

Cassie sighed and ushered Jake inside, closing the door behind him. "Nothing. I'm just tired."

Jake twisted his hat in his hands, his green gaze warm and calming. "Bullshit. You can tell me, Cassie. Hell, you've listened to enough of my life's story to write a novel."

Cassie leaned against the bureau and crossed her arms. Darn, but Jake was a good-looking kid with the presence of a saint. Too bad Cassie was so hung up on his ornery brother she could barely see straight. Too bad her asshole father had messed up her head so bad where men were concerned, she didn't have enough sense to fall for someone like Jake instead of his tough-as-nails brother.

"Jake," she started, wondering how on earth she could broach the subject of Dean—or if she even should. She twisted her hands. "Have you spoken to your brother?" Cassie blurted it out before her reasoning brain could interfere further.

Jake studied her a moment before answering, and Cassie squirmed under his scrutiny, a fine sweat breaking out on the back of her neck. "I did, actually. We're meeting out at the ranch tonight."

His words sent a shiver through Cassie's abdomen. Memories of her and Dean at the ranch in Dean's bed filled her mind. She cleared her throat and turned toward the window, looking out over the town's main street. "It's just that I haven't seen him at any of the meetings, and I wondered if he'd experienced any other issues. . . ."

"Cassie," Jake said softly.

She kept her back to Jake, her fingers gripping the curtains.

"You don't have to hide it."

"What?" Cassie said, her stomach churning.

"Your interest in my brother."

Cassie spun, and her mouth fell open. "What makes you think—"

"Stop." Jake's expression was serious, his eyes warm. "We've been honest with each other, right?"

Cassie nodded.

"I don't want that to change. I feel like I've known you forever, Cass. I can't explain why that is, but from the first time I saw you at the meeting, I knew I wanted to get to know you. Kindred spirits, maybe."

Their gazes met, and a wiggle of understanding worked through Cassie's chest. "I felt that way, too," Cassie whispered.

Jake stepped closer and took Cassie's shoulders. "I know my brother can be a pain in the ass, but he's also a hell of a good guy, and it doesn't surprise me that you two have hooked up."

"Hooked up?" Cassie shook Jake's hands off and turned back to the window. "We have in no way hooked up."

Jake was quiet, and Cassie rocked back and forth on her heels, her heart thumping. She felt like she'd just been caught with her hand in the cookie jar. Finally, Jake laughed.

She turned. "What's so funny?"

"You and Dean. You two are a pair."

"What do you mean?"

Jake grabbed Cassie's jacket by the door and thrust it into her hands. "Come on. Let's talk over lunch. Looks like I have my work cut out for me."

The diner was nearly empty when they arrived, and Lila, the Bar None waitress for nearly forty years, sat them at a cozy booth overlooking the parking lot.

"I don't know what's wrong with me," Cassie said as quietly as she could over her untouched mashed potatoes and shredded fried chicken. "I know this is such a bad idea."

Jake reached out and stilled Cassie's stabbing fork. "Cass, falling in love is never a bad idea. It's the execution that has the potential to cause problems."

Cassie leaned back, blood draining from her face. "What did you say?"

"Falling in love. Ever done it?"

Cassie had to force her mouth closed before she caught flies.

"I take it by your reaction that would be a 'no'."

"That can't be what this is. I've known Dean for only two weeks, and we haven't spent more than four hours together!"

Jake studied her from across the stable, his green eyes steady and shrewd. Cassie realized with some surprise that where life's circumstances had made Dean a tough, driving son of a bitch, they had made Jake patient and wise beyond his years. The two complemented each other perfectly. And where did she fit in?

She *couldn't* be in love with Dean. It wasn't practical.

"Answer me this, Cass. Can you stop thinking about Dean?"

Cassie pinched her lower lip between her teeth and tried to

shrug, but it wasn't happening. She slammed down her fork. "All right! No, okay? No, I can't stop thinking about your stubborn-ass brother."

"Do you worry every minute that you might run into him or that your phone might ring and it will be him? Or, better yet, can you imagine getting back on a plane for Los Angeles and never seeing Dean again?"

The thought created a solid ball of dread in Cassie's gut, and she swallowed—hard. When had things gotten this serious? It didn't make any sense, and Cassie reached for her new friend's hand, her distress inching up into her chest. "Jesus, Jake. What am I supposed to do about this? I don't even think Dean feels the same."

"He does."

Cassie met Jake's open gaze. "How can you know that?"

Jake removed his hand from hers, crossed his arms, and frowned. "Because the son of a bitch is grouchier than a black bear with his leg caught in a trap. It took half an hour of conversation last night for me to figure out what was wrong with him. It wasn't until he asked about *you* that I finally put two and two together."

He asked about me. . . . Cassie felt practically faint with relief. And, just as quickly, abashed by her reaction. "What—what did he say?"

Jake grinned. "His exact words?" Jake cleared his throat and lowered his voice. "'How's that agent—what's her name? Darling or something. How's she making out?'"

Cassie blinked, her mind trying to piece together how Jake could possibly think Dean's offhanded comment was a good thing.

Jake chuckled, and leaned in again. "It was the lamest cover-up ever. You should have heard him clam up when I said you'd hightailed it back to the city."

"You what!" Cassie said, nearly knocking over her soda.

He leaned back, his smile almost as wicked as his brother's, and shrugged. "I couldn't help myself. My brother deserves a little payback. But . . ." Jake reached over the table to take Cassie's hand. "It was all the things he didn't say that gave it away. Look, why don't you come out to the place tonight? Dean and I have a few things to discuss, but afterward we could all have dinner. Maybe having a third wheel there will help you two get over crap you two have created. What do you say?"

Cassie shook her head, her mind reeling. "I can't do that, Jake. If Dean wants to see me he can damn well contact me." Cassie pulled her hand free of Jake's and pushed aside her plate. "I can't believe we're talking about this with everything else that's happening. It should be the last thing on my—*our*—minds."

"Couldn't be a better time," Jake said, finishing off his coffee. "All this worry and bad feelings. It's about time something good happened around here. Besides, you can't control fate."

"Fate?" Cassie said.

Jake took both of her hands and leaned in, his face even with hers. "My mother always said the Great Spirit brings you face-to-face with your worst enemy and your brightest gifts at the same time. The lesson is in how you deal with both and whether or not you can distinguish between them."

"I'm no good at riddles, Jake," Cassie said softly.

Another grin, and Jake planted a kiss on Cassie's cheek before leaning back. "Part of you is, and that's the part that counts."

10

Dean leaned against the outside wall of the diner and fought the red fog that threatened to engulf him.

Jake. Cassie. *Together.*

His mind replayed the image of their hands clasped and then the kiss. Dean's hands curled into fists.

Without turning back for a second look, Dean made a bee-line for Callahan's bar across the street. Luckily the place was open and nearly empty, and no one paid much attention to Dean as he sidled up to the darkest spot on the bar and asked Harry Callahan for a drink.

Harry must've recognized the look on Dean's face because he placed the shot in front of Dean without saying a word. Dean downed it and raised the glass. "Another."

Harry filled the glass and left the bottle. "It's yours."

Now Dean knew why Jake had sounded so reasonable yesterday, so calm and good-natured. Dean gripped the shot glass, his thoughts darkening by the second. He didn't blame Jake. The kid had no defenses against the charm of someone like

Cassandra Darling. Shit, all she'd had to do with *him* was ask if he was going to kiss her, and Dean had practically come in his pants.

"Jesus Christ," Dean muttered as he poured himself a third. Playing two brothers against each other. Question was, whose side was she really on?

Dean downed the third shot and poured a fourth. He scowled at his reflection in the mirror, grimacing as the whiskey sliced a hot channel down his throat and straight into his gut.

A week. A week without a word from Washington, according to Cassie. How *convenient* that was. Maybe Miss Darling wasn't so much about political alliances as she was about playing head games. Maybe she got off on calling the shots or letting people in little Podunk towns *think* she was calling the shots.

Dean stood and smashed his hat back onto his head. "Thanks, Harry." The door swung closed behind him with a crash, and Dean thrust his hands in his jeans pockets to keep them from thinking up other things to do. Like throttling Miss Cassandra Darling where she sat. Like smacking that fine, tight ass of hers.

"Shit," Dean barked into the bright May morning. Thoughts of Cassie's ass were the last thing he wanted to settle on. There were more important things to consider. Like how to get Cassandra Darling out of his and Jake's life and away from Granite Hollow for good.

Cassie looked at her watch again: Eight o'clock.

"You want a refill, sweetie?"

Cassie looked up into the waitress's wrinkled face and smiled. "No, Lila. I'm done. I think I'll just get a cheeseburger to go."

Lila tapped the pencil lodged behind her ear as she followed Cassie's gaze into the parking lot. "Got stood up, did you? Happens to the best of us, sweetie."

Cassie tried to smile. "Yes, I suppose it does." The sixty-something waitress bustled away, shouting out her cheese-burger order halfway to the counter.

The night air was cool and fragrant as Cassie left the diner, and she wished she had a clear enough head to enjoy the evening walk back to her room. Why had she ever let Jake talk her into waiting for Dean at the diner?

"I'll have him at the diner at six, Cass, mark my words. It will work out okay. You'll see."

Three diet sodas later, Cassie was forced to conclude she was a complete idiot for thinking he might come. She crunched the full, greasy paper bag in her hand and considered throwing it away. Her stomach probably couldn't take it, just like her heart probably couldn't take any other risks where Dean was con-cerned.

The sound of an engine stopped Cassie in her tracks. She clutched the greasy bag to her chest and looked around, unable to help her reaction to the sound. A Jeep. Like the one she thought she'd heard the night she came into Granite Hollow and spotted the downed deer. Headlights beamed off the build-ing to her right as the car turned the corner. Cassie stared, her heart pounding.

Not my dad . . . not my dad. . . .

And of course it wasn't. It was Simon Alistair. And someone else. It was too dark to see who sat in the passenger's seat as the faded old Jeep jugged by, but for some reason Cassie was re-lieved when they didn't see her. Their tires threw mud and rocks across the cracked asphalt of the street as they sped past and headed east. Away from the coalition's rented house. Away from the road that led out of town.

Her cell phone buzzed on her hip, and Cassie fumbled it loose from its case to answer, hope burning in her chest. "Jake?"

"They've made a decision, Cass."

"Jesse!" Cassie stopped walking, the sound of her friend's unexpected voice a welcome beacon in an otherwise dreary night. "Sorry, thought you were someone else."

"Doesn't surprise me," Jesse said, and Cassie heard a pointed sigh. "Richard will call you personally tomorrow morning, but I knew you would want to know sooner, so here I am, good news–bad news delivery boy."

Cassie's heart skipped a beat as she tossed the grease-laden bag into the nearest trash can. "Good news first."

"The good news is that they finally got around to discussing your report, and they agreed with your conclusion."

"What's the bad news, then?"

"They didn't agree with your recommendation."

Cassie's stomach fell into her toes. "What did they recommend, Jesse?"

"Extermination—for the pack."

"No!" Cassie yelled and then quickly found a place to sit on the cracked curb, her heart thumping. "Why? If they don't think the pack is stable enough for release somewhere else, they can go back into the captive breeding program and—"

"Stop, Cass." Jesse's firm command halted the tirade bubbling to the surface of Cassie's brain. "They feel the pack is too dangerous to spend time and money on a capture program. They're sending trackers in. They leave for Phoenix tonight and should be there in Granite Hollow by noon tomorrow to meet with you and Simon before they set up. This is Danny's crew. They're good. It won't take them long to start culling the pack."

Cassie pinched the bridge of her nose. "It's just as easy to dart and cage them as it is to shoot and kill them!"

"I know this is rough, Cass, but I thought it would be better for you to hear it from me than from Richard an hour before the crew arrives. And . . . there's something else."

"What?" Cassie asked. "What else?"

"Is there more going on there in Granite Hollow than the situation with the pack, Cass?"

Cassie frowned and chewed her lower lip. "I'm not sure what you mean, Jesse."

"I think you do."

Cassie's gut went cold and her mouth dry. There was no way they could know about her and Dean. Right?

"There's nothing to tell," Cassie said, her eyes focusing on an industrious brown-spotted moth that had landed on her pumps. "Not . . . really."

"Cass. . . ."

"All right. There is this guy, here. We met, he yelled, I gave him my cool and unruffled agent response, and then . . ."

"And then?"

"Oh, Jesus. They know, don't they, Jesse? They know about me and Dean."

There was silence again on the other line and then Jesse's pointed sigh. "They do. They received an anonymous call earlier this week. From what I could gather, the caller stated you'd had 'relations' with this Dean McCabe, who just happened to be the leading opposition to the wolves staying in Granite Hollow and couldn't be trusted to give an impartial report."

"Did—did they believe it?"

"I'm not sure, Cassie, but either way they're pulling you from the case."

Cassie squeezed her fingers into her palm, her mind reeling. "Well, that's that, then. I fucked my career because I wanted to screw a guy I barely knew. I failed everybody, Jesse. The wolves, this town, the agency." *Myself.* Cassie lowered the phone a few inches and stared up at the faded streetlight. There it was. The sad, horrible truth.

Jesse's voice arrowed from the earpiece. "Cassie! Put the phone back on your ear!"

She did, her mind numb, her emotions raw.

"I mean this in a loving way . . . get it the fuck together! I know your recommendation wasn't based off how you felt about Dean McCabe. You're too good of an agent for that."

"Who else will believe that, Jesse?"

Jesse growled, "Who cares? I don't know how strong your feelings are for this guy, Cass, but you owe it to yourself to find out. Ask to go on leave, or take the eight billion weeks of vacation you have saved up. They'll think up some asinine disciplinary action while you're gone. Probably pull you off fieldwork for a while, maybe a cut in pay, but they're not going to fire you over it. You're the best they have, and they know it."

"I don't know if I can stay, Jesse. I do care for him. It's kinda scary how *much* I like this guy," Cassie said, a tiny sliver of hope at Jesse's words already lodging inside of her. "But I don't—"

"Cassie!"

Cassie stood, her eyes widening as she watched Jake jogging toward her. "I have to go, Jesse. I'll give what you said some thought."

"Cassie . . . don't hang up before I tell you who they think—"

She snapped the phone closed just as Jake stopped in front of her, his face flushed. "There's been another killing. Out at the Rocking T."

She took hold of Jake's arm and pulled him down to sit on the curb. He didn't look good. His color was off and his breathing ragged as if he'd just run a mile.

"I've never seen anything like it. They came right into the corral, Cass. Dean and I heard the commotion and the dogs, but by the time we got out there, Remus, our Australian shepherd, was down, killed, and the Lab was cut up bad. I just dropped her off with the vet." Jake put his head in his hands. "I can't believe I'm going to say this, but we've got to stop them, Cassie." His head came up, and Cassie recognized the steel in Jake's gaze. "No matter what it takes."

Cassie squeezed Jake's arm. "We—they—are. I just got word."

Jake sobered, and he focused on Cassie's grim expression.

"They think the best option at this point is extermination."

Jakes green eyes went wide, and his face paled. "That's not what any of us wanted."

Cassie tried to swallow away the lump in her throat. "It wasn't what I suggested they do, I swear, Jake. I asked that they be captured and monitored before considering them for relocation."

"I believe you, Cassie." He paused, and Cassie was struck by the gloomy tone of Jake's voice.

Dean.

Cassie's stomach cramped, and a sick feeling filled her chest and throat. "Where is Dean, Jake? Did he come with you?"

"He stayed at the ranch to watch the horses." He waited a few seconds before adding, "You should know . . . he . . . he thinks there's something going on between us."

Cassie jumped to her feet. "What! Why on earth would he think that?" An instant image of she and Jake in the diner filled Cassie's mind. Of Jake holding her hand, of the innocent peck on the cheek. But . . . how could Dean have seen that?

Standing, Jake shoved his hands in his pockets, his expression confounded. "He was at the diner, Cassie. He wouldn't admit it, but I know he was there to see you. To tell you how he felt. When he saw us, he jumped to the wrong conclusion."

"Don't tell me," Cassie said, her arms crossed on her chest to hide their shaking. "He thinks I'm a manipulative bitch working both sides."

Jake looked sheepish. "Well, uh . . . something like that."

Cassie jerked away, tears burning her eyes.

A hand on her arm pulled her back around. "I told him what a jackass he was for even thinking that."

"And did he believe you?" Cassie said, the pitch of her voice rising, along with her fury at Dean's ignorance.

Jake's silence said it all, and without waiting for an answer, Cassie headed for her car a block away.

"Cassie!" Jake fell into step beside her. "What are you doing?"

"I'm going to go take pictures of what happened out at the Rocking T so I can give them to the trackers who will be here tomorrow. Then I'm going to thank your brother for single-handedly shit-canning my career." She stopped at her car and faced Jake, fighting to keep the tremble out of her voice. "I'm sorry if I ended up causing an issue between you and Dean. You are a great guy, Jake."

Jake put his hand on her car door. "You make it sound like I'm not going to see you again, Cassie."

Cassie took a deep breath and pushed Jake's hand aside. "You won't. As of tomorrow, I'm off the case and out of yours and Dean's lives for good."

11

The Rocking T was dark as Cassie drove up. "Damn you, Dean McCabe, you'd better be around somewhere, or so help me I'll hunt you down."

Fury had gotten her this far, but as Cassie parked in front of the sprawling ranch home, an overwhelming sense of loss filled her. Loss over the outcome for the pack, loss over what she and Dean might have had.

"Get a hold of yourself, girl," Cassie said between gritted teeth, her eyes already misting up. This was no time to feel sorry for herself. She needed to be strong. Pissed off and ready to rip Dean a new asshole for what he did. *God* . . . she still couldn't believe he had been the one to make the call. But who else could it have been? She never would have figured Dean for a vindictive stool pigeon. Which just showed her how much she really *didn't* know about him.

A sharp ache filled Cassie's chest again, and she shrugged it away as she slung her camera strap over her neck and started out, wishing she'd had enough sense to go by her room first and change into jeans and boots.

"Where in the hell are you, Dean?" Cassie muttered as she looked out over the sprawling cluster of lit barns, shelters, and dark corrals that surrounded the house. Her gaze stopped on a gray outbuilding. "The medical room, of course."

With purposeful strides Cassie made her way to the building Dean had taken her to the other night.

Shadows lengthened into vast lakes of inky velvet the farther away from the house she went, and a tingling erupted at the base of her spine. Cassie's gaze flicked from the worn path at her feet to the quiet shuffling of horses ten yards away.

"You're spooking yourself, Cassie," she muttered, the back of her neck pinging with electricity. The closer she got to the medical shed, the more urgent Cassie's footsteps became, and she suddenly found herself running. She ripped open the door without knocking and stumbled inside.

It was dark.

She flicked on a light near the door. The room was empty. A sinking feeling filled Cassie's abdomen, and she took a deep breath as she walked to the freezer. She opened the door but didn't step inside. She could see the body of the shepherd from where she stood, it dead eyes staring into the far corners of the cooler.

Cassie squeezed her hands into her palms and stepped back, closing the door. "This shouldn't be happening. They have plenty of prey. Plenty of range to roam. Why would they be coming *here*?"

Her questions hung silently in the air as Cassie turned and headed back outside, her thoughts spinning. She had to find Dean. Had to tell him that the trackers would be here tomorrow and would do everything in their power to keep something like this from ever happening again.

And give him a piece of her mind. She couldn't lose sight of that.

As the door banged closed behind her, Cassie tried to think

of where Dean might have gone. Into town? To a friend's to enlist help? There was no way he would have tried to track the wolves. Not at night with only a half moon. Not on his own.

Right?

A niggling of doubt made Cassie's stomach roil, and she pressed a hand there as she started back to her car. The snorts and shuffling of the horses filled her ears. She could make out their shadowed forms as they moved from one side of the corral to the other, their unshod hooves throwing up dust.

Cassie coughed and waved a hand in front of her face. Her car seemed a mile away, and the tingling was back. Cassie fought to quell the sudden surge of panic that had infected her.

The red Thunderbird gleamed in the light from the house, but Cassie knew she would never make it. Not now. Not with what stood between her and the driver's-side door.

"Shit," Cassie whispered, easing to a stop.

She watched as one, two, and then four dogs walked out from around each side of her car. Their tongues were lolling, their bodies thin and primed for action.

Dogs. *Wild dogs.*

The enormity of her—and everyone else's—error wasn't lost on her, but she had no time to dwell on it.

"Stay," Cassie barked, keeping her eyes up and making herself seem as big as possible. They stopped. They were large dogs, leggy and powerful. Shepherd and Dane mixes, with possibly some boxer and chow mixed in. A dominant, low growl reached Cassie's ears, and she looked to her left. Out of the darkness slunk a massive animal, its head low, its yellow eyes fierce, and its white and gray coat bristled.

The alpha male. Cassie's gaze darted from him to the pack in front of her, trying to keep them all in her line of sight. "A hybrid," Cassie whispered. Probably shepherd and wolf. Its head was huge, its muzzle long and menacing.

"This is not good," Cassie whispered, her mind grasping for

solutions even as it processed the bizarre set of coincidences that had led to this moment. *How had a group of wild dogs been allowed to roam in Granite Hollow undetected?*

Cassie weighed her options. The house was too far, and she would never get the car door open in time, plus she would have to go through the animals to *get* to her car.

Shit, shit, shit!

She looked at the corral a few feet away and the mass of snorting and seesawing horses pacing nervously in their pen. The alpha growled again as it moved in on stilted legs. Quietly Cassie pushed her pumps off one foot at a time.

The alpha lunged.

Time was up.

Cassie spun and bolted, diving between the wide fence boards and into the churned-up dirt of the corral.

Stay on your feet! Fucking run!

She heard the dogs' mad scramble behind her, and Cassie's legs pumped harder as she sprinted directly toward the shifting herd of wild-eyed mustangs. Out of the corner of her eye she spotted fur, and an audible *snap* at her calf made her pitch forward. Hot breath grazed her thigh and, in sheer terror, Cassie threw herself into the crazed mix of sweating horseflesh and flashing hooves.

"Uh!" Cassie's shoulder was slammed sideways. She caught herself on the rump of a spotted pony. The scent of horsehair and dust filled her nose and eyes, and she lurched around one scrambling, hot body to the other. Hooves slashed the dirt around her legs, and she heard a yelp somewhere within the chaos.

Stay upright!

Cassie spotted a fawn-colored foal a second before it rocketed into her, knocking her flat onto her ass. Her breath whooshed from her lungs, and as her head smacked the lumpy ground, everything went a hazy red. Her vision came back just in time to see the wave of black and white bodies part like the Red Sea, leaving her completely exposed. The foal that had hit her stumbled sideways and froze, its nostrils flaring and its sides trembling violently.

Cassie forced her head all the way up. *Oh, God. . . .*

A blood-flecked muzzle filled her field of vision. She raised a hand to cover her face and—

A sharp clap. Once. Twice. The dog's head plowed into the compacted soil as its rear twisted around, striking Cassie's legs with a thump.

Cassie slapped a hand over her mouth to hold back a scream. More shots. The foal next to her shuddered and then bolted toward the herd at the far end of the corral, its light-colored tail streaming out behind it like a victory banner.

Gulping lungfuls of air, Cassie forced her feet beneath her and stood. The dog was still. She kicked at it. Dead.

She looked up as a massive red stallion jerked to a halt, and Dean vaulted from the saddle.

Dean.

Without thinking, Cassie met him halfway and threw herself into his arms. He picked her up and crushed her to his chest, one hand buried in the hair at the nape of her neck.

"Jesus, are you all right? Did you get bitten or kicked?" His breath blew warm across her cheek as Cassie wrapped her fingers around his neck and drank in his pine and leather scent.

She couldn't speak. Could only feel, and Dean's warm, hard body felt so good. So safe and solid.

"Cassie?" Dean's hands grabbed her arms and he held her at arm's length as his amber gaze roamed her from head to foot, his expression grim. "Can you talk? Are you okay? Jesus, woman, answer me!"

A feeling of calm stole through Cassie, and somehow she managed to disengage Dean's fingers from around her arms.

"I'm fine." Back on her own feet, Cassie fought to keep her balance and to maintain her earlier sense of rage. Of the real reason she'd come to find him. The reason why she'd ended up in the horrible situation in the first place.

Images of the wild dogs slammed into her mind, and she shivered.

Thank god it had happened to her and not to a child or group of children. The thought left Cassie's stomach sour, and she turned away from Dean's anxious gaze. "The other dogs . . . did you see them?"

"I shot two, including this one, but the others ran. Are you sure you're okay?"

Dean stepped closer, and Cassie stiffened. *Don't touch me, please don't touch me. . . .* If he touched her, she would be done. History. A weak kitten in Goliath's embrace.

"Why?" Cassie spun, her chest burning. "Why did you do it, Dean? I never figured you for a chickenshit rat. Not 'Dean the mighty pillar of the community. The man of conviction and loyalty.'" Hurt and rage boiled up to replace the terror of moments before, and Cassie inched closer to Dean's startled face. "Did you know that's what all the people I spoke to said? They went on and on about what a great guy you are. How self-assured and honest. Guess you have all of them fooled, eh? Guess you like to make fools out of the people you care—"

Dean took hold of her face, his hands cupping either side, forcing her to look at him. Keeping her still.

"When I heard you scream, I thought I was too late."

He brushed away the dirt that creased Cassie's forehead then leaned in and pressed his lips against her skin. Cassie's throat clenched, and she had to force her hands to stay at her sides. *Oh, shit . . . he's touching me. . . .*

"Dean, did you hear what I just said?" Cassie said, her skin tingling where Dean held her.

Dean leaned back but did not drop his hands. One eyebrow rose, and Cassie shivered, the look shooting fissures of desire straight through to her clit.

"Yeah, I heard it. I'm just not sure what in the hell you're talking about."

Cassie's vision went red as she ripped his hands off her face and stumbled backward. "Don't pull that bullshit with me! Not after what you did! Dean remained immobile as she landed a blow on his chest. "Goddamn you! I thought maybe there might be something between us. That *maybe* you felt *something* other than lust. And even if what we had *was* just a good fuck, why did you screw me, Dean McCabe?"

Dean was still, his expression unreadable, and Cassie felt the anger drain from her in waves, leaving her empty. Her heart a rotten void. Her mind numb. "Why?" she asked quietly, dropping her fists.

Son of a bitch.

Dean had never felt more like an asshole than he felt at that moment. Cassie's pain was clear, and to think he was the one responsible left Dean disgusted with himself. And damn pissed off. Especially because he couldn't figure out why.

As he stared at her tear-streaked, flushed face, his gut clenched. Jake had been right. What a complete jackass he'd been for figuring Cassie for a game-playing bitch. She might be as cool as a cucumber, but she was also fiercely straightforward. Not the type of person to mince words and play games.

"I'm sorry." The words tumbled from his mouth like hot stones. "Did Jake say—"

Cassie threw up her hands. "Oh! So now it's *Jake's* fault? Is that it? Jake's responsible for you deciding to ruin my career and fracturing my . . ." Cassie paused and turned her face away, her shoulders trembling.

"Fracturing your what, Cassie?"

She shook her head and avoided looking at him, her arms crossed.

Dean took a deep breath, drawing in Cassie's intoxicating scent. Even covered in dust, she was the best-looking woman he'd ever seen. Shit . . . how had he ever thought he could let her go?

Don't mess this up, Dean. . . .

He sighed. For once, he figured he'd better listen to his mother's advice. "Cassie." She didn't turn, and Dean reached out, spinning her gently but firmly to face him. The streaks of tears on her face nearly undid him, and Dean reached up with a thumb to wipe them away. "I know I've been a stubborn jackass this past week. I avoided you because I didn't know what to do with you—with us." Images of their lovemaking filled Dean's mind, and he clenched his teeth, his cock already hardening. "Well, I knew what I *wanted* to do with you, but I wasn't certain how you felt about it."

Cassie scoffed. "*You* weren't certain? What about me? I risked everything, Dean. Granted, it was my risk to take . . . but I thought I could trust you." She tried to pull away, but Dean held tight.

Their bodies heaved with the forces of their breaths, and Dean had to fight the urge to press his lips against her neck and cradle her tits in the palms of his hands. "Damn it, I know I was way off base about you and Jake. But when I saw you two together, it just about killed me. Jake set me straight. I couldn't deny that I'd been an ignorant ass and—"

Cassie's livid expression brought Dean's grumbled confession to a halt. "You . . . he . . ." She took a breath. "You believed Jake when he said there was nothing between us?"

A sickening lurch hit Dean's gut like a fist. "Yeah. Did Jake tell you something different?"

Cassie laughed and pushed hair out of her flushed face. "That little shit." She looked up. "Jake set me up. He told me you didn't believe him."

"Damn kid," Dean said, not really thinking about his brother one way or the other. All he wanted to do was stare into Cassie's blue eyes every morning of every day. The realization made his palms sweat, but he wasn't about to let that stop him from saying what he should have said days ago. He reached for Cassie's hand and pulled her in. "Looks like he did the right thing, then. Because I can't get you out of my head, sugar. You're like a drug, and I'm goddamn addicted."

Dean couldn't stop himself. He cupped the back of her neck and drew her in. Her body was stiff at first, but as Dean's mouth descended, Cassie's mouth parted, and she melded the curve of her body into his. He drank in her essence, his tongue teasing hers as he pressed his hand into the small of her back.

She groaned into his mouth, and Dean growled, deepening his kiss and drawing her in closer.

Cassie gasped and pushed Dean's head away. "Stop! Put me down."

He dropped his hands, his fingers trailing over the curves of her back as he let her go. "Cassie. . . ."

She held up a hand between them as she tried to catch her breath. All Dean could stare at were her beautifully swollen lips, tousled hair, and the ample cleavage falling out of her half-open blouse. "Don't look at me that way, Dean McCabe!"

Dean almost chuckled. Almost. Now would be a really bad time to screw up. She just looked so damn cute pissed off. And her eyes looked green again. Dean stepped closer, and Cassie kept her hand up and stepped back. "What in the hell did I do, Cassie?"

Cassie clenched her fists, her expression going from pissed off to confused and then back to pissed off. "You are either the best liar in the world, Dean McCabe, or you really don't know."

He stared directly into Cassie's eyes. "I don't lie, Cassie."

She met his stare for several seconds and then leveled a fiery glare at the dead dog to their left. "Dean, how do you figure a pack of wild dogs was able to roam Granite Hollow undetected for nearly a month? Anyone in town missing dogs?"

A sickening fury filled Dean. "No."

"Is there anyone you know in this town capable of loosing these dogs to manipulate the removal of the wolves?"

"Not a chance," Dean said, certain he knew his friends and neighbors well enough to make that statement. "I can't speak for the coalition members, but no one in town has that kind of mindset. They would be more likely just to shoot the wolves, and deal with the consequences."

Cassie was silent for a time, as though considering his last words. "Someone called my boss in Washington this week and told them I was involved with you. I've been removed from the case. They're coming in tomorrow to exterminate the wolves."

Cassie's words hit Dean like a blow to the chest. "Jesus Christ. And you thought it was me?"

She nodded, her expression hurt-filled and confused.

Dean ground his teeth, the idea so repugnant he felt like smashing his fist into the face of whoever had actually made that call. "I can't believe you thought I would do that."

"Can you blame me, Dean? You didn't call all week. I had no idea how you felt about things, and then when Jake told me about you thinking he and I were . . ." Cassie stopped.

Dean took Cassie's hand and held it between his own. "No. I don't blame you. I didn't give you any reason to think it wasn't me." Dean took her other hand and brushed the dirt off her palms. "I couldn't do that to you, Cassandra." He looked up. "But I'd like to know who in the hell did, so I can beat the shit out of them."

Cassie shuddered, and her eyes went wide. "Simon Alistair."

"What?" Dean growled. "Simon? But why in the hell would he want the wolves out?"

Cassie walked over to the dead dog. She ran her hand through the animal's coat and around his neck. "This dog's thin but not starved, and even though his paws are calloused, the nails are trimmed, and the animal's been neutered." She looked up. "I would bet my salary for a year that these animals were scheduled for euthanasia. Unadoptable dogs. They were picked up by someone who had some pull and raised to do what they've been doing. Only someone with specific knowledge could do that."

Dean's thoughts tripped through the events of the past month. The sudden killings, the disappearance of the field agent, the lack of actual wolf sightings, and Simon's complete reluctance to request a new agent or to offer the townspeople any reassurances that they could control the wolves. Or even provide a qualified expert to investigate the occurrences.

"That son of a bitch," Dean growled, his hands in fists. "But why the fuck would he want the wolves out?"

Cassie stood. "I thought it was odd when I first heard that Simon had volunteered to head up this release. He's a stuffed shirt, Dean, not a field-operations manager. I was even more surprised when he requested Pete to be his liaison agent for the project. Pete isn't known for his dedication to this cause, although he *is* knowledgeable about wolf behavior. This whole thing stinks."

Cassie shuddered, and Dean pulled her in, nuzzling his face next to her ear. "We'll figure it out, Cassie. My money's on the idea that those assholes had this planned from the start."

"I—I thought I saw lights on the mountain the other day when Jake and I were up there. Near an area Jake said mountain climbers sometimes go."

Dean's hand stilled on Cassie's head. *The old mine.* It hadn't been active since the sixties, and even then had produced only marginal copper veins. And while the demand for copper had risen with the demand for new construction, Dean couldn't imagine it would be a lucrative enough endeavor for someone like Simon Alistair to risk what he had risked. There had to be something else. Someone bigger.

"Goddamn," Dean whispered, the realization hitting him like a brick. He moved Cassie just far enough away to view her gorgeous face. "I bet the asshole heard about the possibility before the coalition was given the land for the release."

"What?"

Dean swung Cassie up into his arms and started toward the house.

"Dean! I can walk!"

He scooped up her shoes in the gravel near the fence and handed them to her. "Not without these on, darlin'."

Once inside, he set Cassie on her feet and went to the glass case in the den. The case in which the McCabe family kept their keepsakes. Jake's baby shoes, their mother's pottery collection, and a few pieces of rock. Dean took a key off a rolltop desk nearby and opened the case. He picked up a lumpy piece of gray and white rock and handed it to Cassie. "This is why."

She turned it over. "What is this?"

He pulled Cassie over to the lamp and turned over the stone to reveal the shaved side. "Opal. Blue opal."

Cassie ran a finger over the milky blue, iridescent center. "It's beautiful." She looked up, and Dean pulled a piece of straw from Cassie's golden hair. "Are you saying there are opals in that abandoned copper mine?"

"My father brought this home one day, spouting off that he and a friend had found it in some forgotten offshoot of the old mine." His gaze flicked to the pictures on the mantel. Pictures of his family, of Jake, and his mother back when there was still hope that they might be a family forever. "We didn't believe him. No one did. He was a drunk, Cassie. We thought he made it up."

Cassie held the stone up to the light, her face creased in thought. "How much would these be worth?"

He moved to the case and picked out a nugget of gold his uncle had given him as a kid. "More than this chunk of gold if the pieces are of good quality, and if there's a lot of them. Blue opal is found in only one other place in Arizona. It could be worth a fortune."

"Unbelievable," Cassie murmured. "I wouldn't put it past Simon to have orchestrated the donation of the land to the coalition just for this reason. The investor would think he was giving it over to a good cause, and, once deeded with all rights, the coalition could damn well do what they pleased with the land if the release didn't work out."

Fury burned deep in Dean's gut. "And the son of a bitch couldn't count on you to insist on the wolves' removal, so he made the call to give himself a little insurance."

"Dean, we can't let them start culling the pack. We have to get ahold of someone tonight. Take in the dogs you killed, and make sure they try to find the others." She slammed the rock onto the table. "And Simon. That asshole fucked with the wrong bimbo."

12

"That's . . . oh . . . god . . ."

Cassie moaned, her fingers gripping the blanket beneath her bare ass, her hips thrust forward to allow Dean better access to her drenched and aching clit.

His tongue flicked and dipped as Cassie stared up at the stars overhead. The swish and sway of the pine trees around them and the deep green scents of the forest filled her senses.

Her vision blurred as Dean suddenly buried a finger in her slick hole. Cassie cried out, her orgasm shuddering through with the force of a freight train. She collapsed back onto the quilt. "You call that a riding lesson, cowboy?" Cassie said breathlessly.

Dean stood, unbuckled his belt, and pulled it off before dropping his jeans. "*That* lesson's just beginning, sugar."

Cassie grinned and sat up on her elbows, ignoring the snort and stamp of their horses tied only a few yards away. "Better make sure I understand all the basics. You wouldn't want me falling out of the saddle, would you?"

As Dean's cock sprang free, Cassie licked her lips, her pussy already aching to feel Dean's rigid length inside her.

"Stand up, Miss Darling," Dean ordered, and Cassie obeyed. Her nipples beaded tight as they made contact with Dean's smooth chest, and Cassie nipped at his shoulder. "Put your arms around my neck." Cassie complied as she twisted her tongue around his nipple. "This is how you mount your stallion, sugar." Cassie squealed as Dean cupped her ass and lifted her up. "And this is how you get off."

He brought her down on his rigid cock until she straddled his groin fully, her legs wrapped around his waist. Cassie gripped the hair at the back of Dean's neck and groaned. "Show me how to ride, cowboy."

Bending slightly, Dean growled in Cassie's ear, "Just hold tight, sugar."

With fast upward thrusts Dean drove his point home, and Cassie hung on, her world exploding in sharp waves of pure ecstasy. Each plunge of Dean's cock sent trills of electricity through Cassie, and she held on to the muscles of his shoulders, leaning back slightly to take him in deeper.

She shouted as she came, not caring any longer who might be within earshot. The sensation was too intense, the pleasure too wickedly perfect. Dean growled as he came along with her, his thrusts continuing until his seed was spent.

He lowered them both onto the quilt, their breaths commingling. "I could do this every hour of every day with you, sugar, and never get tired of it."

Cassie groaned. "I believe you *could* do this every hour, Dean, on the hour, which makes you an extraordinary man I don't ever intend to share."

He rolled them onto their side and pinched Cassie's nose. "That's a mite selfish, don't you think, Miss Darling?"

Cassie frowned and pinched Dean's nipple, which made him

bark with surprise and capture her hands between them. "Yeah, so what? I'm selfish. Deal with it."

Dean chuckled and pulled Cassie into a sitting position until her breasts were even with his mouth. He sucked in her nipple and bit it lightly.

"Hey! Oh!" Cassie said as the nip turned into a series of lazy circles and flicks, and the beaded tip throbbed and ached for more.

After another round of lovemaking, Cassie and Dean relaxed on the quilt and enjoyed the sounds of the forest and the cool perfection of the late summer night. The past two weeks had been a roller coaster of great sex, candid talks, and a truckload of teamwork to drive Simon Alistair out and to gain a reprieve for the wolves and release program in Granite Hollow.

There was lots of convincing to do on both sides. It wasn't until the government-sanctioned trackers found the kennel in the woods where the wild dogs had been kept that both sides conceded there was more afoot in Granite Hollow than a poorly run release and lots of pissed-off citizens.

They never found Pete, the government agent who had been in charge in Granite Hollow until his disappearance, but his fingerprints were all over the kennel area and the old Jeep they found at the site. Simon denied any knowledge, of course, but his reputation was already in shatters. Cassie had had to physically restrain Dean from smashing in his face; for as much as she would have liked to do that herself, neither one of them wanted to spend time in jail for assault.

There were other more pressing things they needed time for.

As they lay back down, Cassie twisted a thick strand of Dean's hair around her finger and realized that for the first time in forever, she was comfortable around a man. She was certain that Dean wanted all of her, not just her body. Certain that her dad had been wrong. And even though her therapist had told her that a million times, it wasn't until now, until Dean, that she finally believed it.

"You're thinkin' again, Cassandra Darling."

The growl in her ear made Cassie smile, and she turned to face her rugged lover, her mind sharp with the feel of his body next to hers, his scent lingering in the space around them. "I am, Mr. McCabe, but this time it's only good things occupying my gray matter. Things like how lucky I am to be here with you."

Dean's expression sobered, and he pulled her in for a long kiss. As his lips left hers, Dean cupped her chin. "You got that backward, sugar. I'm the lucky one. I never thought I would meet someone like you. You're a gift from the Great Spirit, woman, and I need you like I need the air to keep living."

Jake's words at the diner scrolled through Cassie's mind as she stared openmouthed at Dean.

"The Great Spirit brings you face-to-face with your worst enemy and your brightest gifts at the same time. The lesson is in how you deal with both and whether or not you can distinguish between them. . . ."

"Dean," Cassie said, the back of her neck tingling as Dean's amber gaze captured hers. Cassie brought up a hand to trace the scar on Dean's cheek. "I—I have always been my own worst enemy when it came to men. I fucked them first and thought about whether or not it was a good idea from a relationship standpoint afterward. And I did it with you, too. The difference is I knew right away that I'd messed up. I knew I wanted more with you, Dean, but I thought it was too late. I'd already followed the same pattern, and I didn't see how it could work out."

Dean pulled her hand into his chest. "And now?"

She stared into Dean's eyes and smiled. "Now I know I was wrong. *You* are *my* greatest gift, Dean McCabe. You showed me that the risk isn't in finding the right guy to screw, it's in trusting my instincts when they say, 'This might be the one.'"

A sudden howl split the night, followed by two, three, four more, and Cassie snuggled into Dean's arms, her heart full.

"I'm so glad we never had to capture any of them," Cassie whispered. "They deserve to be here. To be free."

Cassie heard a chuckle and felt Dean's lips near her ear. "You captured one, darlin', and he's not looking for freedom any time soon."

Rodeo Man

Nikki Alton

1

The summer twilight, blue, rose, and orange, lasts a long time before sinking fast into the dark that is the outline of the Absaroka Mountains. In Cody, Wyoming, in August, night falls late but moves quickly, and with the last fading color of the sun, the heat of the day fades, too.

Anna Hartley found herself shivering, tugging her jean skirt lower over her bare knees as she sat in the bleachers waiting for the rodeo to start.

She had scored a good seat above the loading chute when she showed her press pass. The woman at the ticket window told her the loading chute was where the cowboys climbed onto the bucking bronc or bull they were going to ride. The outdoor arena was packed, and there were scores of little kids lined up outside in the parking lot, posing for photographs on the back of a well-tethered, sleepy-eyed old Brahma bull; bigger kids were riding a mechanical bull surrounded by inflatable air cushions.

Food stands sold hot dogs and peanuts and cotton candy

and soda, all cheap; Anna wanted a beer, but they didn't sell any, which was sort of the way her entire day had gone so far.

Earlier, the magazine she worked for had flown her from LA to Jackson to review a new spa hotel. It had been a plum assignment, one she supposed she'd been thrust in to only because her boss was too pregnant to fly herself. Considered the junior writer at the LA office, despite past experience covering hard news for a suburban daily, Anna was usually relegated to stories along the lines of diet and exercise, stuff like the pros and cons of spinning classes.

So, Anna took the assignment eagerly, as a step up from her usual fare. Besides, it would feel good to get out of town for a day or two. Her boyfriend was pushing for an engagement, and she was down to holding him off with "I'm just not quite ready." The truth was that the longer she and Steve were together, the less ready she felt. There was something missing, and when she thought about it, that something was passion. Whether passion was that important in a relationship, or just something they talked about in magazines like hers, she wasn't entirely sure.

She'd been thinking about that just this morning, in her enormous, gorgeous, frighteningly sterile black marble and gray fieldstone suite. She had been undergoing the subtle torture of shiatsu and a goat butter and lavender wrap that made her sneeze when her cell phone rang, her boss calling.

"Anna, are you sitting down?"

"Lying down, actually. I'm having a massage of sorts—"

But that didn't deter her boss. Nothing ever deterred her. "Good. Because this may not be a surprise, but it may be a bit of a shock. We've had a visit from our new editor in chief, and a decision has been made."

The magazine had been in the process of folding into the umbrella of a larger corporate owner for months now.

Anna waited for her to go on, but when she didn't, Anna prompted her. "A decision?"

"Yes. It seems that our West Coast women's features are being downsized."

Anna realized all at once that her boss had never liked her, and that she sounded way too cheerful now.

"Unfortunately," her boss went on, "we're going to have to let you go. Effective, actually, immediately."

As a kind of consolation prize, Anna would receive a thirty-day severance package. And, by the way, could she e-mail in the spa story that afternoon. They needed to get this whole issue laid out fast, with the changes and all.

Anna hung up and, despite the protestations of the masseuse, was headed for the shower when her phone rang again.

She saw it was an LA number, but she didn't recognize it, and for a moment there she thought it was going to be whoever it was who had bought the magazine, telling her it was all a mistake. She was staying; her boss, the one who was going to take a paid maternity leave any day now, was out.

But it was Steve, exhibiting his usual bad timing.

"Steve, look, this just isn't the time to talk." She rattled off an abbreviated version of her firing and tried to sound upbeat about it. "I'm sure there're other things I can do with my life that'll be a lot more interesting than—"

"We have to talk now," he said. "You can't keep putting me off."

Steve's voice had an edge to it that made her sigh impatiently. She was wrapped in a towel and covered with goo and she'd just been fired.

"Please," she said. "Not now."

"You've made it clear that you're not ready to commit. And if what you mean is you're not ready to commit to me, then let's just come out and say so."

"Where are you?" it finally occurred to her to ask.

"I'm at—I'm with—" he was struggling. "I'm seeing someone else," Steve managed to get out.

"Since when?" Anna had kept her voice cool and even, but the phone had been shaking in her hand.

"Since the last time you told me you weren't sure—you weren't ready—I guess two months ago."

"And now the other girl wants you to be sure about *her*." Anna sounded remarkably calm, even to her own ears. But inside she was seething, furious, and she wanted to cry.

"I love you," he said, his voice anguished.

Boy, she really doubted that one.

"But you do understand—I have to make a move. If there's no real chance for us—"

"There's no chance *now*," she said, and she hung up.

She had showered and thrown her overnight bag and the laptop in her rented car in less than five minutes; screw the resort review. She had booked right out of Jackson without paying much attention to the direction in which she was going.

She should've taken the 89-A South and headed for the 15 and Salt Lake and that night's Jet Blue flight back home. But instead, she was going north into Grand Teton National Park. Well, she'd always wanted to see it. She had no real reason to drive to Salt Lake, catch that particular plane, go home. She had no office to go into tomorrow. Eventually she would have to go in and pick up her check—if she still got one, because she wasn't going to write that last story. At least not that day, not that night. She could always say she had written it, and that the e-mail got lost. And Steve certainly wasn't going to be picking her up at Burbank.

She had paid the park entrance fee, and she kept driving. Hot tears stung her eyes. She wasn't sure why she was crying. For her hurt pride, maybe. When she came right down to it, she wasn't going to miss her job or Steve, not all that much. When she came right down to it, she hadn't particularly liked the way her life was going at all. She desperately needed a change in direction. She needed to find that missing passion. It was just that she wasn't entirely sure which direction she should go or how she would go about finding it, or even if she would recognize it if she did.

The directionless part had become rapidly and literally true. The mountains were beautiful, so blue and stark and sudden, capped with perfect streaks of snow, no foothills to soften their raw majesty. She just kept driving toward them, taking a turn at a crossroad toward some place called Dubois and then barreling up an unmarked side road that looked interesting, which went from paved to gravel to dirt, and still she kept going as it climbed higher and higher, the car bouncing on the washboard surface.

It was too narrow to turn around without hitting a pine tree or vaulting off the side of a cliff anyway, so she just drove on. The road had to lead somewhere. An hour passed, and the mountain views diminished behind a thick veil of ponderosa pine. Branches were scratching at the side of the car when the road ended in a thicket of disappointing scrub pine.

She'd gone off on an adventure and ended up at a dead end. It was an apt metaphor for her entire life up until then.

She had turned off the ignition and hammered her hands against the steering wheel, beyond frustrated. After a minute her hands hurt, and she drew a deep breath and turned the key again and began to back the car up and inch the front end around by degrees. Minutes ticked by until she finally got the car facing downhill again.

To make up for lost time, and because she was more familiar with the road now and less intimidated by it, she was bumping along quite nicely, almost speedily even, downhill. And then she scraped something with the bottom of the car. She heard a clatter, and that wasn't good. And soon there was a red warning light on the dash about oil and temperature, and then the car started sputtering, and then it died on her.

She had sat there in the middle of nowhere on a one-lane, rutted dirt road with a cell phone that had absolutely no signal bars, a laptop, an overnight bag, and, fortunately, a pair of sneakers to change into. She put on the sneakers, tied her hair back with a rubber band, locked up the car, and started walking.

It was hot, ninety maybe, and where the pines did not cast their shadows over the road, she could feel the sun burning her neck. So much for adventure, direction, passion. What she really wished she had was some water.

"I'm wondering if it's a tie." Grant Olson's friend Chick chugged a glass of iced tea. They were finishing up a lunch of burgers and home fries at Irene's Mustang Diner in Dubois.

"You have probably ridden as many women as I have horses," Grant said, taking a sip of his coffee. "But I keep my horses between my legs longer."

Chick snorted. "Just don't start thinking they're a substitute."

Grant swallowed the last of his coffee. "Much as I would like to hear more of your sage advice, I gotta hit the road," he said. "To make Cody this afternoon—see which broncs they've brought in, get my gear stowed—I have to hustle."

"Don't want to hear no complaining," Chick said, walking him to his pickup. "Wish I had to make Cody. But first I woulda had to make the semifinals."

Grant shrugged. "Next year."

"Gonna look into a job at a ranch up near Whitefish. You interested, let me know," Chick said.

"I will," Grant promised. He hoped he wouldn't be interested. If he took first, he could winter with his own horses and kick back instead of wrangling someone else's livestock. Of course, that kicking back . . . he'd be doing it alone this year. He exhaled sharply.

"Worry about you, buddy," Chick said. "You're not still missing that girl who worked for the park service, are you?"

"Sometimes," Grant admitted. Then he grinned the smile that seemed to get him most of the women he got. "But you don't need to worry. I'm gonna find some new consolation."

Chick punched him on the arm and popped a toothpick into his mouth. "Just make sure," he said, "you're looking at a filly with two legs and not four."

Grant gave him a salute and climbed into his truck.

He drove a long way listening to Dwight Yoakum and the Warren Brothers and just thinking about the rides he was gonna make tonight, thinking how much of a chance he had of taking first and feeling pretty gut sure he had a good one. From there it would be a lock to move in to the finals.

Man, how he loved to ride. And he loved the untamed horses, the bucking mares, geldings, and stallions; he loved the eight seconds riding the broncs' unbroken backs best of all. That was what he lived for.

Mandy, the park service girl, she told him if he didn't settle down, turn off some of the fire inside him, he was gonna burn out. She seemed to think he should get gentled, put a bridle on, get led out to pasture. It just wasn't him.

He took a shortcut he knew and crossed the old fire road near the Gros Ventre slide. It would bring him down the pass to Buffalo Bill Cody Scenic Byway at about Pahaska Teepee, Buffalo Bill's old hunting lodge. He liked the brown hills that made themselves purple late in the afternoon, the Wind River running fast alongside the road up to the Buffalo Bill Dam.

Buffalo Bill. Now there was a man, he thought, who, if anybody told him it was time he stopped living on the road, riding broncs, shooting off firearms, and time to settle down, would've known what kind of a response to make to a woman. If only Grant could just figure out what sort of response that would be and use it himself. He laughed. Here he was wondering what he would say the next time a woman asked him to change his spots, and he didn't have anyone to say anything *to*.

And it was right then, just at the place the fire road crossed his pavement, that he saw a fine example of a woman—just sitting on a rock fanning herself—he knew he would sure like to say something to.

She jumped up and waved her hand at him, panicked that he would drive off without stopping.

He pulled over fast, sending a skid of dust over his truck and the girl. Even through the haze of it he could see she was strikingly pretty, dark hair, green eyes, a little sprinkling of freckles across her cheeks. She had on a pair of tight jeans that cried out "city girl" and showed off a round, firm bottom and a scoop-necked T-shirt that was damp and clinging to some equally round, firm breasts. Her face was flushed, and a thin sheen of sweat glazed her arms and neck.

"Can you give me a ride?" she asked. "My car—it's a rental—broke down up that mountain."

He followed the direction she was pointing. "There's nothing up there but an old fire break. What were you doing up there?" He leaned over and opened the passenger door for her.

"I don't know. I sort of got lost, I guess. I was looking for scenery." She was already climbing in the truck. "Thank you. Not that many cars pass along here, do they? The only other car I've seen in an hour was a lumber truck, and he went straight by me. I thought nobody would ever come. I thought I would be stuck here all night—"

"Do you breathe out?" he asked her, smiling.

She seemed to start to get offended, but she saw his smile and smiled back instead. She put her hand to her hair and tucked behind her ears the ends that had come loose from a rubber band. She ran her tongue over her lips. There were other things he would like to see her run that pretty pink tongue over.

"You thirsty?" he asked.

"Very," she said.

He leaned across her, his arm accidentally brushing her knee, and opened the glove box.

"Help yourself," he said. He noticed she didn't draw back when he touched her. Maybe it meant nothing except she was too worn out to care.

She took a bottle of water from the glove box and drank it straight down.

"I'll take you down to the ranger station," he said. "They'll call a tow truck for you."

"I appreciate it." She leaned back in the seat and closed her eyes.

He looked at her out of the corner of his eyes. A few drops of water had escaped the bottle and spilled onto her shirt, and watching her breasts straining against the fabric . . . How he would like to open up another bottle, and pour it all over her. See how she would look all wet. Even now he could see the faint outline of a nipple. The heat flush on her cheeks—he bet she colored like that all over under the right circumstances. It had been a long time since he'd had any of that consolation he'd told Chick he would be getting. He could feel himself getting hard beneath his jeans, and he shifted in his seat, put his eyes back on the road.

If he didn't have to sign in, check his gear, check out the mounts they'd brought in . . . if it wasn't the biggest purse of the season he would be riding on tonight . . . he would've liked to have waited with her at the ranger station, talked her up a little; a woman that pretty, he would like to see where things might lead.

But, as it was, he took her to the station, apologized for having to move on, and shook hands with her. He let his hand linger just a second or two longer than necessary on her skin, feeling the warmth of her hand in his. Wondering what it would feel like if she ran that smooth little hand over other parts of his body. She was holding his hand just as long as he was holding hers.

There was something about her, he knew there was, something that just clicked with him. She knew it, too. They both looked into each other's eyes for a moment, and they were going to say something, he wasn't sure what it was, but something, until they got interrupted.

The ranger on duty started asking her questions about the color of her vehicle and the license plate—"Just how many sedan cars do you think are abandoned up on that fire road?" she asked, which made Grant laugh—and then he came to his senses and left her there.

The tow had taken a long time to arrive. Anna had sat on a stoop outside the ranger's station, watching other people who hadn't wrecked their cars drive by on the two-lane highway, most of them heading east, the same direction the cowboy went.

At least, he looked like a cowboy to her. She was pretty sure he didn't buy his blue jeans with a hole in the left knee as a fashion statement. She saw how sun-browned and strong his arms were beneath the sleeves of his T-shirt. She let herself wonder what his shoulders looked like, his back. She thought about the way his hand felt in hers, the tapered, long fingers, strong and calloused. She just liked the way his hand felt. She hadn't wanted to let go.

Crazy thought, but it felt like he had wanted to keep on holding her hand, too. Or, maybe he had wanted to do more than that. Maybe she wanted him to do more. It might be nice to feel those fingers moving up her arm, against her cheek, turning her face toward his. He'd had incredibly blue eyes, almost violet. And kind of curly dirty-blond hair. She wondered how old he was. Maybe thirtysomething. He had little crinkles around his eyes from being out in the sun, but this in no way had diminished his attractiveness. And he was very attractive.

It wasn't just how cute he was, though—she wasn't so superficial that just because a guy was hot she was going to start fantasizing about him. Even though that was exactly what she was doing.

After he turned her face to his, maybe he would bend down, or she would lean up—he was at least four inches taller than her five-foot-five—and they would kiss. And maybe it would be a good kiss. A devouring kiss. The kind of kiss that betraying asshole Steve had never given her.

Of course, a guy as good-looking as that cowboy, he was probably married, had a ranch, and had ten kids. But maybe not. She'd felt him looking at her out of the corner of his eye. She liked that. And she liked the way he'd teased her a little; he didn't make her feel stupid the way the ranger had for taking her car off-road and breaking it, like she was a bad child who'd broken a nice toy.

She had not even asked her rescuer his name. All she knew about him other than his looks was that he was driving an old green pickup with bench seats and Wyoming plates. If she'd paid attention to the plate numbers, she would've had a chance of finding him again, but she hadn't. That she even wanted to find him surprised her, but she wished she could. When the tow truck arrived, she had stopped thinking about him.

She had paid a lot for the tow into Cody, and she was going to pay a lot more for the repairs. Neither her insurance nor her rental contract would cover them. She was not supposed to take the vehicle off-road, and if she did she would be liable for a stiff fine, as well as being responsible for any damage. Of course, if she got the damage fixed, they would never know she took it off-road. That was as good as things were going to get.

"This is a Friday. Nobody in town has that part. Gotta come

from the Ford dealer in Cheyenne. And that'll be Monday," the mechanic at the garage in Cody had told her.

She revised her thoughts. Getting the car fixed on Monday and spending the weekend in Cody without any wheels—*that* was as good as it was going to get.

But Cody was a nice-enough-looking town, with restaurants, bars, a world-class historical museum, dude ranches, motels, and a rodeo. A big-purse professional cowboy semifinal and final. All weekend long. So, she wouldn't be bored.

On the downside, the restaurants, bars, museum, and motels were all packed with tourists and rodeo contenders. Anna had called everywhere in the phone book, looking for a room, and then she started over again, looking for cancellations.

At last she found one at a place called the Bear's Den Motel. It was off the main drag on a side street lined with secondhand stores and a tack shop. She had laughed when she saw the room; the queen-size bed nearly filled it, the ceiling fan didn't work, and the bath towel looked more like a hand towel. But still. It had a pool.

"It's your lucky day, sweetheart," the manager told her.

Other than getting fired, and finding out that her boyfriend was unfaithful, and screwing up her car to the tune of eight hundred dollars plus the tow, it had been her lucky day, all right. But, yeah, things could've been worse. She could still be wandering around on the fire service road and out of water. She could be sleeping in her disabled car in the back of the repair shop. She could be married to Steve.

Instead, that night, she would go check out the rodeo.

2

So, there she was, folding her arms across her chest, punked again, this time by the weather, which was cooling off dramatically as the sun plunged behind the hills. She was wearing a sleeveless tank top and an open-weave summer sweater vest with her jean skirt, and she wished she'd brought the sweatshirt she'd left in her motel room. A wind blew up as the moon rose, sending her hair across her face. She pushed her hair impatiently behind her ears. She saw the cowboys down in the chutes jamming their hats lower on their foreheads.

The lights dimmed in the bleachers and came on bright across the arena. "Ladies and gentlemen! Let's hear some noise—for our cowboys!"

A rodeo clown came out in absurdly large boots and a red nose and started clapping his hands and stamping his feet in time to a loud recording of Queen's "We Will Rock You." The bleachers shook and thundered with the response from the crowd.

"Our first event, bronc riding, is brought to you by Zane Chevrolet, right here in Cody. Coming out of chute number three"—right below Anna—"we have Grant Olson, a Wyoming boy holding the championship record for the longest and highest-rated bronc riding in the *naaaation.*"

There were more cheers and applause and stomping, and Anna looked down into the chute as a pretty brown horse was hustled into the wooden box, gated at front and back with metal piping. There were eight chutes, all in a row, and in each one a cowboy was waiting. The only chute with a horse loaded was this one right under her, so she kept her eyes on the action inside.

The horse was stamping and pawing, snorting, shaking its mane back and forth as if possessed. She saw the rider square his shoulders and pull on a pair of leather gloves. Two other guys were holding the horse, which was straining just to break out of there.

Grant Olson mounted up. She watched his muscular legs, taut inside worn jeans, his broad shoulders straining against the fabric of a simple blue denim work shirt as he swung into the saddle. With one hand, he gripped a handle strapped to the horse. He had his other hand up in the air, like he was going to wave at somebody. He gave a nod to one of the guys holding the horse, and the gate of the bucking chute opened.

Horse and rider burst into the arena, the horse trying to throw off the man as fast as it could.

Anna watched, fascinated. What made a man want to do something this crazy? Hold on to a horse that wild, that determined to get rid of him, doing it over and over again for the sport of it . . . And, yeah, the money, but it wasn't like the NFL or the NBA. Most of these guys, even the top performers like this Grant, had a hard time making a living at it. You had to be good and tough and maybe a little bit crazy, she supposed.

Or maybe a lot crazy. There was something exciting about that.

"Eight seconds!" the announcer crowed, like that was a victory.

Grant Olson had just taken a spectacular fall, right off the side of the horse, flipping away in a gymnast's roll seconds before the horse kicked at him, its flank straps trailing. Grant moved fast enough that the horse got only dust on his hooves.

The cowboy's Stetson was lying on the ground, and when he bent to pick it up, he gave a bow to the crowd on the other side of the arena. Anna wished he would turn toward her. She would like to see how he looked. Was he scared, mad, happy? Apparently he should've been happy, because the announcer was practically ecstatic.

"Let's see who's gonna top that performance!" the amplified voice bellowed. "Judges say that scored a nine-two. Nine-two, ladies and gentlemen. Exceptional!"

A couple of guys roped the horse and led it out of the arena. She saw that a new horse and rider were being readied in the next chute down the line.

Her eyes went back to Grant, who was walking with a slight limp as he passed right beneath Anna again, heading through a passage next to the chute.

The wind threatened to lift his hat again, and he put a hand on it. As he did, he turned and looked up in the stands. His eyes met Anna's. They were very blue, almost violet. She felt a start of recognition and pleasure. She felt her heart kind of skip a beat and then hammer on faster. He smiled at her, a warm, self-deprecating, but oh-so-confident smile. She'd seen a glimpse of it in his truck, but this was an even better smile.

She smiled back, just as she had earlier. She felt a heat rise up in her cheeks. She'd found him.

He rode four more broncs that evening, never topping his first record, but taking home first all the same. He was in the calf- and barrel-roping competitions, too, and she liked watching him ride the saddle horses, swirling his rope like it was a living thing he was sending off into the shine of the arena lights.

There were dozens of competitors, some from as far away as Australia, but most of them from Montana, Wyoming, Colorado, and Texas, some as young as eighteen and peaking, Anna noticed, in their early forties. After that, she guessed, it would be harder to heal up after a fall. There were women, too, some of them as graceful as ballerinas doing the roping, the stunt riding. There was one who rode a bronc, and Anna saw, with a wave of something like jealousy, that one of the cowboys holding her mount steady was Grant.

They were all hard and lean and tanned and good at what they did. Confident. Not cocky confident, exactly, but like they knew what it took to do what they were doing, and they were proud of themselves for pulling it off.

Anna watched them all, but, time and again, even when he wasn't riding, she found her eyes drawn to Grant. It wasn't just that he was good-looking, or even that he'd smiled at her the way he had. There was something about him, the same thing she'd felt when he'd given her a ride. There was some sort of heat that drew her gaze to him, something that passed off him in a wave and washed right over her and pulled her in. And she liked the way that felt.

He kept looking at her, too, when he was lounging with the other guys, bumming a cigarette, telling a joke, grabbing a soda. His eyes cut up to her to see if she was watching him, and, of course she was.

She'd never stared at a guy like that in her life. And she'd never had a guy stare back at her. She'd met Steve at a journalism school potluck, and he liked the crust on the takeout pizza she'd brought, which got them started talking.

She had never dated much before Steve, and their relationship never involved anything like him giving off some kind of indefinable heat that made her knees feel weak and her stomach drop.

Both of which were happening now, just because she'd been looking at this complete stranger, a cowboy in a rodeo ring.

She forced herself to look away from him, and looked instead at a vendor selling peanuts in the stands. She waved her arm wildly, as if the peanuts were something she'd wanted all her life and she just remembered how much she wanted them, and she bought a bag.

When she settled down again in her seat, Grant Olson was gone.

Using her press pass like a prop, she looked for him in the tack room behind the arena, but he wasn't there. She waited around by the snack stands until almost all the crowd had emptied out.

Then she walked her lame self through the dusty gravel parking lot and down the highway past the Wal-Mart toward her motel. For a bag of peanuts, she'd thrown away something she really did want a chance at.

The fact that he won first place was a big photo op for Grant, and he posed more than willingly for the local paper, the Professional Rodeo Cowboys' Association's magazine and Web site, and the Cowboy Hall of Fame. Then came the hand-shaking and the beer-toasting and the taped radio interview in the only quiet place they could find, the manager's office. By the time he started packing up his gear, everybody was gone. Including the girl.

Why he thought she would hang around, he didn't know. She had been sitting next to a couple of kids, and they were probably hers. There was probably a husband, too, and he'd missed him. Although why any decent husband would let a girl like that parade around in too-tight jeans in a car not meant for going off-road up in the mountains, he couldn't guess.

Anyway, she was gone. He figured he would take his big silver trophy, and the five grand in prize money burning a hole in the pocket of his favorite shirt, and go on down to the Irma Hotel bar and listen to more people tell him how great he was.

He knew he'd had some damn spectacular rides. He'd placed well in the roping, too. Some of it, he knew, was that he was showing off for that woman he was so sure had come to watch him. Sometimes pride just got the best of you, and sometimes you could use that pride to go yourself one better. He'd done that tonight, but the girl was gone now.

It was disappointing, but he wasn't going to let it get him down. Now Sunday's championship was his; everybody said so. Girls came up to the big hundred-thousand-dollar cherry-wood bar at the Irma—the bar Queen Victoria gave Buffalo Bill because she was so impressed with his performance in his Wild West show. Nobody was giving Grant a hundred-grand bar, but the girls were giving him phone numbers and motel rooms on little rolled-up pieces of paper, and the guys were giving him slaps on the back. They wanted to know how he did it. He laughed, but he never said, because he didn't really know himself.

It was a gift given to him, worthy or not. Over the course of a winning streak and good times that had lasted some twenty years, Grant had come to think of himself as worthy—at least just as worthy as the next guy.

Still, ride after glorious ride, he wasn't so stuck on himself that he wasn't grateful for this long run he was having. It was a perfect life, the horses and the smell of the sage and creosote out on the plains and the pale skies after it rained and the feel of himself just riding, in the arena or out, and there was only one thing that was missing, and of course it was the girl, whatever girl that would be. He knew who he wanted, but she was gone.

Then, there she was again. The one he had picked up on the road, the one in the bleachers right above his starting gate. She was at his elbow now, her cheeks all pink again, but not from a hot afternoon walk this time.

Anna decided she wasn't just going to sulk back to her lousy motel room. She was going to have that beer. There was a Denny's that looked dismal, and there was a steak house that was closed, and there was a sign for a roadhouse that was too far out of town for her to walk to. Then she saw the Irma. It had a plaque on the front porch identifying the building as being built by Buffalo Bill Cody for his daughter Irma. Laughter and country music spilled out into the night, and it sounded welcoming.

She went inside. It was crowded, and the welcoming noise seemed daunting up close. Still, she was inside, and she was going to have her beer. She was always talking about having an adventure or something, and now here she was, intimidated by a crowded, friendly bar. She drew herself up and plunged on in.

There were no tables, so she pushed her way up to the bar. And, standing at one end of it, with his big prize trophy, a beer and a shot glass in front of him, was Grant Olson. Third time, she thought. That had to be a charm.

Before she could feel too discouraged by the fact that most of the crowd in the room seemed to be focused on shaking his hand, she joined the throng and waited, not patiently, until she was just behind him and to the right. She cleared her throat, but he didn't turn; she would have to say his name or touch his shoulder, and either one felt wrong. But she could stand there all night, or at least until someone elbowed her out of the way, and he would never notice her at all if she kept clearing her throat like she needed a cough drop or something.

It flashed through her mind that she could just slink away into the crowd again, and maybe that was the wiser plan. Instead, she gripped the edge of the bar like it was a life-saving device and leaned across the eager young man who was edged up close to Grant, who was laughing at some joke the guy on the other side was telling him.

"You looked great out there today," she said very loudly.

The guy between them frowned, but Grant turned, saw her, and flashed that smile.

"Well, there you are," he said, like he'd been waiting for her all along. "'Scuse me, partner." He edged the young man aside. "Get him another beer." Grant gestured at the bartender, offering the guy a consolation prize of sorts. "You want something?" he asked Anna.

She wanted a lot more than a drink, honestly, but she started there. "Sure. Whatever you're having."

The bartender slipped her a shot glass, brimming with something clear, and a mug of Bud draft, the foam spilling over on her hand as she lifted it to her mouth for a taste. She wiped her hand on her skirt and tossed down the shot. It was Cuervo, and it burned her throat, but at least it gave her a reason for the fire she felt flare up inside her, standing so close to Grant there in the crowd.

"Why do you do it?" she asked him.

"Do what?"

"Ride like that. You got thrown—hard—over and over."

"I've been stomped hard, too," he said, not like he was bragging, just like it was a fact. "Over and over." He tossed down his own drink.

"You do it to win?" She was genuinely curious; maybe it was some latent journalistic skill coming out, now that she'd been liberated from containing it inside questions like "Is the oatmeal scrub or the rosemary herb better for closing your pores?"

"You don't do it for the money," he told her. "You do it for . . ."

"The rush?"

"You do it 'cause it's like love. Feel dead without it."

" 'Cause it's like love," she repeated after him, and her eyes met his, quite direct in what she wanted, and she could see in his eyes that it was what he wanted, too.

It frightened her how much she wanted it. She could so easily excuse herself and slip away and run, not walk, down the dark sidewalk through the all but asleep town to that little motel room, and lock the door, and be safe from whatever it was she wanted, whatever it was she was afraid of. From him.

But she didn't move, because she wasn't really that afraid. And if she was, she didn't want to be. He put his hand on her arm, lightly, and she did not move her arm away while they made small talk about the rodeo tour he was on, how the season was spring to fall, you start out in the small towns, you build up to the big ones.

She asked him why the broncs bucked, and he told her nobody knew, really. "It's like this urge, this strong, undeniable urge."

And his hand was on the small of her back, just like she'd imagined it being, and he was moving it back and forth just a little, and she was all worked up inside, just from his hand moving on her there at the base of her spine. She was having her own strong, undeniable urge.

"An urge?" she said, and her voice was husky.

"To just buck—wildly and wholeheartedly. Why some horses are born like this—seriously, nobody knows. But it's not 'cause they're scared or hurt or anything. The horse just . . . wants to."

Anna could really understand that all of a sudden. There was no reason why she wanted this guy so badly. The good looks, the feel of his hand—those were excuses. The real reason was she just plain wanted him.

He asked about her, and she kept it brief: worked for a magazine, LA really is a great big freeway like the old Burt Bacharach song said, and she was taking some time off—a vacation, more or less—before she messed up the rental car. All of which was true, as far as it went.

Her skin felt so hot where his fingers were touching her.

"You know something funny," he said. "I don't know your name."

"Anna," she told him.

"Almost as pretty as you are." He smiled again, and the smile was so genuine that his words didn't sound like just a line, even though they probably were, and he'd probably used lines quite a bit.

She resisted the urge to throw herself against him, but just barely.

This was turning into a fine, fine night. He was high on the win and a buzz of Cuervo, the look in Anna's eyes, and the sweet curve of her body as she spun that trophy toward her, making the pink neon of the bar sign wash over the trophy like a sunset.

She was smart enough to ask him the kind of questions he actually wanted to answer, as opposed to the silly sort of small talk he brushed off like rodeo dust. Maybe it was because she was so up front about wanting him; there was no game to it. Before he could even order her another drink, she leaned in and kissed him full on the mouth, her lips open and moist, and she said, "Can you take me someplace?"

He could've just taken her back to her motel room—he was sharing his with another rider—but he liked her enough that he wanted to take her someplace that meant something. He liked her enough that he wanted it to mean something to her, too.

Outside, the stars were sugaring the sky; there was a yellow half moon riding low in the hills.

The din from the bar faded away as they walked across the street. When he put his hand on her shoulder, steering her toward his truck, goose bumps shivered over her night-cooled skin, and he saw her nipples harden through the thin fabric of her tank top.

"Got a chill?" he asked her.

"I'm used to LA summers."

"Which are the same as the winters, am I right?"

"That's a common misconception," she said, laughing.

"I'm sure there're lots of things I'm mistaken about," he agreed affably.

"Maybe not that many," she said. She laughed a little more, and she sounded nervous.

He could tell she was going to be fun. He was having fun already just looking at her standing there in that short skirt and that tight white top, the funny little woven thing that passed for a sweater over that, and, beneath those, the shadow of whatever lacy thing she had on for a bra, not substantial enough to hide those erect nipples. It set Grant to wondering what her panties looked like; were they lacy, too? Did they match?

Then there were those long legs of hers—seemed to go on forever, her feet thrust inside high-heel, backless sandals girls called slides. He liked the idea of sliding one foot out and then the other and nibbling on her toes, maybe. Massaging her ankles, calves, knees, following everywhere his hands went with his tongue. Slowly, not too fast, he would move his hands up her fine thighs—muscled but not too muscled—and spread those legs, licking higher and higher until his hands and his tongue both found those panties—they would be lace, he was sure they would be lace—pull 'em on down with his teeth, put his fingers on up in that pussy—it would be soft, it would be wet, it would open right up for him. Maybe she would lift up those legs and wrap them around his neck.

The idea made his mouth dry, and he swallowed hard. He turned to unlock his truck.

One thing he'd learned from the bronc riding: you didn't try to climb on too fast because they would throw you faster. He liked moving slow, anyway.

When he opened the passenger door, she was looking at him, expectant.

He leaned over her and kissed her softly on the lips. "I want you," he told her simply.

"I want you, too. And I want you to—" She didn't finish. She didn't even know what she was going to say. Instead, she reached for his face, pulled him to her, kissing him, ravenous. They kissed until his lips felt hot and raw, and her lipstick was just about gone.

"I don't know what I'm doing," she said when they broke apart.

"Doesn't matter. I do," he said. At least, he sure hoped he did.

He started the engine, backed the truck out of the space, shifted into drive, and sailed down the street past the tourist shops and the gas stations and the bronze statues in front of the Buffalo Bill Historical Center, past her motel and a string of others and out into the unblemished darkness.

Civilization, such as it was, disappeared into a blur of insignificant light behind them. Anna was as nervous as she was excited.

He took a turn up a dirt road and then another turn, and unlike the fire road she'd trashed her rental on, this one led somewhere. They were alongside the tumbling Wind River, its rushing water golden in the moonlight.

"Spring and summer, wild horses come down just about there." He pointed to a wide spot in the river where the current seemed to slow before pulsing on downhill. "It's one of the prettiest sights you've ever seen."

"It's beautiful here," she said. She relaxed a little and inched herself closer to him on the cracked vinyl of the bench seat.

"And not what you expected," he said, sounding pleased with himself.

"In a good way," she said. "Oh, look."

There, in the wide spot upstream, two horses, then a third and a fourth, sauntered out of the moon-swept brush and into the water. Their supple bodies moved with a fluid grace as they bent to drink, as if they'd sprung up from the water, were one with its shining liquid.

They were both silent; she was practically holding her breath, just in case out there in the emptiness, the sound would carry and scare them away. They watched the magnificent horses until they left, slipping out of the water, disappearing, their hooves echoing into the night above the splashing of the river.

"C'mere," Grant said, and he pulled her close and kissed her again.

She pressed her tongue to his, her lips to his; they were drinking in each other, lapping up each other. And while he was kissing her, and she was kissing him, he slipped one hand behind her back, finding that place along her spine she liked. He rubbed there, and she leaned closer, wanting more touch, more touch. How did he know she liked that spot?

Then his hand was slipping under her crocheted sweater and under her ribbed white tank, too, and he just unsnapped the back of her bra. Her bra straps drooped down off her shoulders, and he moved his hand around to her side; his fingers reached through the weave of her sweater, and he lowered the straps a little more.

Then he sat back, just looking at her in the moonlight, his eyes glinting. "Let me just . . . see you like that."

She sat still, embarrassed, smiling. But he couldn't just let her alone. His hand moved to the front of her breasts now, grazed her nipples until they rose under his palm.

"That feels good, I bet?" He had a question in his voice, but she could tell it wasn't really a question in his mind.

"Yeah," she breathed. They were getting started now.

"So you'll let me have my way with you?" he asked.

"Sure looks like it," she replied. Her heart was beating very fast.

Now he moved his hand under her sweater and under her top and under her loose bra, and he rubbed each nipple skin on skin, first one and then the other between his thumb and his forefinger, making them harder still beneath his warm and calloused fingers.

She gasped.

He slipped her sweater off her shoulders, lowering her bra straps more along with it, until both the sweater sleeves and the bra straps were down around her elbows, pinning her arms. Her breasts were constrained only by her top now, rubbing against the fabric.

He leaned in and kissed her lips again, his tongue moving between her teeth and out to trace the outline of her lips. He nibbled on her ear and ran his tongue along the line of her jaw and the tendons of her neck and then lower, shifting between light little kisses, and lapping with his tongue small circles right up to the edge of her shirt.

She was so turned on her breath came in ragged little bursts.

"You like this," he said, not even a trace of a question now.

"Love it," she said. Then, feeling she had to let him know she said, "I don't, you know, usually do things like—"

He kissed her lips again, silencing her. She guessed he didn't care whether she did them usually or not. As long as she did them now.

He dipped his head down lower, kissing her loose breasts through the fabric of her top, his lips sucking on them, open-mouthed, leaving wet marks on her top.

He stripped off his own T-shirt, showing his taut, muscled chest, silvered in the moonlight. His skin was dark from night shadows and summer sun, and she moved her half-bound arms so she could press her hands against his chest, her fingers stroking his pectoral muscles, his shoulders. He bent his head lower against her chest, and she wrapped her fingers in his curly hair and pulled his face up to hers so she could kiss him again, and again.

He drew back enough to work the sweater off her arms and, deftly, tossed it to the backseat.

He stripped off her unfastened bra from underneath her top, and hung it like a talisman over his rearview mirror, freeing her arms.

She laughed. "I'm surprised you don't have a whole mess of bras hanging up there."

"I take 'em down," he said.

She wasn't sure he was joking.

Then he lifted her top over her head and let it fall beside her. He pushed her tangled hair off her face and kissed her forehead, her eyelids, her cheeks, her nose and then her lips again, all the time flicking his fingers against her nipples, rubbing his warm, rough hand across her breasts.

She moaned as he put his mouth on her bare breasts for the first time, kissing and licking them, first one and then the other, the nipple, the aureola, the round flesh, and down to her ribs.

She was enormously excited. She felt like she had a fever, as if some sort of delirium had overtaken her. Beads of sweat broke out along her brow and between her breasts. He licked her there, cooling her, but just a little.

She could still hear the river, but she couldn't see it through the steam they'd made on the windows.

What she saw was Grant's erection pushing at his jeans. She put her hand on his crotch and felt him pulsing under her palm.

He teased her nipples gently with his teeth. Dropping them,

glistening with his saliva, he moved his tongue over the whole of her breasts again, circling them, keeping them hard and wet.

So far, she realized, all the action had been above the waist, except for her own hand on his dick.

Like he was reading her mind, he lifted her hand off him and pushed her skirt up on her thighs and spread her thighs gently. He rubbed his hand up one thigh and then the other, slowly, slowly inching his hands from her knee to her pelvis.

She cried out when he finally reached the corner of her panties and pushed the fabric to the side. He stroked the pubic hair he'd exposed, twined his fingers in it, and then, almost tentatively, stuck his index finger inside her. One finger, just one, and he wriggled it around until he found the right spot and made her slick just from stroking her there. Then he started moving that finger back and forth and sideways.

She twisted around in her seat because it felt so good and she wanted more. He pushed her panties aside a little more and put in a second finger and then a third and then she came, shuddering and crying out into the dark night.

It wasn't like she was a virgin, although she'd been only with Steve before, unless she counted some semiserious groping in the freshman dorm back in college. This felt far more like a rite of passage than sleeping with Steve ever had.

After he gave her the hand job, Grant sat back and watched the flush fade from her cheeks and bare chest and spread thighs. A thin sheen of sweat lay over her skin. Her mouth was just slightly parted, and he touched it with his fingers, still sticky from her cum.

She took his fingers in her mouth and sucked on them.

He wasn't sure how much longer he could hold back, no matter how determined he was to give her a good, long ride.

"You like that, baby?"

"Yes."

No need for the question or the answer; it was just part of the rhythm he was using to hold on.

He turned her torso toward him and lifted her legs high on the seat so they were bent at the knees, her back nearly up against the passenger door. He spread her legs wider. He put one hand under her ass and, lifting her up, tugged her panties down about to about mid-thigh.

They weren't all lace like her bra, but they had trimmings of it over some kind of synthetic satiny stuff. The crotch was cotton, and he felt it, nearly sodden. He inhaled the smell of her sex and her sweat as he pushed the panties down her legs and slipped her shoe off her right foot—and the panties over that foot—and then slipped off the left shoe—and tugged the panties off that foot, too. Then her shoes and her panties were discarded on the floor of the truck. Then he began to kiss her, just as he'd imagined doing, only better, from her firm, trim ankles, up the swell of her calves, behind her knees, and along the inside of her thighs, until he rested his lips inside her other lips, the soft, pink labia, spread her open, so rosy and wet. He sucked on her clit and rubbed his tongue all around until she was even wetter and so much bigger, opening up to him.

He lifted his head just once. "Look at you. You're just dripping," he said.

She did look, and with her fingers wrapped in his hair, just looking, she came then, and again against his tongue, shooting out salty and strong, and again when he sat up and put his whole hand inside her.

Her mouth was parted in a big round "O", open kinda like the lips between her legs. Her lipstick was mostly gone and smeared around the edges, and that turned him on even more because he wanted the last of it gone and he knew how he was going to accomplish that, too.

When he drew out his hand, her body made a little sucking sound, like she wanted to keep him there. Oh, yeah, oh, yeah, she did. But he sat back from her again and slid the back of the bench seat all the way down and unbuckled his belt.

She got the message and leaned over him, unzipping his fly.

"Got a peppermint-flavored raincoat in my pocket," he said.

When she'd suited him up, she took him in her mouth and worked that cock until he was as hard as a tree.

She had her own fingers inside herself, twisting in the pink, wet places beneath the damp curl of her pubic hair, and when she came this time playing with herself, she took him in her mouth deeper, right down to his balls.

As good as it felt, he lifted her lips off his dick and then lifted her in his arms. She felt light as he swung her on top of him, thrust himself between her legs.

She was wide open and loose and ready, and she clamped herself around him, moving up and down on him as he was pushing in and out of her. They got quite a little beat going, thighs slapping together, his cock and her cunny rocking hard.

"Oh, yeah," she said. "Oh, yeah, yeah." And her hands clutched at his shoulders, and they banged together fierce and fine until she let out a long, vibrating cry. She collapsed against his chest, panting, and he let go, too, the cum exploding out of him. They just stayed together, his cock shuddering inside her, her entire body quivering against him like the beating of wings.

After a while she gave a long sigh and raised up to look at him, all flushed, her hair wild. He pushed her hair off her face, smoothed it, and then let his fingers play down her cheeks to her lips. She took his fingers in her mouth again and sucked them, one after the other, moved them in and out between her lips like slender cocks.

"Insatiable," he said, amused.

"You don't know the half of it," she replied, like she was surprised about it herself. She dropped his fingers and climbed off him, pulling down her skirt as she slipped onto the seat next to him.

"We having fun yet?" he asked her.

"Oh, yeah," she said with that same throaty vibration in her voice that she had when she was coming.

He laughed.

She plucked her tank top off the floor and threw it on.

"Don't get yourself fixed up too much," he said. "I like being able to reach over and touch what I see."

She just sighed, but it was a good sigh.

He put his arm around her shoulders, and she rested her head against his chest.

They stayed like that for a while, with the river rushing by outside the truck, and the wind moving the cottonwood trees and the pines along its banks, and the heat of their bodies slowly cooling. The steam crept back from the windows, and soon they had a view again, of the moon higher up over the hills now, rimming the rocky points with halos of light.

She was not herself; she was floating outside herself; she was seeing little colored lights flashing; her ears were ringing; that was how fucking fantastic it all felt. It was like getting struck with lightning bolts but in a good way. She was just shaking with the electricity of it, the way he touched her, licked her, felt her up, put his hands on her and in her. And his tongue—coursing over her skin, pushing between her lips, licking her and stroking her and then moving wet and hot between her legs and up inside her, the warmth of his saliva in the heat of her, his tongue reaming up inside her. God, she'd never had anyone do something like that to her before. He had sucked her clit until it vibrated, and she felt the vibration echo through her whole body until it was almost a sound. And, in turn, when she was sucking him, she wanted to make him her own instrument.

Then when he had lifted her up, opened her up, shoved his dick inside her, it was like a convergence or something, a harmony, a rhythm section just fucking away to the beat. And he was right: She was insatiable. She wanted more. It was like she'd never even considered feeling like this, and now she wanted to keep feeling like this, keep the wildness going, not let it slack off, not calm down, not ever.

Maybe, she thought, this was what he felt on one of those horses. Maybe it was the sheer craziness of it that made him want to take the ride. That was more or less how she felt, anyway. She just wanted to keep him on her, crazy or not.

She just wanted the night to last forever; she wanted nothing more than to feel his skin on her skin, his lips on her lips, his lips all over her body, hers on his. She was so hot, inside and out, she thought she must be giving off steam.

Had she once found this night chilly? Now she was practically incendiary with heat; she wanted to jump in that cool river out there, she wanted to take Grant with her and swim with him somewhere, wherever the current would take them.

She listened to his heartbeat, a rapid staccato. Gradually, its rhythm slowed. Her own heart was still pounding.

"I want to go for a swim," she said. "In the river."

He shook his head. "Baby, the water's so wild they don't take the rafts in. You can't swim there."

But she was already scrambling out of the pickup, barefoot.

She had no intention of really climbing in; she could see for herself how fast the water was tumbling. And at the calm place, upstream where the horses drank, the bank was lost in brush and boulders. But she wanted to at least feel the spray of the water on her burning skin, feel on her cheeks again the cool wind she'd felt back in the rodeo arena. She wanted to let it circle her body, brush between her legs where she was naked and hot and wet beneath her crumpled skirt.

The fever that was consuming her was starting to frighten her just a little. If she stayed in that truck one more second, she would be begging him for more. She wasn't just insatiable, she was shameless. She was consumed by a desire that ached out of a place she didn't know, couldn't name. She didn't think she should let him know how much she was feeling.

She ran down a sharp slope, skipping around rocks and creosote, until she reached the edge of the riverbank. She'd wanted to wade in the water, just put her feet in, but the bank was steeper than she'd realized. It was still a good three abrupt feet down from the cut line. So, she stopped where she was, her toes slipping in the damp mud and sand. She could feel the dampness rising off the river, a mist dewing her hair. It felt good. She just stood there, wriggling her toes in the cool muck. The fever began to leave her, her heartbeat to slow down.

She felt his hand on her elbow. "I was afraid you were insane there for a minute," he said.

"When was that? When I let you undress me and eat me out, or when I was sucking your cock?"

"When you were asking me about swimming in a class-five rapid," he said.

She turned to him, anxious to see his face in the moonlight, but, as she turned, a piece of the bank crumbled under her, and she slipped backward. Not much, but enough that he pulled her against him.

"Be careful there, baby," he said.

"I'm not crazy," she replied, but she sounded a little doubtful, even to herself. "Although this is a pretty crazy night." She pulled away from him a little.

"Just be careful," he repeated.

"If I was going to be careful, I wouldn't be out here with you in the first place, would I?"

She looked up at him, and he scooped her up in his arms and carried her, like a newlywed or an overgrown child, back up the slope of the riverbank. She put her arms around his neck, enjoying the grip of his hard, muscled arms clasped over her.

"Tell me what you want," he said.

"I don't want you to stop. Not tonight." She closed her eyes. That way, if this was all a dream or something, she could keep it going.

3

Driving back to town, they were pushing it as far as they could, pawing at each other, wild. It was like they wanted a piece of each other to hold on to.

He lifted up her shirt and licked his fingers and rubbed them against her.

She stroked his thighs and then his balls, squeezing just a little, brushing her fingers up and down along his dick until she felt him throbbing and swelling between them.

They kept kissing and necking, leaving little love bites on each other's necks and shoulders.

He took her motel-room key card, and they fell through the door; he already had his shirt off, and they were tearing at what was left of each other's clothes.

They stumbled to the bed, leaving the door hanging open behind them. He pulled off one of his boots and threw it at the door, and that closed it.

They were lying on that lumpy queen-size bed in her motel room, a faint blue light reflecting from the pool just outside her drawn curtains, splashing over her body like she was underwater.

And she could've been, because moving under his touch, she felt as slippery as a pale fish.

He didn't bother to take her shirt all the way off again; he just pulled it off her shoulders, with her breasts pushed up through the top, and he was licking them, keeping her nipples wet and hard.

Her skirt was bunched up around her hips, and he had his hand inside her—not just a finger, which he'd started with, but his whole hand now—playing with her, keeping her wet down there, too.

Her panties and bra had long since disappeared, the bra still hanging like a prize from the rearview mirror of his pickup truck.

She cried out again and rocked back and forth against his hand. Her feet, muddy from the river, left dark prints on the sheet. Her head arched off the mattress and then fell back. "Again," she exhaled, panting.

He laughed, a wonderful laugh, muffled against her chest. "I never met anyone I could make come so many times," he said.

"Top your record," she gasped.

He ran his free hand through her tangled hair, moved his lips off her breasts and onto her lips, pushing his tongue between her parted teeth, both of them tasting of Cuervo and beer, of him and of her.

He was on top of her now, naked, his hard chest pressing against her, his strong legs pinning her down as he stuck his cock inside her again. She was so loose and open, and he just moved in and out and in and out, so slippery and smooth. He was hitting all the right places, his hips locked against hers.

His lips moved down to her tits again, and he nibbled on her, pulling up her nipples like bullets between his teeth. He put one hand under her ass and held it tight while he fucked her; she could feel his balls up against her pussy and her buttocks at the same time. The cheap bed creaked and sighed beneath them, and somebody's TV hummed through the walls.

He flipped her over, lifting her bottom off the bed. He did her from behind now; she could feel his long, powerful strokes, his dick coming out far enough to brush against her thighs. He put a finger inside her anus, and then another, and moved them with the same timing he was using on her pussy, so she felt like he was screwing her in both places at once.

With his free hand he was stroking her breasts as they hung down, pendulous.

Then all at once he pulled out, both of them gasping from the surprise of it. He tossed her onto her side and pulled her skirt off at last, throwing it on the floor, tugged the tank top off again, roughly. She felt the seams rip as he pulled it off her arms.

When she was naked, he started kissing and licking at her clavicle and moved down from the base of her neck, tracing her bones, her veins, licking her all over like she was ice cream, and she was sure melting inside when he lapped at her between her legs again.

Then he rose and took her by the arms and plucked her off the bed.

"What are you—" she began, but he had moved her against the dresser so they could watch in the mirror, his skin tanned and dark against her own white torso, his dick impaling her from behind, her body glistening with his saliva and their sweat, his blond hair dark with sweat. They bucked and rocked so much the bottom drawers in the dresser sprang open and hit their ankles and calves.

Then he had her down on the bed again, on her back, her legs spread wide. He lifted her feet until they were resting on his shoulders, and then he had at her, pounding into her deep, and she sucked on his shoulder, on his arm, on his hand, and she cried out with her lips buried in his chest, and then he cried out, too, and they both collapsed there on the damp sheets of their underwater bed, arms around each other, side by side.

He woke at ten in the morning to the maid knocking on the door. "Later," he called out and the knocking stopped, leaving only his heart pounding in his chest.

He'd thought maybe he was dreaming Anna, but there she was beside him, her hair tangled across the pillow, her fine, firm, naked body curled against him in a square of sunlight. Like he'd told her, he'd never met a woman who could come so many times before. It was as if she'd been saving up just for him. He liked thinking that, anyway. He'd also never met a woman this wild before; she was like a beautiful, untamable mare; she was like the turbulence in a summer sky right before a storm, electric, exciting, and—he knew it damn well—unpossessable. Except he was possessing her now, and for now, that was enough.

Putting his arms around her, he slipped his dick inside her again.

"Oh," she gasped, and that was how he woke her, moving in her, barely penetrating at first and then diving deep inside her.

He pulled out of her and rolled her onto her back. "Mornin'," he said.

And she smiled. "It seems like a good one."

"It's gonna be." He kissed her tits and her belly. "Wish I could keep you lying there like that, just lying there, all day," he said.

She stretched and yawned and crawled down between his legs like a cat. "Why can't you?" she asked.

Before he could answer, she had his cock in her mouth. He

hadn't dreamed her, but he might as well have—the world might end before he ever had it this good again.

He was pulsing inside her, trying to hold back. She raised her face to his, her lips all wet and open. "You like?"

"You have to ask?"

Time melted by, with the sun spilling in wider patches across the twisted sheets, and she kept on working him until he couldn't wait any longer, and he shot off in her hot little mouth. She sucked him dry, did not lift her mouth from his dick until every last drop quivered out of him.

She slipped out from between his legs, then, and just fell back across the bed. "You believe I never sucked a guy off before?"

He laughed, "You're a natural at it, then."

He touched her lips gently with the tips of his fingers, wet them with his own saliva, and traced a moist outline around her mouth. He kissed her chin and her cheekbones and put his tongue in her ear and made her giggle, sucked on her earlobes and left little love bites along her neck. It was only fair; it was her turn now.

He put one of her nipples in his mouth and rubbed at the other one with his hand and then lifted his face and switched nipples. He slipped his free hand between her legs and rubbed at her until she contracted around him, shuddered against him, and cried out. Then he put his fingers inside her, got her off four or five more times just like that. He could feel his dick already starting to stir again. Maybe she was right; maybe they could just lie here all day and touch other, suck each other, fuck each other.

Except that he had to take a run down to the state fair in Green River, sign some autographs, shill tomorrow's rodeo a little. He got paid for doing it, but when he'd agreed, it wasn't for the money, it was for something to do between the Friday night semifinals and the Sunday afternoon final. Keep him from obsessing about the ride too much. He never thought he would have something better—something like this—to do.

He broke the news to her, couching with it the promise of breakfast and his fervent hope that she would enjoy coming along.

She laughed. "You have to ask?"

They shared the cramped shower, soaping each other. The hot water sent steam rising all around the bathroom, thick as fog.

She had given up all pretext of playing it cool—had she ever been cool? Maybe for a few moments before she started touching him, sucking him, wanting him so badly she felt like her head was going to explode, her heart burst right through her chest. Right now, for the record, she was done with any pretense of composure. She had wanted passion and adventure? She'd found them in him, and now she just wanted to make sure he found them in her, too.

She wanted to see just how recklessly far her desire would take her, what she would let him do, what she would do to him. She was sure there were endless possibilities.

She ran her hands over the hard muscles of his buttocks, the lean sinews of his thighs. She knotted her fingers through his curly wet hair, watched his beautiful smile spread across his face as he blew a soap bubble off her breast.

She found herself laughing out loud, and then he was laughing, too, hoisting her soapy hips around him. He knew just what she wanted. She knew what he wanted, too. The shower drummed down on her back as he fucked her, sliding her up and down against the slippery tiles.

It was noon by the time they left the steamy bathroom. They day was hot and still. Bouncing along the highway in his truck, she was glad she was wearing only sandals and a sundress, pale blue with thin straps, and a camisole under it.

They'd dressed up for each other. She'd put on lipstick and earrings and did her best on her hair with the anemic motel hair drier. He'd shaved, put on some sweet-smelling cologne, a crisp white T-shirt, and tight Levi's that made her want to run her hands along the fabric, to feel his thighs pressing beneath the denim. His curly hair shone angelically golden in the sunlight. Still, she didn't think of him as an angel, exactly, not when he already had her dress hiked up around her waist, and his fingers were stroking her thighs.

They swung east out of Cody, stopping at a roadside place called the Home-Style Café. It had a sign in front proclaiming BREAKFAST SERVED 6 TO 6—BEST PANCAKES IN WYOMING!

It was a little wooden cottage with ten red-checkered tables and a lunch counter in front, and, down a narrow hall, a bar with red plastic booths in the back. The place was empty except for a cook behind the pass-through window at the counter and a lone waitress, slumped on a stool, who looked bored with her chewing gum and her magazine. She told them they could sit anywhere, so they picked a booth in the back, carrying their own menus.

The waitress sighed over the long walk from her stool to the booth they'd chosen, but Anna noticed she didn't look quite so bored when she got a good look at Grant. It wasn't just how handsome he was—even though he was definitely hot—it was a certain reckless confidence in the way he looked you right in the eye, appraised you, summed you up.

The waitress was younger than Anna, and she certainly had bigger breasts, but Anna knew Grant wasn't interested, wasn't even considering the possibility of being interested. She felt herself tingle, quite literally from head to toe, knowing that Grant had already appraised her, summed her up, and found in her all he wanted.

Grant ordered pancakes, bacon, scrambled eggs, hash browns, and coffee for both of them. Ordinarily Anna was more of a fruit-and-cereal or bagel-with-light-cream-cheese kind of person, but she was too hungry to object. The waitress poured their coffee and left them alone.

Anna liked just watching Grant's long, strong fingers wrapped around his mug while he told her about the cabin he owned near the Montana border, how he was planning to spend the winter there this year, how beautiful it was in a high valley full of birches where the snow sometimes fell as early as October.

She told him in LA it usually rained in the fall, causing traffic jams on the freeways that made a fifteen-minute drive to work an hour or more. And then, without meaning to really, she admitted that she didn't have to worry about driving to work right now, anyway; she'd lost her job. Before he could even sympathize, she blurted that her fiancé had just left her, too, but truly and honestly she wasn't sure losing either one was that great a loss.

"The only thing is," she said, trying to laugh it off, "I don't really have any idea what I'm going to do next."

Grant kissed her tenderly on the lips. "You must have some idea," he murmured.

For now it seemed the best idea was just to keep kissing him.

The waitress came back, rattling a tray of condiments—pitchers of syrup and honey, packets of butter, and jam. They didn't stop kissing until minutes later when she slapped down their plates.

They both tucked into their food, then, devouring their bacon and eggs.

"For a city girl I first saw in skinny jeans, you do enjoy a meal," he said, amused.

"I'm starving," she admitted.

"It's all the exercise we've been having," he grinned.

She scooped up the last crumb of her hash browns; sated, she pushed away the side plate with her pancakes on it.

"Aw, you're skipping the best part. Gotta have a bite or two of the 'Best Pancakes in Wyoming'!" Grant teased. He applied liberal amounts of syrup and butter to her untouched stack, cut off a piece with his fork, and held it out to her. "C'mon, baby bird."

She opened her mouth, and he fed her.

A drop of syrup slid off the fork and rolled down her chin. Grant leaned in and licked it off.

"Delicious," she said, moving her lips to his again.

He fed her another forkful and ran his tongue across her sticky lips. Her tongue met his, playful.

"Don't know about the pancakes," she said. "But I do like the syrup."

He set down the fork and dipped his finger in the syrup, drew a line of it across her lips, and licked that off, too.

"Wish I could lick it off all over you."

"Why don't you?" she suggested.

"Well, then," he said.

He dipped his finger in the syrup again and ran it down the side of her neck, following with his tongue. He let a thin line of the stuff drip off his finger and run down the front of her throat to her cleavage.

Again his tongue followed the trajectory of the syrup, sliding down between her breasts. "Mmm, very tasty."

She felt that fever coming over her again, and it didn't frighten her now. In fact, she welcomed the rush.

"More," she murmured. She dropped her hand lightly over his cock. She could feel him stir under her touch, so she touched some more.

"The lady asks for more," he said, a devilish gleam in his eye.

She watched him press his fingers into a pat of butter. She gasped as he spread her legs and pushed her panties aside and rubbed it in her pubic hair, making it slick and shiny. He took more butter and pushed it up inside her, where she was hot enough that it melted and ran down her thighs.

"Oh," was all she said.

He went back to the syrup again, swirling his sticky fingers inside her. The suction made her come fast and hard against his hand; he had to put his other hand over her mouth to stifle the cry she made.

"Shhh," he said. Then, "You still want more?"

She managed to nod. "Lots more." The raw urgency in her voice surprised them both.

He took her at her word. He painted her arms with syrup, stroked it down inside the front of her dress, and then set about licking her.

"I look like I bathed in breakfast, I guess," she said.

"Not quite."

He couldn't seem to stop himself now; he slid the straps of her dress low and rubbed at her nipples with butter and more syrup, popped her gooey breasts all the way out, and buried his face against them, all the time licking and kissing her.

She unzipped his fly, rubbing a pat of butter between her own hands and sliding them up and down his cock.

She wriggled out of her panties and climbed on his lap, pushing his cock inside her. The butter and syrup on her legs rubbed off on his jeans and her syrupy breasts left smears on his T-shirt. He ran his sticky, buttery hands through her hair.

They were out of syrup now, and it was orange marmalade she rubbed on his cheeks and licked off, grape jam she painted on his fingers, which he stroked across her shoulders. She wanted to roll with him in a whole vat of syrup and butter and jam.

They came together, arms wrapped tight around each other. They couldn't move at all for a moment. Then she climbed off his lap and tucked her breasts inside her dress and pulled down her dress. He zipped up his jeans. They looked at each other and just laughed.

The waitress sauntered down the hallway past the bar. Her eyes went large looking at them, the syrup dripping off the ends of Anna's hair, the stains on Grant's shirt and Anna's dress, the jelly on his cheeks.

"Had yourselves a little food fight, I see," she said matter-of-factly and slapped down the check.

Grant left a big tip to make up for the messy table and in thanks to the waitress for not calling it exactly as she must've seen it.

They could hardly stop laughing just looking at each other. They cleaned up as best they could in the cold-water restrooms behind the restaurant, both of them emerging with wet hair, clean hands, and only faintly improved clothing.

"It sure is fun to buy you breakfast," he said, helping Anna into the truck.

He'd promised to be at the fair by three, so he had to gun it through the red dust of southern Wyoming, with her pressed up against him, both of them singing along with anything that came on the radio: Brad Paisley and Toby Keith on FM country, and, when they lost that, ancient Petula Clark, crooning "Downtown," followed by the instrumental theme from *The Good, the Bad and the Ugly* on the static-ridden AM dial.

They made it in time, even with a detour to the Wal-Mart in Thermopolis for a clean dress for Anna and T-shirt and jeans for Grant. When they arrived at the fairgrounds, he popped a peppermint Life Saver in his mouth and his Stetson on his head. Anna stayed in the truck, saying she wanted to fix herself up a little. He looked back as he crossed the parking lot and saw her applying lip gloss to her pretty lips, and he almost turned back around just to kiss it off her again.

Instead, he settled himself at a small table between the cattle and horse barns next to Ag Hall and signed black-and-white glossies of himself astride a bronc. Everyone was wishing him luck in the finals and promising to drive up to the Stampede and see him make good for every local boy in Wyoming.

Anna slipped into the crowd around him and handed him her own photo to sign. He wrote *Just wait'll dinner* on it, and she laughed.

She'd pulled her hair into a ponytail, the way she'd had it when she first met him, and her makeup was perfect again. She watched him signing for a while, and then she went off and bought herself a Coke and left one on the table for him and sat down on a bench in the shade in front of the barn. All he could see of her from there were her legs, crossed ladylike at the ankles.

Three hours hurried by, and his teeth hurt from smiling so much, and his hand ached from signing his name over and over, but the promoter was happy—good crowd—and he gave Grant two hundred, said he'd sold a lot of pictures. He wanted to talk about bull riding and calf roping and a lot of other stuff, but Grant said he had a friend waiting and took off at a jog around the barn to where Anna was sitting, shaking the ice in her cup, which was all that was left of her soda.

That cute little nose, those freckles, those lush lips. Her new sun-dress was yellow and straight-off-the-rack crisp in spite of the heat, and, man, how he wanted to grab the fabric in his hands and crumple it up around her hips and have at her again.

Beads of perspiration clung to her forehead and to the shallow of her flesh between her breasts. He wanted to wipe it away with his tongue, but there were people walking by.

"It sure is hot," she said, crunching some of her ice.

"We're down in the plains here, that's why," he said. "Sorry I left you to sit out in the heat all this time."

"Don't be sorry. I've kept myself busy."

"Doing what?" He'd seen her legs; he knew she hadn't moved since she brought him the Coke.

"Thinking about all the fun we're going to have at the fair." She uncrossed her legs and spread them just a little at the knees. Looking down, he could see she'd taken off her underwear.

You wouldn't figure it, her sitting there all nice and proper, her hair in that girlish ponytail—you wouldn't figure it, from what she'd told him about her ex-fiancé and her routine life in the city, but this girl was wild. Best of all, she was wild for him.

"You're crazy," he told her.

"About you," she replied, her eyes shining with the truth of it.

"Crazy about you, too." He put his arm around her shoulders, and she put her arm around his waist, and they walked around the fair.

He bought them a couple of cold beers and some popcorn, and as the warm summer twilight fell in golden, rosy shades around them, and dust rose up from the fairgrounds in little dry puffs and clung to his boots and her toes, he thought he was maybe the happiest, most foolish, most turned-on cowboy on Earth. And he was gonna take first in the finals tomorrow, for sure. And she was gonna be there watching him.

Anna knew she'd crossed some kind of line, gone over to a place where all she wanted was Grant. All she wanted was to be with him, touch him, feel him, have him touch her. She felt electric, intoxicated, insatiable, alive. She was ready and eager for anything, and now she would show him she was.

She sat on his lap on the Tilt-a-Whirl while he spun the wheel in their car faster and faster, making her dizzy. In the House of Mirrors, he bent her backward and posed with her like a swashbuckling silent-film star; she was in a swoon in his arms even before he slid his hand under her skirt and stroked her bare bottom with his warm, dry fingertips.

On the midway, with his arms wrapped around her, he helped her shoot out a target with an air rifle. For a prize she got a shiny purple bear—and the sensation of his stiff cock pressed against her from behind.

He rode a mechanical bull just for laughs, blowing the mind of the kid running the thing and drawing a crowd. The ride was spectacular enough that he won her an even larger stuffed bear. Some people recognized him, so the two of them gave both prizes to a couple of little kids and hurried into the dark of the Haunted House.

Anna screamed for the first time when a glowing skeleton dropped down right in front of her; the second time, Grant made her scream, slipping his fingers in and out of her.

They listened to a bluegrass band and danced under a wide sunset sky, with the lights of the midway spinning around them. Grant kept a hand on the small of her back, in that spot she loved, steering her easily around the dance floor. Then he moved her behind the bandstand and probed her pussy with his thumb.

On the Ferris wheel they necked and groped, and she took out his cock and just stroked him lightly with her fingers.

Afterward, they drifted past giant pigs and woolly sheep and big-eyed calves with blue ribbons hooked on their pens. In the air-conditioned exhibit halls they lingered over beautiful hand-sewn quilts and jewel-like jars of preserves and enormous pick-les, which she whispered to him, were not quite the size of his enormous dick.

They had their handwriting analyzed: true love was pre-dicted. Then, as the moon rose yellow and fat in the sky, they succumbed to the heavenly aroma of barbecue. Grant filled a big cardboard tray with ribs, corn on the cob, more beers, a slab of hot-fudge-slathered brownie, and pale pink orbs of cot-ton candy.

"I don't know if I can eat all that," Anna protested, laughing.

"My mama always told me to be good, and clean my plate. But I won't mind if you wanna be a bad girl, and play with your food," he said.

A heat rose in her, consumed her like a wave. She was ready for anything, and she would show him she was.

Grant found a picnic table at the dark edge of the fairgrounds ringed by generators running the rides and sheltered further by a large spreading oak. The buzzing and humming of the generators overpowered the screams and laughter from the midway, just as their bulk blocked out most of the light.

They sat down on the bench, their knees touching, his heart pounding with how much he wanted her, but he enjoyed waiting, too, waiting for her to maybe make the move.

"Messy," Anna said, licking some of the barbecue sauce off her fingers, eyeing him mischievously. "Don't you think?"

That was enough of an invitation for him. He slipped the straps of her dress off her shoulders and lifted her beautiful breasts out into the warm night air. He tasted them plain and then with a little bit of spicy barbecue, with the warm, oily butter for the corn, with little puffs of cotton candy smeared on them.

They fed each other chunks of brownie with their fingers, licking the fudge sauce off each other's hands.

"You'll let me do anything I want?" he asked her, but it wasn't much of a question, because he already knew.

"I want you to do everything you can think of," she murmured.

She spread her legs for him, and he went down in the dust on his knees and painted her thighs with butter, rubbed it down her calves and knees and even between her dusty toes. He took a handful of the cotton candy and decorated her pussy with it, a cloud of a pink muff covering her thick, curly brown one.

"I can't keep my hands off you," he admitted.

"Or your tongue. And, please, don't stop, okay? Please don't, ever."

And there he was with his face inside her again, getting the butter he'd left on her legs all over his last clean shirt; there she was licking warm fudge sauce off his cock, giving him head again.

And then he spilled her back against the table, her ponytail falling into the last of the cotton candy, and he fucked her so hard and so fast one of their beers knocked over and sloshed against them. He rode her like he would a bronc, even lifting one hand up, showing off, sweat pouring off his forehead and into his eyes. How long could he last, how long? It was a grand championship ride, that was for sure; she was bucking and throbbing under him, she was laughing and she was crying, and they both finished at once as they were learning to do. He rolled off her and lay down next to her, panting on the tabletop.

"That was—" she began, but she stopped, at a loss for words.

"It sure was," he agreed.

She swiped at her face with her hands and discovered the cotton candy in her hair. He had a time getting it untangled, but then he kept getting distracted from his purpose by little bits of the stuff falling off onto her shoulders and breasts, and brushing it away from her warm skin before it melted, and then watching it melt and pulling her nipples out hard, covered with the stuff like taffy, and all the time she was sucking on his fingers and his face.

There were still little bits of it in her hair and on her arms and cheeks and all over him when they left their alcove and the fair, stumbling through the dark parking lot, furtive, like they'd stolen their loving, so nobody would see the state they were in.

The moon was high in the sky now and even brighter than the midway lights. It was after midnight, and there was a chain across the end of the gravel road Grant had picked up off the highway. A sign alerted them: NO SWIMMING AFTER SUNSET.

He lifted the chain, and they ducked under, hearing only crickets, the occasional car back on the main road, and their own footsteps. Holding hands, they ran silently down to the lake. She kicked off her shoes and Grant pulled off his boots and stripped off his shirt, jeans, and boxers like they were all one thing, a second unnecessary skin he was removing.

Anna just stood for a minute, admiring his broad, strong chest, the muscles rippling in his arms, the tight, hard curve of his thighs, all silvered in the moonlight.

A cluster of tiny bats glided low over the wind-rippled water, and a few fireflies darted along. Raw rock slabs rose from dark hills like prayerful hands reaching for the sky.

It was a beautiful place, and Anna was utterly content; she could not think of a single thing more she wanted. She walked down to the water's edge and waded in. She thought of something she wanted, then. She wanted the water not quite so cold.

Grant plunged past her. "What're you waiting for?" he asked, diving in.

"It's cold," she said, having made it up to her knees.

He swam back to the shallows, reared out of the water, and lunged for her, pulling her into his arms and all the way in.

"Why'd you do that?" she gasped.

"You were having second thoughts," he said. "No second thoughts allowed."

She realized she hadn't had any at all until now. Not one.

The shock of the cold against her skin receded; the night was still and warm. They splashed and swam; she shook out her ponytail and rinsed the cotton candy from her hair. Small silver trout brushed her ankles. The sky was full of low, bright stars.

"God, you look good wet," he said, admiring her breasts, transparent through her soaked dress.

They swam together to a sandbar in the center of the lake. He scooped her up in his arms again and lifted her out of the water. He laid her gently on the soft, fine sand, stripped off her dress in one careless motion, and climbed on top of her.

His cock felt hot inside her after the cold, clear water. She wrapped her legs around his hips, and they rocked together, slow and steady.

She touched his balls with the tips of her fingers, felt his dick tremble in her when she squeezed gently. She grabbed his buttocks as he rolled her over on top of him.

Dripping like a mermaid, she sat on his cock and deliciously rocked herself back and forth. Then he grabbed at her and held her down tight against him, his wet skin slapping against hers, and they both came at precisely the same, screaming second.

Well, she was the one who screamed. She threw back her head and cried out, her cry echoed by something that sounded like a coyote.

They both saw the lights snap on in a cabin across the lake.

"I don't think it's just the coyotes you woke. Park ranger lives over there."

They heard a car engine start, and at that they sprang up, racing into the water again. Grant grabbed Anna's dress from the sandbar; she gathered his clothes on the shore; they forgot her shoes.

They dove naked into his truck and hightailed it out of there, watching the headlights of the ranger's truck swing out on the lake road as they hit the highway.

They stopped at a pull-out, and he tugged on his jeans, and she threw on his T-shirt, her dress too wet to manage. She rested her head on his shoulder and closed her eyes, utterly fulfilled, slipping in and out of sleep. The day played back in her mind in a long, sensual blur, and she felt half drunk on the heady imbibing of him.

4

The finals were playing out exactly as he wanted. Grant made it to the top three with little effort, and he felt like he could stay in the ring all day, taking ride after glorious ride, the sun catching on little motes of dust and making rainbows. He was getting solid nines, and the crowd in the arena was going wild, chanting his name. But the horn sounded; it was down to just two of them, and time for intermission.

His eye scanned the crowded bleachers, the judges' stand, the sponsor booths draped with flags and banners, until he found Anna there in the front row right above his chute.

She waved, smiling radiantly. She was so sleek and beautiful and didn't much know it, didn't know the power she had over him, didn't know how much he reveled in claiming her, making every inch of her his. He loved fucking her, he loved doing things to her, stuff nobody else he'd met would ever dream of doing, and he loved just being with her, too; holding hands, riding in his truck, watching late-night TV—even doing their laundry this morning was a blast. He was probably falling in love with her.

One of the wranglers socked him on the arm. "You're kicking ass out there."

Grant grinned; he knew he was.

"It gives me a thrill, watching you, Grant." This was the dulcet voice of a pretty nineteen-year-old cowgirl in a white-sequined miniskirt, one of the sponsor flag bearers, just mounting up to circle the arena. She brushed her lips against his cheek.

One of the guys he had known on the circuit years ago used to joke that Grant always had a blonde on his arm. And when he didn't, he was looking around for one, like a guy who misplaced his car keys. This girl would've fit the bill, if he'd still been looking.

But the truth was he'd always been more of a quality-not-quantity kinda guy, even in his younger days, and Anna—she was definitely quality. She was what he'd been waiting for. She was all bottled-up passion, all explosive desire, all he could ever imagine wanting, and here she was wanting him, too.

He clattered up the metal steps into the bleachers and took her in his arms. She felt as good as he imagined she would feel, maybe even better.

"How'm I doing from your perspective?" he asked.

She teased him. "Maybe a little too good. I saw that girl put her hands all over you. . . ."

"You know what I'm talking about," he said, while he put his hands all over her.

"Nobody has anything on you," Anna murmured.

He kissed her and lifted her soft hair, nibbling on her neck. She gave a little shiver as he pressed his lips against her skin. He liked that. He wanted to make her shiver some more.

But she pushed him away, playful. "Come on, Grant. There's something like three thousand people out here."

"That doesn't turn you on?" It did him. He fiddled with the strap of her dress. It was another little dress like the yellow one she'd worn over nothing but her skin yesterday. He realized with disappointment that she was wearing a bra and underwear today.

He rubbed his hand along her back, found her bra hooks, and started disconnecting them.

"Right now I better turn you off." She laughed, pulling away.

"S'not what you said last night. You said, 'Don't stop. Don't ever, ever stop.' Said it like you meant it." He turned serious for a minute. "Did you mean it?" he asked her.

Before she could say anything, there was applause from the bleachers, and the announcer boomed over the loudspeakers. "Rick Ryan's the man of the moment—narrowly edging up to our hometown favorite, Grant Olson, overall nine-two to nine-one. That makes it a tight two-way contest for first place!"

"Better get saddled up," Grant said. "I gotta ace this." He knew he would; didn't matter how close the score.

"You will," Anna said confidently.

He felt himself swell like a rooster strutting across a barnyard. "After I collect my winnings, we're gonna have to do something about this excessive amount of clothing you're wearing," he teased her.

Two top riders left, two rides each. A hush fell over the crowd as Rick Ryan took his first ride, and a pretty damn nice one it was, Anna had to admit. Still, he was lacking something—Grant's grace, his firm self-assurance.

"And now, the hottest cowboy in town tonight!" the announcer crowed.

As Grant bolted out of the gate, Anna's cheeks flamed. The hottest cowboy any night; she would bet on it.

She was getting the hang of the rodeo now; she knew before the time was called that Grant had claimed his bronc not just longer, but with better form than Ryan had his.

When he was thrown he rolled away in a catlike curl as

though the blow was meaningless. She was up on her feet with the rest of the crowd, cheering—when the horse came charging back at him and kicked him twice, hard in the chest, even as three other strong-looking cowboys were pulling it away.

The cheer she was about to let loose died in her throat.

"Ladies and gentlemen, we have an injury situation here. This cowboy is down. Our rodeo doctor is riding out into the ring this minute to look him over."

A chunky older man careened into the arena on a dappled horse, dismounted fast, and bent over Grant. Grant wasn't moving. The handlers and the other cowboys—his rival, Rick Ryan, too—closed ranks around Grant, shielding him from the eyes of the crowd, from Anna.

"Let's everybody say a little prayer for this fella," the announcer said, and there was a long silent spell in the stadium, and then some fiddle music started up on the speakers and Grant was being ferried out of the arena on a stretcher.

"We'll be taking our boy Grant backstage for some medical attention, and hopefully he'll be able to participate in the last round of riding. Be a shame for forfeit, when Grant had, according to our judges, a solid nine to Rick's eight-nine in this round, making it still a close contest. Keep your fingers crossed for him, ladies and gentlemen, and turn your attention now to Clarence our rodeo clown in his barrel-roping debut."

Shaking, Anna ran down to the tack room.

The cowboys wouldn't let her in at first. They wouldn't let her in when she brought out her press pass. She had to explain she was Grant's "girlfriend," and even then she got incredulous looks.

"Yeah," one of the wranglers spoke up, finally, the one who'd socked Grant on the arm, "I seen him up in the stands with her just before."

So they let her in. Grant was propped against a hay bale, pale beneath his tan, his brows furrowed.

She swiped tears away with the back of her hand so he wouldn't see how upset she was. "Jesus, Grant. I—I'm so sorry," she stammered.

"Just a little bit of bad luck, baby." He managed to flash her a small but amiable smile. "Got a couple of broke ribs, nothing worse."

"Lift your left arm," the rodeo doctor ordered.

She saw Grant wince as the doctor wound thick adhesive around his chest.

"Are you in a lot of pain?" she asked anxiously.

"Nah. Doc just gave me a shot for that. Don't feel a thing hardly."

"Shouldn't he go to the hospital or something?" she demanded of the doctor.

The doctor cocked one eyebrow at her. "Not if he wants to ride in the last round."

"How could he do that—" she began, but Grant interrupted her.

"I got a nine, baby. I'm not letting this one get away from me." He was already struggling to his feet.

"Hang on there, partner. Not finished yet," the doctor barked.

"Rodeo riders don't give up easy." Rick Ryan had Anna's elbow and was leading her away.

"This one's gonna hurt," the doctor said, and it must have, because Grant let out a cry that was like a distorted version of the shouts he sometimes made making love to her.

Anna felt sick and pressed her fist to her mouth.

"You just go get yourself a soda or something," Ryan said, propelling her toward the door. "Much as I hate to admit it, he's probably gonna take first. Less he dies trying."

These were not the most reassuring words she'd ever heard, but when she turned around to protest, she found the door locked against her.

So she went back to her seat, digging her nails into her palms.

"That cowboy's gonna be just fine, sweetie." An elderly woman leaned in from behind and patted her shoulder. "They're used to hard knocks. This is what they live for."

The intermission seemed endless, interminable, and looking at her watch, Anna saw that twenty minutes had indeed stretched to thirty-five. She wondered if the delay was getting Grant ready to ride, or trying to convince him not to.

The rodeo clown came out and made everybody in the arena but Anna laugh, and then Rick Ryan took his final run at the championship and drew a solid nine.

"Now, let's give a fine round of applause to Cody's own Grant Olson—he's coming back for more."

The roar from the crowd was deafening.

Anna watched Grant mount his horse down in the chute. He was stiff-legged and his face was drawn, the pallor under his tan still clearly visible. She wanted to call out to him, to stop him, to at least whisper a little prayer for him, but all she could do was sit there frozen, with the announcer's words, the cheers of the crowd, the clatter of the chute gate opening—all of it softened by a rushing in her ears.

Then he was out there in the arena, and he was riding his heart out, and his form was perfect, and you would never have known he was hurt, at least until the moment he was thrown and he grew paler still, and one of the wranglers had to help him off the ground. Grant leaned on the kid like a crutch, hobbling back to the sidelines.

He slouched against the arena wall, face barred from her under the slant of his hat. But when the announcer read the judge's score as nine-one, he straightened. He turned then and looked up at Anna, a triumphant smile creasing his face ear to ear.

She screamed for him; she jumped up and down and clapped

and yelled. Ecstatically happy for him, she ran into the arena and kissed him, and then she stood off to the side and watched him mug for ESPN2, pose for photographs, and finally accept a trophy—larger and shinier than the one he had earned in the semifinals—and that coveted prize money.

"You doing all right?" she asked him softly.

He gave her a dazzling smile. "All right? I'm great, baby. Why wouldn't I be? I had a great ride, and that's everything. Everything."

And she knew then, no matter how good she made him feel, no matter how good he made her feel, no matter how much either one of them cared, what this man lived for would never be her. For the moment, she didn't even really mind. But she knew unequivocally that for Grant his life was now and would always be the ride.

5
————————

"You're gonna have to come to me tonight, Anna, honey." Grant was lying on the bed in her motel room, pillows propped behind his back, a bag of ice tucked against his throbbing right side.

He had a beautiful woman hovering over him, a twenty-five-thousand-dollar check in a white envelope on the night table, and ten round orange pain pills in a tiny manila envelope next to that. He hadn't touched the medication, and no matter what the doctor said, he didn't plan to. He preferred the flask of whiskey he'd picked up, along with the ice and whatever ministrations and distractions he was sure Anna would offer.

Nothing was gonna stop him from wanting Anna every which way he could have her tonight, too. Still, he would be a liar if he didn't admit he wasn't exactly at the top of his form.

She lay down on the bed beside him, stroking his fingers and laying soft kisses across his forehead and against his cheeks and lips. Not the top of his form, but still he felt himself grow tumescent inside his jeans.

He passed her the flask of whiskey he was working on, and

she took a long swallow. He could taste it on her lips when she kissed him ever so gently.

"You don't have to treat me so delicate." He laughed, pulling her face against his. "This wasn't, well, my first rodeo."

They kissed long enough and deep enough that he started thinking about other things they'd be doing soon, and he felt his cock stiffen and swell like it was going to burst right through his jeans. He lifted her hand from his hand and placed it over his crotch so she could feel him.

"If I'd checked your vital signs like this before, I wouldn't have worried about you at all," she said.

She unzipped him and drew his sex out between her hands. She bent over him and licked him like a lollipop until he was hard as a fucking rock.

"You gonna nurse me real good tonight?"

"I'm your own personal Florence Nightingale," she told him.

"Then undress for me," he said. "Do me a real, you know, dance."

She got up off the bed and stripped off her dress, trying not to laugh. She left on her high-heeled sandals and her bra and panties. He passed her the whiskey again, and she took another drink, and then she unsnapped her bra and slipped it off slowly, one arm at a time, and tossed it to him. He made a one-handed grab for it and missed, and the garment impaled itself on his dick.

They both laughed then. She plucked it off him and tossed it across the bed and peeled off her panties, twirled them around her hand, and threw them, too. They landed on a lamp shade.

"I'm not that good at this," she said.

"Oh, yes, you are," he replied, licking his lips. She looked so good he could almost taste her. She twirled around, naked, humming a little. She lifted up her breasts and thrust them near his face, but not quite near enough to touch. She rubbed her hands over her hips and thighs and mound and bent over and waggled her buttocks in his face.

He applauded. She kicked those high heels off last and knelt down on the bed beside him.

"Your wish is my command," she said, a little breathless.

Grant finished off the whiskey, felt it burning his throat and the desire he had for her eclipsing that, burning some place deeper and a lot stronger.

"Never quite understood that expression," Grant told her. "But I think it means if I wish you to do something, you'll just do it."

She gave him a mock salute, and her breasts bounced. "Aye-aye, cowboy. You better believe it."

"Wouldn't that be 'aye-aye, captain'?" Grant asked, but she made no reply because she was licking at his cock again. Just licking, not sucking.

"Can you help me get my clothes off, darlin'?" he asked after a while.

He was already barefoot. She unbuckled his belt and tugged down his jeans, pulling them off one leg at a time. Then she worked off the boxers, licking at his balls now, rubbing his cock between her palms.

"Oh, yeah," he said. He wanted to tell her how great she felt, how great she made him feel, but sometimes words were just pointless. She had to know already.

She moved between his legs and took him full in her mouth now, bobbing her head up and down so her tits brushed up against his balls and thighs. He clamped his legs around her, holding her fast.

"Touch yourself," he whispered. "Do me another little show."

She put two fingers in her pussy. He could hear the soft wetness lapping against them. She shuddered when she came and swallowed his cock deeper in her throat.

"Fuck my leg," he said, and she mounted herself over his

thigh and humped him. He could feel her wetness on his skin. He flicked a finger in and out of her; he could smell the tang when she came. Man, he just wanted to nail her right that second.

Still, tonight he had to take it slow. And besides, it was the long ride that hooked her, wasn't it, and how many times he got back in the saddle.

He laughed at himself for thinking in those terms, but he just couldn't shake the rodeo tonight. You could take the cowboy out of the arena, but you couldn't take the arena out of the cowboy. Somebody said something like that to him once.

Anna rolled off his leg, and, carefully, her touch featherlight, she set the bag of ice on the night table and peeled back his shirt.

He had two cracked ribs, and he was bound up in adhesive like a mummy, from his breastbone almost to his naval. A map of blue bruises were swelling along his right side. Still, with the shot the doc had given him, he wasn't doing too badly. He had no internal injuries the doctor could detect, and he'd been through this kind of thing enough in the past to know he could skip the emergency room. It was all about the healing now. And Anna was sure gonna help with that.

She made little murmurs of commiseration and kissed his pectorals, ran her tongue over his nipples, brushed her hands softly across his belly.

"Lemme tell you, if you have to get messed up, this is the kind of nursing care a man likes. You're doing me more good than twenty doctors," he told her.

"I can see that." She smiled. His cock was sticking straight up in the air.

"So climb on."

She straddled him, crouching, keeping her weight off him, just moving him in and out of her. He appreciated her gentleness, but he wasn't going to slip up on satisfying her.

"Come again," he said. "Will you? I love watchin'."

And she touched herself, and she did come, her pussy sinking deep, swallowing his shaft to the root.

"How about you roll over on your side?" he suggested.

She slipped off him. Moving carefully, he turned, too, so that they were pubic bone to pubic bone. He stuck his dick back inside her slippery pussy and thrust one and then two fingers in her anus. He could feel that tight little hole contract around him when she came again.

She was just getting warmed up now. Her eyes were closed, and a line of perspiration trickled down between her breasts. He pulled out of her again, and she moaned. He inched his face between her breasts and licked off the sweat, and then he spilled the last little drops of whiskey from that flask where the sweat had been, and he lapped that up, too.

"Bartender. Give me another round," he joked.

"I'll give you something better," she said, sliding down in the bed. She pressed her breasts around his cock, confining him. She rubbed her nipples up and down against him.

"Come on me," she said.

"Yeah?" His voice was thick.

"Yes, all over me," she insisted, and she kept on rubbing her soft breasts and those pebble-hard nipples against him until he shot out on her chest.

She pushed herself back up on the pillow beside him and rubbed his semen across her skin so that it glossed her arms, her breasts, her belly.

"I'm drinking you in," she said. And to prove her point, she lowered her lips to his cock again and sucked out the last few drops of cum. He realized they were long done with the peppermint-flavored raincoats, and he wasn't quite sure when they'd given up playing it safe. Maybe when they started painting themselves with pancake syrup. Maybe when they knew they were it—they both knew they were absolutely it—for each other.

"Sit up here on my pillow," he suggested.

She curled up so he could reach inside her with his lips and tongue and make the little sucking circles he knew drove her wild. She gave the cry that woke the coyote and the park ranger over at the lake, and he wondered if anyone was hearing her now through the motel walls.

"I knew I could do it," he crowed.

Laughing, she rearranged herself on the bed and rubbed his shoulder. "I knew you could, too. You're damn good at doing it."

"I meant the ride, baby," he said, because his mind had flashed back to the rodeo ring. He felt the sweet ache of triumph wash over him again.

Anna nodded like she had known what he meant all along. "Sure. I didn't have a doubt there either."

"You get it, don't you, why I love the thrill?"

"I do," she said. "Although I never felt it myself. Except now, with you."

Man, he liked this woman. He squeezed her hand.

"I'm still wired," he said. "You mind staying up?"

She yawned. "No."

He tickled her along the inside of her arm, and she giggled and stopped yawning. He grabbed the remote, they watched a black-and-white gangster movie until it ended, and then he flipped around and found some stupid infomercial about yoga. The positions this one guy and girl got themselves in gave him the idea they should sixty-nine, Anna's mouth on his cock, his lips on her clit, and Anna was, as ever, game. It was in that wonderful, ludicrous position that they fell asleep.

When he woke it was full morning, but he was ahead of the maid. Tentatively he flexed his chest; he was stiffer and sorer than he'd been the night before, but nothing hurt too badly.

He ran his fingers across his ribs and more gingerly along his side. He'd always been a fast healer, and the lure of great sex sure took his mind off his injuries.

The infomercial was still playing; apparently the same thing played over and over on that channel. Just like he was on continuous play, too, he went right back to licking at Anna until she woke up, and she played along and sucked him, her teeth grazing his cock a little each time she came, and she came a lot before he lifted his dripping face and kissed her.

With no further regard for his accident, he thrust her legs wide apart and pounded into her, and since she was upside down on the bed, her feet thumped against the headboard over and over like the beat of a drum. It made him happy just to hear that banging while he was banging her. It was like the sound of a parade coming, some kind of celebration. He bet even Buffalo Bill had never had himself a celebration any finer than this.

And, it was safe to say, as he collapsed against her, he was no longer feeling anything remotely like pain.

"With this money in the bank, we can go on up to my cabin, lay back all autumn. I wanna do the big rodeo at the Vegas convention center New Year's Eve. Purse is even bigger there. Get a lot of hotshots from Australia, New Zealand. Doesn't mean I can't win it, though. Missed the last couple of years, working another guy's ranch, but this year—I'm gonna rock it. Then we can go on back, just watch the snow fall."

They'd packed up and checked out of the motel, grabbed coffee and doughnuts, picked up her car. When she saw the mechanic's tab, she had an expression on her face almost like the one he must've had when he saw that horse wheel back around and kick.

But she shrugged it off and followed him over to the arena, the plan being he would pack up his gear and follow her down to Salt Lake so she could return the rental car and then head up to his place, maybe stop for the night at some motel along the way.

He realized he'd never officially asked her if she wanted to spend the next four months at his spread. He just took it for granted that if he wanted to her come, and he did, she would go. She'd done everything he wanted to do up until now, anyway.

The parking lot was empty except for his truck. Everybody else had been and gone, he supposed. He called to the cleaning crew sweeping up in the stands, and they unlocked the tack room for him.

It was stripped bare except for Grant's gear, his saddle and blankets, stirrups and bridle, ropes and hat. There were a couple of notes tucked under his hat. One from the doctor, a prescription refill on the pain pills Grant wasn't even taking, a request from the ESPN2 reporter for a full interview, which made Grant smile, and one he crumpled up—from a girl suggesting the kind of nursing care Anna was already providing.

He took a quick look at her to see if she had noticed it, and if it was bothering her at all, but she was busy folding one of his blankets and was seemingly sanguine. He couldn't wait to get her up to that cabin, couldn't wait to take her riding and fishing, couldn't wait to ride her all over again. He was ready to do that right now. But he collected himself and started in on coiling his ropes.

Anna saw the girl's note, but she wasn't jealous. She knew she wasn't in competition with her. What she would have to fight was the rodeo itself, the thrill of the ride Grant lived for.

Not that she wanted to fight the rodeo, because if she did, and she won, and Grant lost that thrill he loved so much, he wouldn't be the same; he wouldn't be the same man she wanted so much.

She had to accept it. His passion was the rodeo; hers was—

him. The question was, could she hold on to him the way he held on to those wild horses, live for him like he lived for the rodeo, just because she loved the ride with him?

Here, right now in the empty, dusty room that smelled of horses and sweat and cigarettes, she thought she could.

She felt her breath catch in her throat and a melting heat welling up inside her, just watching him coil those ropes.

He looked up at her like he could sense what she was thinking, and apparently he could. Flashing that smile of his, he uncoiled the rope he'd just wound. It was lassoed at one end, and he tossed the loop over her and gently reeled her in.

She was wearing the tank top and jean skirt she'd worn when she first hooked up with him at the bar. She remembered how wild he had made her feel from the first moment he'd touched her on the small of her back. It was like he'd found the secret spot that unlocked everything she'd been holding back inside. Maybe she wasn't the only one remembering because he was touching her there now, she could feel all her doubts dissolving. Maybe this was enough; maybe it would always be.

"Just 'cause I missed a lot of the celebrating around here last night," he whispered, "doesn't mean we can't celebrate now."

He lowered the lasso around her hips, drew it tighter. "We don't need," he said, "to throw confetti. We've got other things."

Holding the end of the rope in one hand, he stripped off her tank top with the other hand and tossed it away.

"Boy, I like seeing you trussed up with your shirt off," he told her, licking his lips.

She licked her own and leaned in close, pressing her mouth against his.

Deftly he unhooked her bra and let it fall to the floor. He stopped kissing her, bent to run his tongue quickly across both nipples. She felt them harden just at the proximity of his breath.

He unzipped her skirt, and it slid off her hips, and she stepped out of it. There she was in just her panties and heels, his rope scratching not unpleasantly against her belly.

He dropped down on his knees and looped the rope around her thighs. He knotted it, and threw the end down.

"Can't leave now," he said.

She didn't want to.

He pushed his fingers inside her panties. Just as she was coming, he shoved the fabric aside and sucked on her. She dug her hands into his shoulders, bunching up his shirt in her fingers.

"Oh, we liked that," he said.

She laughed "Well, I sure did."

From outside they could hear the conversation of the clean-up crew. Grant strode over to the tack-room door and threw the bolt closed.

He unzipped his jeans and circled her, his cock enormous. He brushed it against her buttocks, thrust it between her bound legs, rubbing it against her twisted panties until she came again.

"Doesn't take much," he noted.

"Just you," she agreed.

He kissed her again, and she kissed him like she would swallow him up if she could; she kissed his lips, his cheeks, his neck, and back to his lips again, pushing her tongue between his teeth, locking on.

He had her breasts in his hands, twirling the nipples between his calloused fingertips. Just that touch made her come again.

Pleased with himself, he moved his hands between her legs. "I love it when your panties get all wet," he said. He wriggled his thumb inside her and pulled it out all slippery, rubbed her cum across her tits.

"You're gonna have to untie me now," she murmured.

"Why's that?"

" 'Cause you gotta take off my underwear and fuck me before I fucking explode," she gasped.

"Not quite yet," he said.

His saddle was lying on the ground, and he led her over to it, tossed a blanket on the floor, and lowered her down so that her head and shoulders were resting on the saddle, her hips on the blanket. She closed her eyes, absorbing the heady aroma of their bodies, the leather and oil of the saddle, the wool of the blanket, the warmth of the sunlight through the dusty tack-room windows.

He tied the free end of the rope that bound her around the saddle horn and stepped back.

"Oh, the things I can do with you now," he said.

He knelt down next to her. She raised her head just enough to take his dick in her mouth.

He rubbed at her through her panties and probed her beneath them until he could fit all four fingers inside her. She arched back against the saddle, and when she came that time he took her breasts in his mouth, first one and then the other.

He lifted a bridle from the pile of his gear near the saddle. He unhooked one leather strap. Lightly he wrapped it around her wrists and fastened it, binding her hands.

Anna was so turned on she could feel herself coming again. She was in his control now.

"I can see it on your face when you get off. You open your mouth just a little, and then your cheeks get . . . all flushed."

He sounded almost awestruck, like he was watching falling stars.

She was trembling all over, just trembling.

"You gotta fuck me," she said.

"Yeah, now I'm gonna explode," he agreed.

She thought he would have to untie her to remove her underwear, but instead he reached up and just ripped her panties off her right hip, left them hanging there, damp against her left thigh.

He touched her inside with just the head of his dick, rubbing it against her, barely probing her, and then pushed deep, rocking her from side to side, pulling out and then driving inside her. *Oh, yeah,* she thought, *he's going for the perfect ride again.*

When at last he did untie her, they were both shaking; it was that good. Before they dressed again, she kissed his ribs, his side, his hip, all the places with the bruises and the tape.

"I don't want to leave this room," she said, and she meant it, too.

"Could just tie you over my saddle, and ride you off into the hills." He grinned. "But taking our vehicles would be a lot more practical."

With her suitcase already in the trunk of the rental car, it was easy enough to change her clothes and reapply her makeup. It was much harder to regain her composure, harder still to say what she felt she had to say.

Grant had his truck packed up, and he was leaning against the driver's side, one foot on the running board, cool and relaxed, waiting for her.

To look at him, she couldn't tell he was sporting broken ribs; to look at him, she couldn't tell this man was the wild man who'd bound her and consumed her on the tack-room floor. But, then, to look at her, nobody would know she was the wild woman begging for more, either. There were probably many things neither one of them could tell about each other just by looking.

She walked over and stood next to him in the shade of his truck.

"Ready to roll?" he asked.

She wasn't. She wasn't ready at all. She shook her head.

"It's already two. If we're going to make my place by—"

"I can't." The words just slipped out before she wanted to say them. But, then, she really didn't want to say them ever.

"You can't." It wasn't a question, it was a statement, and there wasn't even that much surprise to it. "Here it comes, I guess. I thought you were different; you sure seem different, but I guess you want me to settle down, give up the circuit—"

"Grant. I don't want to change you, I want to change me, my life."

"Your life. Why?"

She struggled to explain. "I told you last night. Nothing's ever meant to me what riding means to you. Until now. Now you—you could easily become kind of what I live for."

"That's a bad thing, I take it?"

"Bad for both of us. It's asking too much of you and not enough of me. You see that, don't you?"

He shook his head. "I see a lot. I see how good we are together, how absolutely fucking fantastic we are, how we've just begun to explore the depths of our desires, and I believe they go pretty damn deep. We have a little cabin up in the woods, just waiting, where nobody'll care if you cry out so loud you wake the coyotes. I see you want to go there just as much as I do, but you *think* throwing me over is what you want. Or what you should want, anyway."

"I'm not throwing you over," she insisted.

"You're not so different from those broncs, are you, baby? I feel so good just claiming you for a while, and I guess it makes you feel good to buck me off."

"No—" she protested, but he overrode her.

"I'm not faulting you. It's an instinct. Remember, a bronc doesn't buck because it's afraid. No, baby, that horse'll throw you because he *can,* because he wants to. I ride as well as I do 'cause I work with that instinct; I convince that mount he doesn't really want to do what he thinks he does. I didn't realize I had to work you the same way."

"I need to go back to LA. I'm out of work, I have rent to pay—"

"LA isn't going to disappear on you. Maybe you can find something you want to write about without even being there, anyway. And I bet you could pack up everything you really need from your apartment in an hour."

"Don't make it harder. I don't want to leave you. I don't want to get in that car and put distance between us. I want to be able to just reach out and touch your arm. Kiss you. Put your cock in my mouth."

The mood lightened between them. He smiled.

"And I want to be able to put my fingers in your hot little pussy," he said. "And my tongue deep down in your—"

"But I *need* to go, Grant," she said as firmly and resolutely as she could. Still, there was a catch in her throat, and he heard it.

He looked at her for a long time beneath the shadow of his Stetson. He lifted her chin, wiped away the tears spilling from the corners of her eyes with his fingers.

"There's no such thing as knowing how long you can take a ride. Sometimes you just have to hold on as hard as you can, and see what happens," he told her.

"It has to be more than just a ride. For me, anyway."

He shrugged. "In my experience, life never stands still long enough to harness long-term."

"Will your life stand still long enough that I could come visit you in that cabin of yours?"

"I'll be there, yeah. I'm not changing my plans," he said, and he took her hand in his and just held it.

"And New Year's—you were talking about Las Vegas. That's only forty-five minutes on a plane from LA."

Grant kissed the top of her hair. "You'll be with me, but on your terms. That about right? At least until I can convince you that we don't need terms at all?"

She managed to nod. He released her hand.

"All right, then. Might've busted a few ribs, but I guess I've missed getting my heart broke. By a narrow margin."

He reached in the backseat of his truck and plucked a rodeo flier and a pencil from the heap he'd made of his belongings. He scribbled on the back of the flier. "That's the address. That's the phone number of the bar I go in for a beer or two every Saturday night. I don't have a phone up there at the cabin."

She snatched the pencil, wrote her own phone number on the bottom of the paper, ripped it off, and passed that piece back to him.

"Don't lose it," she said.

He tucked it inside his jeans. "I won't. Don't you lose that— that virginity of yours."

"Virginity?" she raised her eyebrows.

"You're still pretty untouched by this love business. Keep it that way till you see me again."

She kissed him, and he returned to her a sweet, soft kiss. He let his lips trail down her neck and onto her bare shoulders, but there he stopped.

"Better not get started. You won't leave. We can't have that. Gotta make sure you leave so you can come back again."

"If I call you at that bar—say, next Saturday—will you be there?"

"Yeah. Lookin' at the pretty girls."

She glanced away from him.

"Hey." He tilted her chin back toward him. "I said lookin', not fucking, and you want to know the truth? That bar, it's mostly filled with railroad men and lumberjacks and their old ladies, and I wouldn't call most of 'em pretty."

"So you'll be bored till you see me again?" she asked hopefully.

He cocked his hip and adjusted his belt. "Bored *stiff*, I imagine."

On her laugh, he stepped away from his truck and walked her to her rental.

"And you?" he said. "I mean, no strings or anything. Ropes okay— no strings, though, to tie you down."

She wanted him, frankly, to bind her to him, and hold her fast, and forget all the reasons, all the sane and sensible reasons for leaving, forget that he had a life and she was afraid she would have just . . . him.

"No strings, but . . . I've never known any other guy— maybe I never want to know any other guy—like you. For what it's worth, you absolutely possess me."

A small satisfied smile played across his face. "Go on, then. Drive on back to the real world. I'll be around a while, waiting to possess you again."

She opened the car door and slipped behind the wheel, but she still didn't start the engine.

He leaned inside her open window. "I decide I want a beer earlier than Saturday, I walk down to the bar, I call you tonight, say. You be home?"

"Late," she said. "I didn't—I didn't confirm a flight."

"Still not that sure, are you?" He smiled. "Well. I am. I climb back on even after I'm thrown. You know I do."

He turned away and walked to his truck, his hips swaying slightly, his walk jaunty, his broad back straight and proud. If he turned back, and she saw those golden curls and that wickedly beautiful smile, if he turned back and she saw those full lips and thought about all the things he could do with them, if she saw his tanned, rough hands and thought about all the places he touched her with them, if she saw his deep blue-violet eyes . . .

Anna put the key in the car's ignition, turned the motor over, and sped away, her wheels kicking up gravel in the parking lot.

Hot and gold, the light of the summer afternoon trailed her

through the Absaroka pass. With the car windows open, the sun spilled in on her and scorched her skin until the mountain shadows draped over her, leaching the color from the sun and fading the heat of the day.

She could still feel the weight of Grant's kisses on her bare shoulders. No matter what else happened, she would keep her promise to visit. And if she found herself a life she loved as much as he loved his rodeo, maybe someday she would even make a promise to stay. She just had to find the passion she was missing. Even if she wasn't entirely sure how she would go about finding it, or even if she would recognize it if she did.

She was already four hours south of Cody, Wyoming, and crossing over the Gros Ventre slide, when she turned the car around.